# OH WRETCHED MOON

KATE RAMSEY

ISBN: 978-0-578-76497-9

www.TalesMustBeTold.com

First Edition

Editing by LH Editing

Book Cover Design by ebooklaunch.com

# CHAPTER ONE

*H*ad it been any other day, she would not have seen him die. Instead, Vesper would have been summoned to William's offices by frantic servants and informed of the tragedy along the way. On a normal day, she would not have sought him out. Vesper thought it was a small, frightened love that could not bear to be apart from its object and accordingly, she and William spent most of their days busy about their separate tasks. Even when the day's work was done, they often entertained guests and were not alone together until it was very late, though Vesper preferred the nights when they could walk together in the gardens after supper and early to bed.

On the day her beloved died, she could not wait until the supper tables had been cleared, the songs sung and the household prepared to retire before giving him her news. By the time Fina appeared at the doorway to inform her the solicitor had gone, Vesper felt she had waited more than long enough. In her haste, she sprang up before putting her embroidery down and was forced to disentangle herself as a spool rolled down her skirts and bounced across the room, trailing crimson thread in its wake.

At last! The solicitor was the last in a string of appointments William had that day and she knew he would now be alone, writing. She could not wait another minute to see him... to give him the gift that had simmered in her breast for days, harbored there until she could be certain. Now that certainty had come, Vesper felt sure that if she did not share her joy with him, it would burst out of her chest and she might never be able to gather it all in again.

"Thank you Fina," she said and swept past her into the hall, making no attempt to temper the radiance of her smile. As she neared William's office she relished every step that led her toward him – toward the sunrise on his features when he heard the long awaited news.

The door to the office opened as Vesper approached and she faltered slightly when an unfamiliar servant emerged carrying an empty tray. The girl nodded respectfully as she passed and for a fleeting moment, something inside Vesper turned inexplicably cold. The girl's glance, connecting with her own for only a hair's breadth, seemed not to glide over her as it passed, but to slither.

As quickly as it had come, the feeling was gone. Vesper paused and called to the girl — presumably the cook's daughter, whom they had agreed to employ for the winter. The servant turned and Vesper saw no hint of mischief in her gaze as it settled on her once again.

"Is his lordship in?" Vesper asked.

"Yes my lady. Only, he has a terrible headache." She gestured to the empty tray. "He called for a draught of wine and hellebore to relieve it."

Of course. Poor William was frequently afflicted with unbearable pain, especially on the days the solicitor visited. There was nothing at all unusual about his calling for a pain draught in the late afternoon, yet Vesper found herself in the sudden grip of wild, irrational fear. She dismissed the servant and turned toward the heavy door of William's office. Surely her racing heart was only nerves, she told herself, brought on by the day's anxiety.

Slowly, Vesper opened the door. There he was — her William, the sunlight of her days, seated with his back to her, bowed over the account books as if engrossed in a particularly troublesome sum. There was no relief in the sight. She took in everything at once; the tension in his body, his hands clutched to his stomach, the unnatural pallor on his face, where beads of sweat had formed. She saw the cup, drained and placed back on the table, perfectly mundane, perfectly innocent. She saw the bile, soaking into the rug near his feet. This, at least, gave her a shred of hope.

"William!" She rushed into the room, falling to her knees at his side. "William," she cried again. "Can you hear me, my love?" She put her hands on his face, turning it toward her own. His eyes were clouded with pain, his skin feverish and slick with sweat, as though his body sought to expel the poison through every pore. Perhaps if she could induce him to vomit again or empty his bowels, the poison would not have time to seep into his veins.

William's eyes seemed to clear for a moment and he saw her at last. He offered a rueful smile and reached to touch her face. She thought he meant to caress her cheek, or hair, as he was often wont to do, but his fingers only grazed her skin before his head fell forward and he retched fruitlessly.

"Fina!" Vesper screamed. She knew her lady's maid was not in this part of the house, but surely her scream would draw someone to help. "Help! Fina! "

There was no answer. No hurried approach of footsteps in the hall.

"Get up William," she commanded. He cried out as she lifted his arm and placed it around her shoulders, wrapping her own around his waist. Vesper pushed her bodyweight into him, forcing him to stand. "Get up!" She was frantic now.

No help, it seemed, was coming.

She could run and find a servant in only a few moments, but her heart warned her that to leave him for even a moment would be to leave him forever.

She could think of nothing else but to take him with her — perhaps the walking would loosen his stomach and help rid his body of the deadly tonic. They stumbled together into the hall. Vesper paused, looking frantically around as if she had never seen the castle halls before.

*Why were they so empty? So silent?*

"Come, my love," she said. "Only a few steps. Come with me, my heart, my William, only a few steps more," she had begun to babble, urging him on as if her words alone could hold him upright.

"Vesper," he whispered, but she would not hear him.

"It'll be alright," she told him, now all but dragging him down the hall. "It will be alright, it will be alright, you only need a draught of bryony and you will be alright..."

"Vesper."

She stopped this time, turning to look at him. It wasn't the pain or fear in his expression that would haunt her in the new, dark world she would inhabit before night fell, but the apology.

As if he was failing her and that knowledge, rather than the poison, was killing him.

William reached for her again and this time she caught his hand before it could falter, brought it to her face and kissed his palm through salty tears. He held her gaze a moment longer, then lurched forward. With a cry, Vesper caught him, lowering him gently to the floor.

"I'm sorry, dearest," he said. She shook her head, begging him not to be sorry, not to go at all, but not to be sorry for what he could not prevent.

His face was ghostly white, his beard wet with sweat and bile, but as he smiled again, Vesper kissed his hand, his forehead, his eyes, his mouth. She felt his muscles relax beneath her fingers and as she drew back, she watched the sun set in his eyes, until at last no light was left in them. Those eyes, once so humorous, once so soft as he caressed her face and laughed, had emptied out til they became something else. Something that was nothing. A void.

Then the rest of the world began to grow dim,

It seemed only right that all the light in the room should follow her beloved's soul wherever it should go, as if the void that filled him was spreading — reaching out with dark tentacles to pull the whole earth into itself. As the darkness embraced them both, Vesper felt, for the first time, the flutter of movement within her womb.

VESPER HAS KNOWN since the day she arrived that something is wrong. Some vital element is absent from the place she has made her listless home, though her room lacks no luxury. The carpets are lush and strewn with meadowsweet, the air is warm, undisturbed by drafts. The steam from her baths is scented with oils. She reclines on soft couches, wrapped in soft furs, attended by sweet music, savory food and strong wine.

It was not until she awakened from her faint some time after William's death that she understood it had not been the light in the halls that had fled with William, but her own sight. The physicians attributed her sudden blindness to shock, assuring her that sight would return with time, but the darkness has remained with her since then.

When news of the tragedy reached the surrounding countryside, she had found herself compelled to greet and entertain a steady stream of well-wishers who came to mourn with her and offer their aid, but far more who came to walk in her gardens, fill themselves at her table and rest in the castle's luxurious suites.

Vesper had borne their company graciously but grew more fatigued every day. The flutters of the little one inside her brought some comfort, but also a different kind of grief. So it was that when Fina delivered a letter from the widow of a wealthy duke inviting Vesper to rest at her country castle until the child's arrival, she accepted without hesitation. Vesper had only met Lady Watho once or twice, since the duchess' castle was inconveniently far away in the desolate moors. Of course there were the rumors — whispers of other reasons Lady Watho might avoid society, but Vesper had never been one for gossip and the offer of solitude awakened, for the first time, some hope of comfort to her aching soul.

The day after the letter's arrival, Vesper had begun her journey to the place she would never see, but has since come to think of as her home while her child grows. Lady Watho, kindly, leaves her mostly to herself, visiting only now and then to make sure Vesper's needs are met and occasionally to read her a story when the silence becomes too oppressive. The stories are always sad, but Vesper thinks that is appropriate. Occasionally, Vesper joins Watho in the dining hall, but since she cannot see, rarely leaves her room for any other reason. Falca, Watho's aging lady's maid, attends to her comforts, brings most of her meals and summons musicians to fill the darkness with sweet, sorrowful hymns.

She knows that something is missing, but the knowing is a butterfly's wings beating against a window; persistent — urgent, even — but faint. Like everything else, it lies beneath a shroud of grief.

Once it would have mattered. Vesper's mind was once curious and animated, but that time is long past. The world is dark and Vesper is alone. In the shadow of such towering grief, no butterfly spending its strength against the unyielding window pane can be of any consequence.

Watho is brooding.

She sits in her window seat, gazing out over the gardens, which are pleasant during the day, but take on an entirely different kind of splendour in the pale moonlight. Not that she cares for splendour.

It has been days since Felnys made an appearance and Watho can feel his absence in the straightness of her shoulders, the ease with which she moves. She finds that she stands taller when he is gone, as if simply being near him robs her of her natural poise. That his presence has the power to affect Watho at all annoys her, but that she has no real control over his comings and goings annoys her even more.

*Unless you have power over him, he has power over you*, her father's voice echoes in her head. He was a great believer in power. The lessons he taught on the subject still linger, like the ghost of bruises on her arms.

Sometimes Felnys reminds her of him.

No, that's not right. She dismisses the thought with an irritable shake of her head. Felnys may be a puzzle — unpredictable at times, even worrisome — but he's a puzzle of her own choosing. Her feelings about him may conflict from time to time, but Watho does not allow herself to be ruled by feelings. She chose him and she can dismiss him at will. She is the one in control.

She glances down at the book in her lap. The margin is thick with notes and spells overlapping with the charts and constellations on the page. She's been studying the movements of the stars for weeks – how they might be used to thwart the plans of mortals, or make them succeed. It matters little which, the important thing is to see what they can do. What she can *make* them do.

She snaps the book closed and tosses it aside, unable to shake her restlessness. She catches a glimpse of herself in the looking glass across the room and smiles grimly. Watho knows she is beautiful, but there is no vanity in the acknowledgement. She is still dressed in the green satin with gold lace trim that she wore to dinner with Vesper, rich red hair piled in intricate coils atop her head and her black eyes glitter with cold calculation.

Her mind wanders as she examines her reflection dispassionately. The pieces of the experiment are nearly all assembled. Vesper is settled in her comfortable, if crypt-like room deep in the castle's bowels. Tomorrow, Aurora will arrive and

Watho will station her in the balcony rooms overlooking the garden and the hunting plains.

The groundwork is more tedious than she likes, but if the experiment succeeds, the payoff will be well worth it. She will have proved what she has long suspected and what her father never knew: that true and lasting power is achieved not by violence but by manipulation. People, she posits, can be designed like art and cultivated like flowers. When a person is so fully in another's power that they believe it is their natural state, that is a power no sword can rival.

"I see your machinations are proceeding as planned," a low voice growls, mimicking her thoughts.

Watho's smile widens, infused now with a touch of genuine pleasure. She turns slowly toward the fireplace, where an enormous wolf has appeared and now stands facing her. His thick, brown fur shines in the firelight, rippling with the movement of powerful muscles as he begins to slowly pace. Felnys' dark eyes mirror her own.

"Back from your wanderings, are you?" she asks. "What have you been doing all this time?" Distantly, she is aware that her shoulders have already begun to sag, as if the very air in the room is weighed down by his arrival.

"I'm always about my mistress' business. You know that." His voice sounds like velvet.

Watho dislikes such comments. The more respectfully Felnys speaks, the more mockery she hears behind the words. She opens her mouth to rebuke him but thinks better of it. She will not be baited.

"When I send an invitation," she probes, "I usually expect the messenger to return *before* I receive its acceptance."

"Indeed," the wolf says and curls up comfortably on the hearth rug.

Watho wants to press the issue. She does not like to go unanswered, but she likes even less the thought of appearing to need him too much. She shrugs and turns back to the window.

"The plan is proceeding smoothly, yes. Aurora will arrive tomorrow."

Felnys snorts but says nothing.

"Tell me," Watho says, "Why you felt it necessary to kill the young lord?"

"You think I should not have?"

"His life means nothing to me either way."

"Then why does it trouble you?" Even without looking at him, Watho can hear his derisive smile.

"It doesn't trouble me," she snaps, irked with herself for feeling defensive. "I ask to satisfy my curiosity. You know as well as I do he would have been called away to war with all the rest. So why kill him, unless you just enjoy dressing up as a house maid?"

"You could never have made her blindness last while he lived. As it is now, she will not resist the magic. She prefers the darkness."

This is why she endures the uneasiness of Felnys' presence. Somehow, he understands how her magic works and anticipates exactly what she needs, sometimes before she herself knows. There is something eerie about this prescience. She can identify any other witch she meets by the way their magic feels, as though each one has a unique scent. Felnys, though... he's different. His magic is as familiar as her own. Perhaps it's different with wolves, Watho muses. She's never met a wolf with his own magic before, but perhaps they are not so easily identifiable.

Whatever the reason, having Felnys' power at her disposal is both fascinating and useful enough to quell her objections to his impertinence.

As Watho turns back toward the window, her eyes slide past her reflection again. She's a little surprised to see how deeply her shoulders are now hunched. It's as if a monstrous weight — the weight of the wolf himself — has settled onto them. She consciously straightens her back and looks away.

THE MORNING AFTER FELNYS' return, Watho visits the tower after breakfast. The castle has several towers, but this one is the highest, affording a spectacular view of the heavens and the countryside. The tower is home to her most prized possession: a large, shining obsidian telescope, surrounded by a dizzying array of golden knobs and switches. It is the only one of its kind anywhere to be found.

Watho makes the arduous climb to the telescope's station several times every week. She could ease the climb with magic, but she prefers to store up her power for emergencies. Anyway, expending magic only results in a different kind of fatigue. In fact, she has become uncomfortably aware that even simple spells take more of a toll than they did only a few years ago. She tells herself it must be the result of so many continuous strands deployed to keep the castle running, but still Watho is uneasy.

After a brief pause to catch her breath, she peers through the telescope's eyepiece, adjusting the angle and fiddling with the dials and wheels until she can see far beyond her castle's valley, into the surrounding forests. After a few more adjustments, a horse-drawn coach comes into focus, bouncing along on the forest trails. Watho is pleased to see only one coach and two soldiers on horseback riding behind it.

*Good. The silly woman is not bringing her entire household.*

Another tweak or two and now Watho can see inside the coach, where a young woman sits gazing dreamily out the window. Aurora has deep blue eyes and fair hair that looks as though it wants very much to escape its prison of pins and fasteners. She is dressed sensibly in a periwinkle gown with a light gray traveling cloak.

One gloved hand holds an open book, temporarily forgotten, while the other rests on her rounded belly. As Watho watches, the hand begins to move softly, absentmindedly, over the bump and a misty smile haunts the young woman's lips.

Watho watches her contemplatively for a while and then begins to make adjustments again. She has to make quite a few of them, but in a few moments another view comes into focus. This time, she is looking not across the valleys and forests, but deep into the mountainside beneath her. The lower reaches of the castle were dug out long before Watho came to live there and some of the ancient passages and chambers buried at the heart of the mountain remain a mystery to her. A number of these unexplored or long forgotten rooms pass under her eye before it settles at last on the room which Vesper now occupies.

Vesper, like Aurora, is beautiful, but is otherwise as unlike her as any woman could be. She is tall and delicate, with skin like dark satin and black hair that cascades loosely down her back. Vesper's eyes are black and, as always, lowered in restless grief.

Vesper paces slowly, barefoot, on carpets so soft she could easily throw herself down on them without injury. Sometimes she looks as though she wants to do just that, but instead she wanders, dreaming, Watho supposes, of brighter days. With a minor tweak of the telescope's controls, Watho can hear her faintly humming to her unborn child; a sweet, sad song, that the soft carpets and couches soak up into themselves so that it is barely audible.

Watho realizes that Felnys has joined her on the roof only when he speaks. The wolf enjoys coming and going in silence, keeping her always on guard.

"Are you satisfied with what you see?" he asks.

Watho bristles. She hates the amused tenor of his voice, as if she were a small child playing with her toys. Stepping back from the beloved telescope, she turns slowly and fixes him with a withering gaze, which leaves him entirely unruffled.

There is not another wolf in the country that can match Felnys for size and strength. When both the witch and the wolf stand facing each other, he is more than half her height. They each possess the power to strike fear into the hearts of men with only a look, but neither ever seems able to frighten the other. She studies him, wondering why she's never noticed the faint auburn tint to his sleek coat, which is evident in the morning light.

"I feel your guest approaching," Felnys says at last. His voice is low and hungry and Watho feels his hunger reflected in herself.

"Yes. She'll be here before nightfall." She smiles, triumphant. "Once she is here, you must only be seen in human form, or not at all. Come, let's walk in the gardens together, until then. You'll have little enough opportunity to stretch your legs soon."

The wolf bows his head in acquiescence and follows her silently out of the tower.

Aurora sets her needlework down atop her ever-expanding belly and laughs at it. She is prone to laugh at most things, but she always finds the use of her belly as a makeshift table especially amusing. She takes a sip of wine before resuming the needlework, her fingers working swiftly as she gazes out the window.

At times, Aurora misses the trees that grow so plentifully around her own manor and the bustle of servants and stewards and nobles coming and going. She even misses the smells of the city — sometimes putrid, sometimes sweet, always pungent — and the shouts of the merchants, chambermaids, cooks, and children. The longer she stays in this quiet castle on the moors, however, the more infrequent those pangs of homesickness become. Everything here is so bright that it has taken Aurora some time to adjust. Her rooms face east and feature the largest windows she has ever seen, so that there is no corner of her quarters that escape the morning sunlight. The moors beyond the castle are likewise shadowless, golden, so warmly lit that Aurora sometimes thinks they look like an extension of the sun itself, or a cape, trailing behind her as she races across the sky.

Aurora is, by nature, a creature who thrives in warmth and light, so as time passes and the strangeness of being away from home subsides, she is learning more and more to rejoice in the brightness of her rooms and view. Every day, the chambermaid brings new assortments of morgunn, hemera, and zinia and Aurora delights in the way the flowers lean toward the window, glorying in the light.

She thinks now, as she mindlessly works her needle and watches the hunting party racing across the plain below, in pursuit of what she cannot tell, that she is glad she came. When she first received the invitation from Lady Watho to come and stay with her, Aurora had been inclined to refuse. Her husband had been called away to war, but she could not know how long he would be gone and she was loath to be found absent upon his return.

As the conflict dragged on and showed no signs of conclusion, however, her resolve began to waver. Eventually, it was not his absence that drove her to accept Lady Watho's invitation, but an increasing concern about her ability to provide her husband with a son when he returned. They had been married only a few weeks when he was called away, yet the earl (she still cannot think of him as Hugh and likely never will; Sir Hugh, perhaps, but never Hugh) had left with serene confidence that his son was growing in her belly. He had postponed their wedding night for three days after the actual wedding ceremony, waiting for the most auspicious alignment of the stars. The very next morning he had announced that she was pregnant with a son and had immediately written a letter to his uncle the Duke of Alton, to inform him of the happy news.

Aurora does not share her husband's confidence in the power of the heavens to ensure a male progeny. The few pieces of correspondence she has received from the front have primarily concerned the earl's plans for the boy's education and future, such that Aurora has grown steadily more fearful of his anger should she fail to produce the expected heir.

Lady Watho had sent her invitation so soon after the earl's departure that Aurora wondered if she had known of the war before the king himself did. She remembered later that the eccentric duchess was rumored to do a little magic. Aurora had always dismissed these rumors, but as she felt the quickening of the child in her womb, they came again to her mind. If Watho *could* do magic, she had reasoned, perhaps she could set Aurora's mind at ease – give her some potion or teach her what to eat to ensure the child would be born a boy. At the very least, the duchess could definitively predict the child's sex and bring an end to her uncertainty.

Thus Aurora had arrived, with five months left of her pregnancy, to avail herself of Lady Watho's hospitality. In the months since then, she has come to love the little castle, reclusive though it is. She finds peace in its quiet isolation and often feels a pang of guilt that she does not look forward to her husband's safe return with joy.

Watho visits her often in the afternoons and the two of them bask together in the sunlight that pours in through the airy windows, reading to one another and laughing, or writing letters in companionable silence. Every afternoon, a chambermaid brings them wine, sugared almonds, cheese and bread, then timidly curtseys and flees the room as if a wild animal is on her heels. Aurora watches her bemusedly sometimes, wondering if she has done something to frighten the girl, but a joke from Lady Watho usually drives these thoughts away.

Still, for all her host's charm, Aurora cannot bring herself to ask the question she has come to ask. She does not want to offend the duchess by accusing her of witchcraft if the rumors are false and thus finds the subject difficult to broach.

She finds, when she considers it, that despite the duchess' hospitality and easy grace, there is something unsettling about her, something ever so slightly wolfish behind her friend's eyes. On the few occasions when Aurora almost decided to ask the question that brought her here, she looked up to find Lady Watho looking at her in a penetrating way that was not at all pleasant. Very soon after Watho's nightly departure, Aurora usually begins to feel unbearably tired and is often sound asleep within an hour. She had realized within a week of arriving that the chambermaid was putting a sleeping agent in the afternoon wine. By this point her pregnancy has become uncomfortable and her anxiety about the earl increases daily, so she has decided to consider this a mercy.

*Surely,* a voice inside her occasionally whispers, *it is a sinister hostess who gives her guests a sleeping draught without their knowledge.*

*On the contrary,* another voice counters, *that's just what a courteous hostess would do to ease her visitor's discomfort without having to be asked.*

Watho's visits have begun to come earlier in recent weeks and Aurora nods off to sleep well before the setting of the sun. The first voice returns from time to time, asking her if she really ought to ignore this, but usually the second voice chides the first until it quiets down.

As much as she loves the brilliant sunlight in which she is ensconced at Astarsaga Castle, Aurora finds relief for her turbulent mind in the darkness of sleep and is thankful that the drug keeps any anxious dreams at bay.

Now, as the door behind her opens to admit the duchess, Aurora takes a deep breath. Today, she tells herself firmly, she must make her inquiry.

Lady Watho favors Aurora with a warm smile as she enters, wearing a white gown of light, gauzy material that seems to float when she moves. Her striking red hair is swept up into a loose coiffure that allows wispy tendrils to escape.

"Have you decided to ask me at last?" she asks, seating

herself casually on a chaise lounge and taking up her own needlework.

Aurora stares, forgetting courtesy. Watho looks amused, but says nothing.

"Have you known all this time?" Aurora asks at last.

"Is that not why you came to me? Surely you wouldn't ask a person to predict your child's future who could not also predict the question." She glances up from her needlework to wink at her guest.

Relief floods Aurora. "Then you do know the answer? Please, Watho, I am so afraid." She has never given voice to her fear before and finds she is ashamed of it.

Watho's fingers still and she is quiet for a moment. Her smile remains, but she appears to be struggling with herself. Aurora feels her fear sharpen, but the possibility of bearing a girl into his lordship's arms no longer seems to be its focal point. Perhaps there is some terrible ritual that will need to be endured before she can know the answer. Aurora knows very little about witchcraft. She forces herself to wait.

At last, Watho seems to make her decision and meets Aurora's eye. Aurora is startled to find her hostess' black eyes more disconcerting than ever.

"The child in your womb is a boy," Watho says. Before Aurora can respond, her hostess rises abruptly although she's only been sitting for a moment and this time her smile is all cheer. "I apologize my dear, I won't be able to stay this evening. I've forgotten an appointment I must keep."

Watho has delivered the news Aurora has been waiting so anxiously to hear, but as she watches the door close behind the duchess, she finds her foreboding has only increased.

One thing she understands with terrifying certainty: her friend has not told her everything.

AT THE FIRST tightening of her belly, Vesper wakes and lies breathing quietly as she counts the minutes until the next.

The contractions come ten minutes apart at first and she monitors them drowsily, drifting in and out of sleep. Eventually she rises and begins to pace the length of the fur rug, humming softly to herself. Vesper has no need of light and rarely lights the lamp which Falca tells her hangs from the ceiling of her room.

In her months of blindness she has, however, become familiar enough with her quarters that she can light it with little trouble and she does so now to prepare for the midwives when the time comes to summon them.

She sings softly to her little one, feeling for the first time in months the warm glow of love unmixed with grief. Soon she will hold her little one in her arms. Later, she knows, the grief will come again as she aches to share her joy with her William, to hand his child to him, to see his glowing face doting over its little hands and feet and nose. Later, but not tonight. For now, all her love is focused on the little one, who will, Vesper is determined, be welcomed into its mother's warmth and kindness, if not the light of her former life.

The pains begin to increase and the spaces between them grow shorter. Vesper at last rings the bell for aid. In a few moments, she hears the door open and Falca's familiar footsteps approach.

"It's time," Vesper says, a little breathless, but smiling. "She's coming today."

"What makes you so sure it's a girl?" Falca asks, in her typically direct manner and foregoing as usual the formal address Vesper's rank merits.

Vesper only smiles again. "I feel it in my bones," she says simply. "Send for the midwife."

Hours later, the scents of meadowsweet and incense and the midwives' ointment thick in the air, Vesper feels the first twinge of uncertainty. Everything seems to be going smoothly and lady Watho, who arrived at some point, assures her that the time is short, but some nagging sense — the one that has plagued her since she arrived — tugs at her concentration.

*It's a butterfly* she thinks, incoherently, *trying to get in through the window.*

The pain must be confusing her thoughts.

At the midwife's urging, Vesper begins to push and something wrenches cruelly inside her. Vesper cries out in shock and pain as she feels blood begin to flow down her thighs and the midwife's hands grasping her daughter from between her legs, hears her rubbing the baby's body, working to draw forth breath.

"What does it want?" Vesper gasps.

"What does who want?" Falca demands.

"The butterfly at the window."

Suddenly, she understands what has been bothering her about her rooms. She understands and almost laughs — it is such a small thing, after all — but she feels only horror. In her blindness Vesper has learned every inch of the room she inhabits; the couches, the beds, the tapestries, the tables, the vanity, the rugs, the vases, the lamp and the useless mirror. The realization settles on her now, with suffocating certainty, that she has never once in all her months of pacing, encountered a window.

Her room, which before had always seemed so spacious,

now feels like being buried alive. She must be underground, deep in the belly of the castle. The weight of it threatens to crush her now and Vesper feels a desperate urgency to get the baby above ground, as if the whole castle might cave in on them at any second.

She feels hands pressing on her belly and shoulders to make her lie back, hears the urgent whispers of her attendants, feels the sheets soaking up the life that leaves her body. She hears the midwife patting the baby's back and hears the little lungs take in their first gasp of air.

At the moment that William's daughter opens her eyes on the world, Vesper herself passes into the next.

# CHAPTER TWO

*F*alca stumbles, groggy, toward the unpleasant sounds coming from the baby's cradle. For nearly seven nights she has been entombed in Vesper's windowless room, attending to the newborn's constant demands.

That Falca herself has been saddled with the child's care might be less of a burden had she been allowed to care for the baby from the comfort of her own quarters. She hates the dark crypt in which Vesper lived. Her eyes cannot adjust to the dimness and she has begun to lose track of the days. Watho, however, is insistent. The girl is never to leave her mother's room. As a result, Falca, too, is banished to the castle's gloomy bowels, save when she can enlist another servant to help for a few hours here and there.

She lights the dim lamp and scoops the squalling child out of the crib. She does not have a gentle nature and has never felt a maternal stirring of any kind, but she is nothing if not efficient and a few days with the newborn has taught her that gentleness has its uses.

The baby quiets at once and Falca glares at the tiny face,

like Vesper's in every way except for the eyes. The innocent trust with which those disconcertingly bright blue eyes look back at her annoys Falca.

"Why must you always be hungry when decent people are sleeping, you little tyrant?" she grumbles.

Falca has been in Watho's service for nearly twenty years and has performed her share of unsavory tasks, but this is by far the worst of them. There is no escape from the little wailing creature she never intended to adopt, or from the endless, *endless* darkness.

"Your mother was blessed to be blind," she tells the baby gruffly and rings the bell for a servant. The servants know by now that a bell at 2 o'clock in the morning means goats' milk for the baby and spiced wine for Falca.

While they wait, the lady's maid and her unwanted ward pace back and forth, Falca humming tunelessly and barely noticing the little fingers wrapped tightly around her own.

"It's one thing to be sent to hex people's houses and sprinkle spells in their gardens" she tells the baby irritably. "But I really think this is a bit much."

The baby gurgles agreeably.

"You can wager," Falca continues, "that the lady's maids in other great houses are not imprisoned in windowless caverns, caring for unnatural little creatures with alarming eyes. A woman of my stature ought to be dressing a duchess and arranging her hair. Not stumbling about in this cursed dark with a wretched, wiggling thing."

The sparkling eyes stare adoringly at her in response. Falca's own eyes narrow and she stops pacing.

"Really! It's *too* much," she snaps, depositing the child

roughly back into her cradle, whereupon the baby begins to wail passionately.

A timid sound from behind her causes Falca to whirl savagely on the approaching servant girl.

"Took your time, didn't you?" she barks, though it has been only a few moments.

"I'm sorry," the girl murmurs, glancing around for a place to set the tray so that she can scuttle off. "Where shall I put this?"

To the girl's apparent dismay, Falca snatches the wine from the tray and marches sullenly toward the door without answering.

"Falca?" There is now a note of real alarm in the servant's voice. "What about the baby?"

"Are you deaf?" Falca shouts over her shoulder. "Feed it, so I can have some peace."

She leaves the crestfallen servant and the baby to work things out between themselves and storms back to her own rooms, which she has not seen all week.

"If I wanted a child I'd have gone and gotten one," she declares, tossing the wine goblet back in a single gulp. "I'm damned if I'm going to play nursemaid to a little orphaned waif because my mistress has had a whim."

She says this last part quietly, however, knowing that Watho's quarters are not far from her own.

It has been three months since Aurora's grief-stricken departure from Astarsaga Castle. The many-windowed walls of her vacated rooms still drink the sunlight greedily and when the sun completes its journey each day, lamps and candles are lit so that the room is always bathed in brilliant light. The shadows are few and those that remain are banished to the farthest edges of the room.

It is furnished in bright colors, its tables and shelves painted dazzling white. Mirrors hang at intervals on its lemon walls and between them paintings of vivid flowers — citrine blossom, lumebud, morgunn, and hemera in splendid hues of yellow, cream, and fiery saffron.

In the center of the room where the sunlight is brightest, on a soft yellow rug, a baby coos appreciatively at a rattle clutched in his fat fist.

He is nearly a perfect picture of his mother, with fair skin and flaxen hair, though the resemblance stops at his eyes. While Aurora's eyes are deep blue, baby Aethon's are black as a moonless night. They are like his mother's in one respect; they sparkle often with laughter.

A few feet from where he wriggles, sunlight pooling in his golden curls and around his dimpled ankles, Watho sits with her needlework, as she often did during his mother's stay. She watches the baby with interest and even pride, but without affection.

The boy is flourishing, as she knew he would. Already his fair, soft skin has a constant warm glow, as if it has absorbed all the sunlight it can and is beginning to overflow. Watho gazes at him, curious, wondering that the brightness does not hurt his eyes.

*How quickly one can cultivate them.*

A knock at the door interrupts her musing.

"Enter," she commands.

The door opens and Fargu, her head huntsman enters. He is tall, muscular, and golden-skinned from long days in the sun.

Watho suspects his impassive countenance conceals a formidable mind; a thought she finds disquieting.

Fargu glances at the baby, but his face registers neither surprise nor curiosity. He has surely heard rumors from the other servants about the baby in the sun rooms, but still, it must come as a shock to have them confirmed. His stoic acceptance is irksome.

"That," she says, pointing at the baby, "is called Aethon. From now on, it shall be your responsibility."

She is pleased to see a flicker of alarm on the man's face.

He composes himself quickly enough. "Yes, my lady," he says, but after a pause, adds, "erm... is it chiefly, the child's education you wish me to see to?"

Watho smiles, gratified by his discomfiture. "I am concerned, chiefly, with its entire upbringing, which I now place in your capable hands."

"With respect, my lady," Fargu suggests, "there may be hands more capable than mine. I have brought up no children of my own. I would gladly teach him to hunt when he's of age. That is where my true skill lies." The huntsman's eyes gleam slightly at the thought of his first love.

"You will do that and more," she replies. "To walk, to ride, and to hunt. You will see to its education as well. It ought to be trained in history, literature, language, agriculture, and politics. Hire tutors if you must, but make them keep quiet. No one is to know of the child's existence who is not absolutely necessary. See that it grows strong in body and mind."

"I see," Fargu says. His face remains expressionless, but Watho knows he is none too pleased to find himself an unexpected parent. "Will that be all, my lady?"

Before she can answer, there is another timid knock at the door. Watho turns as a pretty young maid curtseys in.

"This," she says, gesturing to the maid, "is the child's nurse-maid, Lucy. She will stay on until you no longer require assistance."

She smiles grimly at Fargu's apparent relief.

"One more thing." She pauses, to be sure that the two servants properly understand the weight of her final command and sees them exchange a brief glance.

"The child is absolutely never to see darkness."

At last, Fargu looks thoroughly startled. Lucy, already acquainted with this strange rule, gives him a sympathetic look.

"My lady?" Fargu asks.

"Look at it!" Watho points to the baby, who is lying on his back in the gleaming light, trying to stuff his toes into his mouth. She already feels the glow of exultation, though her experiment is in its early stages. "It flourishes in the sunlight and in the sunlight it shall stay. The lamps in this room will be lit before sunset and stay lit while it sleeps, lest it wake in the dark. When the child gets older and begins to go out on the plains with the huntsmen, it must return here before sunset. Dress it in bright colors and give it bright toys to play with. If so much as a dark shadow falls upon it, I will know." She turns sharply on the two servants so they cannot miss the danger in her eyes. "Have I made myself clear?"

"Clear as day," Fargu says, a little too boldly for Watho's taste. Her eyes narrow, but she says nothing.

"See to it."

She sweeps from the room, leaving baby Aethon, his startled new guardian, and his nursemaid to themselves.

Falca smiles as she walks into the dark tavern. She looks around at the worn furniture and greasy patrons with real pleasure that is impervious to the vaguely threatening looks they give her in return.

Falca's visits to Harthwaite are infrequent, especially in the months since the baby's birth. The village is a two-day ride from the castle and Watho had resisted allowing Falca to be gone from the baby's side so long, but Falca had insisted that if she was to raise a little girl, she would need more resources than the castle could afford. Eventually Watho had relented, allowing Falca the occasional visit to the Cirice of Dael, a temple charity, to acquire old toys, clothes, and other necessities.

She is under strict orders to go about her business and return home at once, but the farther Falca gets from Astarsaga Castle, the more the spell of her mistress loosens its grip. She is not a poetic woman and cannot give words to the feeling of lifted oppression — does not even try — she knows only that in town she is easily prone to small acts of rebellion, like visiting a tavern before returning home.

Falca orders beer and a pork pie from the tavern's proprietor, a girl who could not be older than 20 and looks as though she would be far more comfortable in a library than an alehouse. Falca likes the girl at once. She has a rebellious lift to her chin and the other patrons seem to regard her with respect.

When the food arrives, Falca begins to understand why. Even in the castle kitchens she's never seen such a perfect pork pie and the aroma overpowers the scents of sour sweat her fellow travelers have brought with them.

Falca glances up at the girl's retreating back just in time to see a tall man duck through the tavern door and look around as she herself did a few moments ago. She smiles broadly and waves to catch his attention. Fargu grins back at her and makes his way to her table where he sits across from her and immediately helps himself to a portion of the pie.

"Get your own, lout!" Falca laughs, attempting to bat his hands away. Fargu laughs too and Falca sees her own relief reflected in his face.

Like her, Fargu is bound to Watho's service by magic. The details may be different than her own — *was it a carrot or was it a stick?* — but the contract is, nonetheless, ironclad. In Falca's own case, it had been a carrot. She was desperate for work when Watho found her; put away without recommendation by the noble family who employed her, accused of theft. Practically a death sentence for a lady's maid.

She smiles bitterly at the memory. She did not commit the crime her mistress had accused her of, but she was guilty of drawing his lordship's eye a little too frequently. When Lady Watho offered her a place at Astarsaga Castle, Falca had needed little persuasion to sign the magical agreement requiring her loyalty on pain of death. After all, she had reasoned, if she didn't sign she would starve to death anyway.

"I didn't think to find *you* here," Fargu says, leaning forward with a conspiratorial air. They know they can speak more freely here than anywhere on castle grounds but one can never be too careful.

"I hear congratulations are in order. Is it true?"

Falca raises her eyebrows. "Is what true?"

"They *say*," Fargu answers with an eyebrow waggle of his own, "that you recently acquired a bouncing baby girl. And that our illustrious mistress keeps the both of you locked away in the crypts without so much as a window to let air in."

Falca suddenly feels tired again. "Aye. It's true. You're looking at the proud nursemaid of the night girl." She raises her beer as if to toast. "These aging eyes see the daylight so rarely I nearly forgot what it was like."

Fargu smiles ruefully. "I wouldn't trade mine for yours."

"What, your eyes?"

Fargu's eyebrows arch again, this time in real surprise. "You didn't know? You're not the only one in the castle who's come into possession of an infant."

"*What?*" she says a little too loudly, before glancing around nervously.

"I've got one too." Fargu seems to be enjoying her shock. "A little golden child. He lives in the balcony rooms and the mistress won't let him see a hint of darkness. You know I love the sun as much as any man could, but I *pray* for the moment he goes to sleep and I can slip out into the night."

Falca is, for the first time in recent memory, too surprised to speak. Fargu takes advantage of the silence to order another pork pie, having put a significant dent in Falca's.

"I don't understand," Falca says at last, "what she's playing at."

Fargu shrugs. "I know better by now than to ask. You should see the way she looks at the child though. Like she created it with her own two hands. She *studies* him."

"Really? She hardly ever sees the girl. Sometimes I wonder if she even remembers that the two of us exist." Falca can't decide whether to be envious or thankful that Fargu's ward occupies so much of their mistress' attention.

"What's his name?"

"Aethon. He seems like a smart lad, too. Lucy — that's the nursemaid that helps me with him, since I don't know the first thing about babies — Lucy says he's too fearless."

"Lucy, eh?" Falca grins. "I know her. Sweet girl. Pretty too."

Fargu ignores this, but Falca notes the faint color that rises in his cheeks.

"What's yours called?"

"Luna."

"Fitting."

Falca shrugs. "Not really. You'd think she'd be called something darker, wouldn't you? Not named after the moon."

"Why's that?"

"Well," Falca pauses. She has never given the topic much thought before, but as she gives voice to her questions, Falca realizes it has vaguely bothered her. "You say the boy... Aethon is it? The boy isn't to see so much as a dark shadow, yes? The instructions for the girl are just the opposite. She's never to see daylight at all, nor much light of any other kind. She's allowed a single lamp because it's impossible for either of us to live completely in the dark, but I think if we could do it, we'd be made to."

"So?"

"So, why should she be called by the name of the moon? Oughtn't she to be called 'Dark Cloud' or 'Shadow'?"

Fargu looks thoughtful. "I suppose," he says slowly, "that it depends on the purpose of the experiment."

"Have you any idea what that might be? I can't think of a single thing."

"Nor I."

"Anyway, she's a troublesome little thing," Falca says

without conviction. "Squalls at all hours of the night. She'll be the death of me and you can mark my words."

After another moment of silence, Fargu asks, "Have you considered leaving?"

"What, leaving the mistress' service? Who hasn't?" Falca lowers her voice as she utters the treacherous sentiment. "You know it's impossible. You've seen what happens to those who try."

"I know," Fargu nods. "It's just... it doesn't feel right. These little ones have mothers somewhere."

Falca looks down at her beer, avoiding his uncomfortable gaze. Vesper's final, pained cry rings in her ears. "We can't do them any good if we're dead."

"I suppose not."

"Anyway," Falca adds after a moment's pause. "I feel a duty to the child now. Heaven knows I didn't ask for a squirming little moon girl. But seeing as I have her now. I shudder to think what might happen to her if I weren't there."

"I know what you mean," Fargu says and she can see that he does.

A few minutes later, they pay their bill and set off together for the castle. Falca's eyes briefly connect with the narrow-eyed gaze of the young tavern mistress as they go and her heart gives a small lurch. How much had she heard?

The girl glances away quickly.

Falca looks back at Fargu, who has stopped walking and is staring at her curiously.

"It's nothing." She smiles, hoping her words are true.

# CHAPTER THREE

"*Please* Falca!"

The little girl clasps her hands together, her wide, imploring eyes searching for any weakness in her guardian.

"Isn't it enough that I read to you every day, against the express wishes of my mistress?" Falca demands. "Or have you no concern for your old governess?"

Luna remains unmoved.

"But Lady Watho hardly ever comes to visit! And anyway, we always have a warning when she does. I hear her footsteps coming from just over *there*." She points at the tapestry which Falca knows conceals the door leading to her own and Watho's quarters. The revelation is a startling one. The door itself is shielded by a spell that prevents the child from noticing either Falca or Watho's entrance and up to this point it had never occurred to Falca that the child might hear them.

"You're too clever for your own good already," Falca laughs. "You'll have hard work before you if you intend to persuade me you ought to be cleverer still."

"Just think!" Luna says, trying a new tack. "If I could read the stories myself, my 'cessant questions wouldn't be the death of you."

"Oh, yes they would. Only you'd store them up to hurl at me all at once instead of interrupting me every third word to ask them."

"I could read to *you* so you could rest your eyes! Aren't you always complaining that your eyes are too weak to read?"

Falca has known since the beginning of the discussion that she will be conquered.

*The poor little moon sprite*, she thinks. *A child isn't meant to be shut up in such a place as this.*

She doesn't remember when Luna became a little moon sprite in her mind. It may have been because of her name, or perhaps because of the way she becomes enraptured by the lamp from time to time.

This love of the lamp worries Falca. She still has no guess what her mistress' intentions are by shutting the child up in the dark, but she has no desire to be blamed should the witch's plans fail. Watho means for the child to know only darkness, but the presence of the lamp in the room seems to be teaching Luna more about light than about the dark.

Falca does what she can to keep Luna occupied with games and music, though Watho has forbidden any education beyond that.

Still, in the nine years since Luna became her charge, Falca has grown to feel affection for her, precocious little thing that she is and cannot bear to see her languish from lack of stimulation.

Luna is petite and seems frail to Falca. Her skin is dark like her mother's but has nonetheless an unhealthy pallor from lack of sunlight. Her dark hair hangs long and thick around her soft face, from which those disconcerting blue eyes sparkle and rarely blink.

When, some time ago, she exhausted her own creativity and found that Luna was still restless, Falca began to sneak books from her own library into the little cave and read them quietly to her.

She is terrified of being caught at this, but comforts herself with the knowledge that Luna has no frame of reference by which to understand what she hears and will be thus unable to repeat it. Luna loves the gentle cadence of her guardian's voice reading ballads and romances that are far beyond her young comprehension.

The girl frequently interrupts to ask questions, but Falca only answers those that she feels are harmless enough, such as what is meant by terms like "spindle" and "horse".

She has wondered from time to time if Luna doesn't retain much more than Falca gives her credit for, but what can an old woman do with a restless little girl locked up in a castle?

She considers that Luna's last point is her most compelling. Unlike Luna, whose vision is like a cat's, Falca's eyes have grown weaker from her years in the dark. Reading in the dim lamplight strains them and she frequently goes to bed with a headache.

"Oh very well," she relents. Luna squeals endearingly and claps her little hands.

"But," Falca cautions her, "not right away. If you're going to learn to read, we must start you on the right books. Certainly none of mine will do."

Luna's face registers disappointment for only a fraction of a second before she favors Falca with her most winning smile. *She knows*, Falca thinks, *the power of her own sweetness on an old woman.*

"Oh thank you Falca, *thank you!*" Luna cries and performs an impromptu little dance that draws a smile from Falca's lips.

～

"WHAT'S WRONG? MY LADY?"

The alarm in Violet's voice shakes Aurora from her daze.

"What?" She turns to her lady's maid with a tired smile. "No, I'm fine. I just... I thought I saw something."

*What did I see?*

Aurora hadn't particularly felt like walking in the garden today, but Violet had insisted and as usual, Violet turned out to be right. The warm sun, fresh air and exercise had been doing wonders for Aurora's mood. Until she saw the creature by the gate.

*Or was it a man?*

She shakes her head slightly as if to clarify the image in her mind. The girl she once was — known for the constant laughter in her eyes — now feels like a stranger and she passes most days in a fog.

Back in her own manor, an imposing edifice whose ornaments are expensive and impersonal, her mind still daily wanders back to Astarsaga Castle, where the last remnant of untainted joy and her first taste of grief had met and kissed.

As Watho had predicted, she had borne a son at midday. The unforgiving sun had streamed into the windows, filling every space and for the first time since her arrival, Aurora had longed for a reprieve from the unwavering brightness, but her requests for curtains to be drawn had gone unheeded.

Aurora remembers every moment of her lying-in as if it is distilled in time and nine years later her questioning heart still gently probes at the memory, looking for answers that will not come.

Her labor had gone smoothly from start to finish. She felt no hint of urgency, no wrongness in her body's responses from the first tightening of her belly to the final push. The midwives' oils brought comfort from the pain and their soothing voices stilled her mind. She laughed between contractions. She gloried in the sound of the first tiny breath she heard her newborn son draw.

Then, everything changed.

That breath was the only one she heard. She saw Watho's face loom over her own, brows knit with concern.

*What's wrong?*

*Where's my baby?*

The midwives gently hushed her but did not meet her eyes. One of them rushed from the room with the little one swaddled in her arms. Watho stroked Aurora's brow and murmured gently. She persuaded Aurora to take a little wine to ease the pain and almost at once, Aurora drifted off into a troubled sleep.

The earl had been furious.

She had turned to him for comfort despite the newness of their acquaintance, as her husband and the father of her son. Her letter to him expressed hesitant vulnerability, an invitation to share her grief and to find solace in each other. She received no reply. When at last they stood face to face, his was cold, unyielding. She searched his eyes for some answer to her own grief but saw only seething rage behind them. It frightened her.

The earl never once spoke of their son and never allowed her to do so in his presence. He did not inquire about her health or her heart. She felt the punishment in his silent fury and her shame nearly suffocated her. Perhaps, after all, it *had* been her fault. She ought never to have traveled so far during her pregnancy. She ought to have objected to Lady Watho's sleeping draughts. Perhaps it was the excess of sunlight. Whatever the cause, her husband had blamed her for the child's death and her own aching heart had accepted the verdict.

Three days after his return, the earl visited her chamber and informed her, in a tone as impersonal as the manor, that she would bear him another son. They were the only words he spoke to her before leaving her room twenty minutes later, having approached his task with detached efficiency.

When her second son was born, healthy and red and squalling, she found she had still not earned her husband's approbation.

The child was beautiful and full of life. His giggles and dimpled fingers brought Aurora endless joy and helped heal her bruised heart. Her reprieve, however, was short-lived. When Hugh, named for his father, was five years old, the earl announced that he would begin his formal education. Impervious to the pleas of the child's mother, the earl hired a tutor and a governess of his own choosing, allowing Aurora to see her son only occasionally and rarely alone. Hugh grew up worshipping his father and mimicking him with all the vigor of childhood, much to his mother's alarm.

When he turned eight, Hugh was sent to apprentice with one of the king's knights, a thoroughly unpleasant man whose acquaintance the earl made during the war.

Bereaved a second time, his mother retreated into herself until she was rarely seen outside her own quarters, where Violet, her lady's maid, was her only companion. The one mercy in which she has found solace is that, having acquired the son he demanded, her husband's visits are rare and brief.

Aurora has never been prone to despair by nature, though it has been so often forced upon her since the exuberance of her youth. She began her alliance with the earl as a hopeful girl, certain she could turn their marriage into one of love. The intervening years have taught her otherwise. Now, she hopes only to survive with some of herself intact.

She devotes her time to charitable work, attending the beds of the sick when she is able and working with the Sentras — clergywomen who manage the Cirice — to distribute food to the poor. Violet is her constant companion and a quiet voice of comfort. They outwardly maintain the appearance of servant and mistress only for the sake of the earl, who places great stock in hierarchy.

The two of them spend many afternoons wandering the gardens, talking, reading to each other, or walking in amiable silence. A moment ago, they had been deep in conversation about the stratification of social order — with Violet siding with the controversial Sage Einarsson, and Aurora taking the more traditional view — when Aurora had stopped short with a startled look toward the garden gate.

Turning to follow her mistress' gaze, Violet saw only the rows of hyacinth, hemera and proud larkspur lining the empty walking paths. Dimly, Aurora is aware of her quizzical look, but she still stares into the distance, trying to make sense of whatever arrested her attention.

For a fraction of a second, Aurora thought she saw an enormous man (*or had it been a beast?*) watching her from the garden gate.

She shakes her head again, casting a final glance toward the empty paths before taking Violet's elbow and resuming their walk.

"It was nothing," she reassures her friend again. "Just a movement in the corner of my eye. My nerves are playing tricks on me."

She laughs and Violet smiles in response, but a dark foreboding she has not felt in nine years closes vice-like around her chest.

# CHAPTER FOUR

"*H*is name is Fiain," Aethon says. It is an observation, not a decree.

Fargu's eyebrows arch. "The wildest of the spirits. Are you certain that's a good idea?"

Aethon casts an appraising eye at the pony, which lowers its head to meet his gaze with unmistakable challenge.

He's leaning back against the fence, having rushed out to meet the pony the second he was released from lessons. Aethon's lessons in the sun room consume the better part of the day and by the time he is allowed to put down his books and abandon his recitations, he is always champing at the bit, much as the animal before him does now.

"I don't think it *was* my idea."

This elicits a laugh from Fargu. "I suppose if there's anyone that could commune with such a beast, it's you."

Fiain is the latest in a string of ponies with whom Aethon has been paired. Each time he makes himself a creature's master, it is retired and replaced with one larger, more stubborn, and more unwieldy than its predecessor.

Aethon considers this process of conquering each new steed and meeting its successor one of the chief joys of his 9-year-old life. He can see that Fargu is mildly alarmed at the speed with which he masters each new pony, but cannot understand why he should be.

Fiain has a dangerous glint to his eye, as if he is itching to face his would-be rider in the arena. The pony is lean and strong, gleaming white like all the others before him and full of pent up power. Aethon knows the pony would trample him with no hesitation, given the opportunity and at once feels a surge of fellow feeling for it.

The pony shakes his head furiously and rears, while Fargu braces his feet to keep his grip on the lead rope.

Aethon laughs and brushes unruly blonde curls out of his eyes. His guardian has begun teaching him the principles of hunting, but Aethon is not yet allowed to accompany the hunters out onto the plains – that will have to wait until he has broken his first full-sized horse. Fargu has promised him that on that day, he will be welcomed into the hunting party with open arms and Aethon has set his face like flint toward that objective.

He often watches the hunts through a spyglass from his room and he can feel the violent chase pulsing in his blood, calling to him as the men ride out to meet their quarry. This latest untamed pony is merely the next obstacle to be overcome so that he might be allowed to join them.

"May I take him now?" Aethon asks, reaching for the lead. Fargu smiles and holds it out of his reach.

"Tsk. You know better."

Aethon does know better. The routine is always the same. He meets the new animal in the afternoon and is allowed only to observe it from the pasture fence for the first day or two, learning its habits. Before he begins to work with a pony he should be able to describe its temperament with alacrity — whether it demonstrates aggression when unprovoked, or only in response to the threat of being mounted, how it responds to being called, if it's easily spooked, and whether it prefers oats or alfalfa.

The limitation rankles.

"But *why*?" Aethon demands, crossing his arms over his small chest and stamping his foot. "I'm ready *now*!"

"Then you'll be more than ready when you've gone through the steps," Fargu says without looking away from the creature in question.

"But it isn't *fair*!" This is not the first time Fargu's immovable boundaries have stoked Aethon's sense of injustice. He can see no reason for the rule to exist, much less for his teacher's insistence on such rigid adherence.

Reaching into his shallow arsenal of retorts, Aethon seizes upon a favorite entreaty of Lucy's toward himself.

"Why must you be so stubborn?"

Fargu only snorts. Of all Fargu's shortcomings, Aethon finds his habit of laughing off his righteous anger the most intolerable. His mounting frustration is only seconds from boiling over into outright fury, when the pony rears violently in an attempt to cast off the bonds of its own oppression.

Aethon watches with keen interest as Fargu wrestles the enraged creature, his own indignation giving way to excitement once again.

"Someday you'll meet a beast that you can't bear to be patient with any more than I can," he tells his teacher when the pony has been subdued.

"I've been acquainted with many a beast in my day and have yet to encounter such a one."

Fargu leads the pony, bucking and writhing in protest, through the pasture gate and Aethon closes it behind them and fastens the lock. He watches as Fargu grips the lead rope, pulling the outraged Fiain's head down, unties the halter, and narrowly escapes a kick to the wrist as the animal twists away from him and tears across the pasture, shaking his mane and snorting.

Aethon feels such communion with the beast that for a moment he feels the wind blowing through his own mane. He laughs again, his anger forgotten, and launches himself over the fence to stand beside Fargu.

"This one won't take me long," he says.

Fargu's brow furrows. "No," he says after a moment. "I don't suppose it will. You have the same look in your eye that the beast has in his."

Aethon recalls some years ago overhearing his tutor, Master Cardaisseau, telling Lucy that he had sunlight in his veins. He had at first imagined that 'veins' had something to do with his hair and for weeks had not allowed Lucy to touch it, for fear she might comb the sunlight out.

After a particularly explosive row which found Lucy laughing through tears at the end and saying "you little goose, your veins are *inside* you!" the matter had become moderately clearer.

He nods sagely and says, "He must have sunlight in his veins, like me."

He is gratified when Fargu, sounding mildly surprised, replies, "Well that's quite a way to put it. He just might."

AETHON IS LEANING over the balcony, a spyglass clutched in his small fist, by which Watho knows it must be a hunt day. The boy is so still, one might think he is lying in wait for prey himself.

He is tall for his age and lithe, with sun-kissed skin and a thatch of wild hair that sticks out in all directions. He has dimples when he smiles and his dark eyes sparkle with adventure and good humor.

Watho watches him approvingly as he draws in a sharp breath to mark the instant the hunter's spear strikes its target. When he turns at last to face her, there is naked thirst on his face — as if he wishes to drink the sun, the plains, the conqueror, and the slain in one draught.

"Are you so anxious to shed blood, then little one?" she asks with some amusement.

The scornful expression that crosses his boyish features is so comical that Watho bites her tongue to keep from laughing.

"The hunter's aim is not the kill," he recites what she feels sure are Fargu's words. "It's to meet a worthy opponent and look him in the eye."

"Is that so?" she lowers herself gracefully into a chair and motions for him to come near. "Is the hunt over? I'll watch it with you."

"They've killed a buffalo," the child declares exuberantly, handing her the spyglass.

Raising it to her eye, she scans the plains, searching for her huntsmen and their quarry. "Have they indeed. And what makes the buffalo such a worthy foe?"

"He's a mighty warrior! The height of a man, the weight of ten men, and just as brave."

"I see."

Watho hands the spyglass back to him as a servant appears bearing a tray of peach juice, candied almonds, and cheese, her young ward's favorite repast. Aethon runs back to the railing to watch the hunters again.

"Then it's the beast's strength and courage you respect."

"Well it wouldn't be much fun to chase a cowardly, gentle animal," Aethon says.

Watho nods again. She is glad to see Aethon beginning to look on weakness with contempt.

*You are either predator or prey,* her father used to say.

"But you will be the strongest of all the beasts, is that it?" she probes.

Aethon flexes his arms comically and grins. "I will be as strong as the sun, racing across the heavens!" he proclaims.

"Have some cheese, mightiest of hunters," Watho laughs.

Aethon makes his way to the table in a series of somersaults. He is always bursting with energy, for which he can find little outlet when he is not with Fargu or the ponies.

"How are you progressing with your new pony?" Watho hands him the promised cheese.

Aethon's eyes flash. "Brilliantly. He's tried to buck me off, smash me against the fence, and trample me. Nearly succeeded too!"

"But you feel yourself to be nearly his master?"

Aethon's grin is almost predatory. "Oh yes."

Watho smiles at Aethon's confidence, in such sharp contrast to his childlike mannerisms as he wriggles in the chair.

"Perhaps it's time you had a real horse. What would you say about that?"

Aethon beams. "Oh *please* say you mean it!"

"Don't beg," Watho says sharply. "Women and children beg. Men do not."

Aethon puffs out his small chest, affronted. "I *didn't*!" he protests.

"You did. You'll have your horse when I can be confident you are a man. Men ride horses. Little boys beg for them."

She feels a twinge of regret at the boy's deflated countenance, but quells it. Mercy annoys her as much in herself as in others. Her father would never have stood for such childishness.

"If you wish to prove your worthiness to me, I wouldn't start by pouting," she snaps.

Aethon is seething. "I'm not a child and I'm *not* a woman," he shouts. "I *am* ready for the horse and I shall prove it."

*Good.* She had, for a moment, thought he might cry in his disappointment. Anger she can forgive, but never tears.

She responds with a single sharp nod. "Very well. I look forward to your doing so."

"Watho?" Aethon asks after a moment and she sees that the indignation has drained from his countenance, his mind having moved past humiliation to curiosity with the alacrity of youth. "Do you ever beg for anything?"

"Certainly not!"

"But you said that women and children do it," he says, looking at her with such innocently wide eyes that she knows he means no insult. A proud smile lifts the corners of her mouth.

"I am fortunate to be immune to many of the curses of my sex," she tells him. "I am a powerful witch, after all."

Aethon only looks thoughtful. "Lucy never begs either," he says matter-of-factly.

Watho looks at him sharply, searching for intentional defiance in his comparing her to a servant. Finding none, she recomposes her face into a gracious smile.

"You know," she says, "a man who believes himself ready to hunt on horseback is not much in need of a nursemaid. I think it's high time you learn to do without one."

Aethon's eyes widen in horror and this time real tears begin to well up in them, until Watho fixes him with a look so contemptuous that he blinks them rapidly away.

"You wanted to prove to me that you are ready for your horse, didn't you?" she asks. Aethon straightens his shoulders.

"I am. You'll see," he says and Watho is pleased to hear no trembling in his voice.

"ENTER!" Watho barks.

Instantly, she's annoyed with herself. She does not make it a habit to shout at her servants, finding that there are more dignified means of striking fear into their hearts. Shouts and open threats are the tools of the fearful. However much her father despised weakness, he so often let his temper get the better of him that remaining in firm control of her own emotions has become a point of pride for Watho.

Today, however, she is in a bad humor. Felnys has been gone for days, without a word as usual. She knows that he will not return until the fancy strikes him and that he will not be forthcoming about where he has gone.

The only thing Watho finds more intolerable than not

knowing where he's been is the indignity of trying to make him tell her. Worse, she has begun to develop fearsome headaches when he is gone too long, one of which is threatening to descend on her now.

She is sitting behind the ornate desk in her office, where she has been trying to modify some of her more advanced spells and finding herself completely unable to focus.

The door opens to reveal Fargu, looking as impassive as ever.

"What do you want?" she demands.

A flash of uncertainty crosses his face and is gone. "I was told I had been called for, your ladyship. The messenger must have got it wrong." He bows slightly and turns to go.

Watho is surprised to feel grateful at his attempt to let her save face. She had, in fact, called for him and almost immediately forgotten.

"That's alright, come in," she says more gently. "I have been wanting to talk to you. Tell me how Aethon is progressing with the pony."

Fargu looks as if he is trying to choose his words carefully. "He is attempting to break the beast with even more than his usual enthusiasm, my lady."

This amuses Watho. "And why do you think that is, Fargu?"

"He is bound and determined to prove himself ready for a hunting horse. I worry that he might be just a little *too* fearless, though. He could do himself harm in his quest to prove himself a man."

Watho dismisses this with a wave. "Have I not given him a competent guardian? I have no fear of harm coming to him while he's in *your* care, Fargu." She sees the distress in his eyes at this and allows herself a small, private smile. Can it be that she's created a creature that frightens even the unflappable Fargu?

"As you say, my lady." He accompanies the concession with a submissive bow.

"I've decided to send Lucy away," Watho says abruptly. "It was only my own weakness that allowed the boy to be coddled by a nursemaid for so long. He has no use for her now."

By Fargu's unchanged expression, she guesses that Aethon has already warned him of this eventuality.

"She's been a great help to me, my lady, especially on hunt days. Pardon the impertinence but might you be induced to reconsider?"

"Certainly not," Watho says. "A boy who is ready for a horse is in no need of a nursemaid. I made this decision days ago and have only delayed its execution so that the child may say his farewells."

She returns to her spell book, signaling the matter closed.

"Yes, my lady. Er... when you say that she is to be sent away... may I be so bold as to ask where she's to be sent?"

"What does that matter to you?" Watho glances back up at him in some surprise.

"Well it's only this, my lady. Lucy and I have been caring for the boy together for quite a few years, as you yourself know and we've gotten to be quite good friends." He pauses and Watho motions impatiently. *Get to the point.*

"That is, not friends, as such... the truth is, my lady, I've asked Lucy to marry me and she's accepted."

Watho is amused to find that the idea of her servants becoming friends with and marrying one another has never once crossed her mind. For one brief second she is tempted to thwart their happiness for no other reason than that she can. She has, however, little taste for cruelty for its own sake and will still have need of Fargu's service for some time to come.

"Very well," she says. "If you're expecting congratulations for having procured the favor of a servant girl, I'm afraid you'll be disappointed. Do what you wish with her, it matters not to me. Only she's not to see the boy again."

Fargu clears his throat.

"She's very fond of him, my lady. Might she see him from time to time, even..."

Watho cuts him off with a cold stare. "Is it not enough to presume upon me to continue housing a servant of whom I have no more need so that you may enjoy domestic bliss, Fargu? Must I also seek your approval in the raising of my own child?"

Duly chastened, Fargu bows again. "No my lady. To be sure, I'm more grateful than I can say."

"Get the boy his horse," Watho says by way of dismissal. "The best that can be bought."

# CHAPTER FIVE

*A*lyvia does not have time for a kitten. She hardly has time to manage a bustling tavern and care for her ill mother. The little black shadow that keeps appearing on the tavern's back step, however, does not seem to be concerned with her schedule. He first appeared a few days ago, a pitiable little creature, underfed and bedraggled.

In a moment of compassion, Alyvia put out a bowl of warm broth for the tiny visitor and she's been unable to rid herself of him since.

She has always had a soft spot for strays, of both the human and animal variety. Her reputation for kindness to the former, along with her legendary cooking skills, has earned her tavern a respect afforded to few other establishments in the district.

She is thinking about the kitten as she ladles spiced rabbit stew into bowls. If only she had the time to attend to it. She wants to leave some stew on the step for him, but that will only encourage him.

"Tell me you are making pork pie tonight," says a gruff female voice behind her.

"You're not at your mother's house and I don't take requests," Alyvia says with a wide grin, turning to greet the patron.

Falca only visits the tavern once a year or so, but Alyvia is always pleased to see her. The woman first dropped in nine years ago with a brawny, good looking man she now knows to be Fargu.

The conversation between the two had smacked of mystery from the start — she considers eavesdropping to be a perk of tavern proprietorship — and the tidbits that she was able to pick up over the clamor had only increased her curiosity.

After their departure, she'd made what inquiries she could and discovered little more than far-fetched rumors: the two were fugitives who would kill anyone who found out too much, they were members of a secretive cult, they were magically indentured to a reclusive witch. Even with her considerable network of sources, she never found anyone who knew either of them personally.

She didn't see either again until a year later, when Falca came in seeking rest and sustenance before continuing whatever journey she was on. Alyvia quickly struck up a conversation with her and found the woman to be an eager interlocutor – it seemed the poor thing had little opportunity for real conversation in her regular life.

Still, try as she might, she could draw nothing like substantive information from her. In the intervening years, Falca has made it a point to visit the tavern when she comes to town, sometimes bringing Fargu with her and the three have become friends, in a manner of speaking. She never has found out anything about them, but they are both intelligent, cheerful, and eager to hear about the goings on in the kingdom at large. Alyvia has come to love these unexpected appearances.

"I think you'll find this does you quite as well as pork pie, or better," she says, pushing a bowl of stew across the counter.

"There's little from your kitchen that wouldn't," Falca rejoins. "Have you time for a jaw?"

"If you can wait just a bit I will," Alyvia says.

Twenty minutes later, she lowers herself with a sigh of pleasure into a chair opposite Falca.

"How's the stew?" she asks.

"Gone," replies Falca, who is now cradling a pint of beer and looking entirely satisfied.

Alyvia smiles. She knows her own skill, but still derives great satisfaction from the fruits of her labor being properly enjoyed.

"I thought it was about time for a visit from you. What brings you to town this time?"

Falca's deft avoidance of this question has become something of a joke between them, so she is thoroughly surprised when Falca answers, "I need a favor, actually. From someone... er... discreet."

"Discretion is the tavern mistress' highest virtue," Alyvia says. "What can I do?"

"I need a few children's books."

If the woman had requested a dancing bear, Alyvia would not have been more mystified. "What for?"

"For a child, obviously."

"Is it for *your* child? I'm sure the Sentras have some."

Falca is shaking her head before Alyvia has finished speaking. "I can't go to the Sentras. I need someone who has no connection to my employer."

"Your employer?" At last, Alyvia is learning something of Falca's mysterious life and still, none of it makes any sense.

"Yes, my employer. The Sentras will tell her and I can't have that."

"*Her?* It's true then? About the witch?"

Falca glances around nervously and looks as if she regrets having said anything. "If you can't get them…"

"I can! And I won't tell a soul, I swear it. What kind of children's books? How many? How old is the child?"

"She's nine," Falca says in a low voice. Her eyes are sharp with fear. "But she doesn't know how to read. I intend to teach her."

Alyvia's heart is racing now. *Nine?* Then whatever brought Falca and Fargu to the tavern the first time must have been connected to this mysterious child.

"Hm," she says. "I'm no authority on children, but I may be able to find something. Let me think," she taps her bottom lip as she considers. "How long will you be in town?"

"I can stay only one night," Falca says, looking more nervous than ever.

"Ah, mysterious demands and no time in which to meet them," laughs Alyvia. "Stay at the inn tonight and I'll meet you tomorrow morning with anything I can find."

"Bless you!" Falca cries, her face glad with relief.

ALYVIA IS as good as her word.

The next morning she arrives at the inn and proudly presents two little books full of fables, proverbs and poems, both of which once belonged to the tavern mistress herself.

Before the lady's maid takes her leave, Alyvia reaches into her satchel and surprises Falca very much by producing from it a small, confused, wriggling animal.

"What's that for?" Falca demands.

Alyvia looks sheepish. "I thought the little girl might like it. If she's in need of company. It's been hanging around the pub looking for scraps the last week or two."

"I can't bring home a kitten!" Falca exclaims. "My mistress would have me pickled and served for dinner."

Alyvia shrugs and nearly has the poor creature stuffed back into the satchel when Falca stops her.

*After all*, she thinks, *Watho may have already forgotten the girl for all the attention she gives her. And the poor little moon sprite could use something to talk to.*

"Give it here," she sighs.

Falca used to believe that Watho had some magical means by which she could see anywhere in the castle she chose, but after her time reading to Luna in their little tomb, she's concluded that her mistress either can't see them or doesn't care to.

When Falca presents the kitten to Luna, her small face glows with delight.

During the trip home, she had begun to worry that the child might be frightened. Luna has, after all, never met an animal of any kind and only knows of them from the murals on her walls. She needn't have worried. The child's ecstasy is so great that the new books lay nearly forgotten on the table for days while Luna and her new companion become acquainted.

Together, Falca and Luna decide to call him Nox.

"He is the color of my eyes just before sleep," Luna says,

holding him up in both hands, with her delicate nose touching his whiskered face.

"Your eyes are blue, moon sprite," Falca corrects her.

"But I don't *see* blue with them," Luna explains. "I see what the lamp shows me, until I close them and then I see only blackness until I begin to dream."

"I see what you mean," Falca nods. "He resembles the darkness itself. Mayhap even my mistress would be pleased with him."

"Master Aethon, please sit up straight."

Master Cardaisseau's nasal voice intrudes jarringly on Aethon's private thoughts. He is slumped over in his chair, tuning out the droning intonation of his tutor's lecture on the inherent hierarchies found in nature.

Since Lucy's dismissal, Aethon's lessons have felt even more unbearable than they were before, now there is no prospect of a cheerful playmate waiting for him at their end. To make matters worse, it has rained for the entire week she has been gone, leaving him confined to the indoors.

If he could spend his time on horseback in the sun with Fargu and Fiain, the afternoons might be more tolerable, but as it is, the world is bleak in his eyes. He is forbidden from trespassing the bounds of his own wing of the castle and so must wander between his chambers, the sunroom, and the library where there is precious little to arrest his attention.

The unnaturally bright light in these rooms does not bother him at night, or when the sunlight is streaming in through the windows, but against the steady syncopation of the rain on glass, invisible behind a wall of thick, white drapes, the light feels abrasive.

He scowls and straightens his posture against the uncomfortable chair back.

"What did I say just now?" Master Cardaisseau asks, a frequent test he administers to determine whether Aethon is attending.

"That colo'zation is a natural process seen in flora and fauna," he mutters, though he hasn't the foggiest notion what the words mean.

"Colonization. Very good." Master Cardaisseau gives him a hard look, then sighs. "I suppose that's all I'm going to get out of you today."

To Aethon's relief, he begins to gather up his papers and books, signaling the lesson's close.

Master Cardaisseau seems as discomfited by the gloomy weather as Aethon is. The tutor is constantly squinting as if the lights irritate his eyes and has been uncharacteristically anxious to end the day's work.

After he leaves, however, Aethon finds his mood much unchanged. If Lucy were here, the two of them would play a game of buncles in the library, or run laps the length of the room, or curl up by the fire and read adventure stories while eating warm brie on toast and drinking spiced tea.

Without her, none of these activities hold any appeal.

So far, Aethon has successfully held his tears at bay when he thinks of her, Watho's admonition constantly at the front of his thoughts. He has become convinced that the longer he misses her the longer it will be until he can have a full-sized horse and be allowed to join the huntsmen. Thus, he has told himself repeatedly, he does not miss her, because he is not a baby anymore.

"Where is Fargu?" he demands aloud of the silent room. "It's not as if *he* can go out in the rain either. He could at least come to visit me."

This neglect on the part of his other guardian suddenly seems monstrously unjust. Hot tears spring to his eyes as if they've been hiding just around the corner, waiting for the chance to strike. Ashamed, Aethon looks around wildly for some other outlet for his feelings and his eyes settle on a crystal vase that sits atop the hearth. It is full of bright citrine blossoms, which seem insultingly cheerful in the face of Aethon's misery. Before he fully knows what he is doing he has seized the vase and hurled it across the room. It shatters against the opposing wall with a satisfying crash, leaving a wet splash across the bright white paint and damp yellow blossoms scattered among the shards on the floor.

This has such a marvelous effect on his mood that he at once seeks out another object to try it on, this time a bright white clay pot with golden edges that adorns the center of a nearby table.

The more items he finds to break, the more frenzied he becomes, until at last he collapses on his bed and finds that the sadness he sought to subdue has only been delayed. The tears have waited patiently for his outburst to spend itself and now that it is over, they flow freely, dampening his pillow and the golden curls around his face.

By the time he hears the footsteps of the chambermaids in the hall, he has sobbed until his head feels thick and he wants nothing more than to drift off to sleep.

~

Aurora feels hands gripping her shoulder, shaking her.

For one muddled moment she thinks her husband must have come to pay an unexpected visit and groans. He rarely calls, but when the mood strikes him, he does not allow the fact of her being already asleep to deter him.

"Aurora." The voice is gentle, concerned. Not the earl, then. Slowly she blinks her eyes open and sees Violet's worried face inches from her own. "You were dreaming," she says.

Aurora groans again and sits up as bits of the dream seep back into her consciousness.

"I'm sorry. I didn't mean to wake you."

"You didn't?" Violet asks with a sardonic arch of her eyebrows. "I assumed you were pretending to be stalked by dream monsters so as to rob me of my own sleep."

"It's too early for wit. I won't have it," Aurora says. "If you have no mercy for my fears, at least be decent and pour some wine."

"Gladly." Violet bounds across the room with far more energy than Aurora approves of anyone having in the middle of the night. "What was it you were so frightened of?"

Aurora suppresses a shudder. "I think it was a wolf."

"Bless me. Only a wolf? From the way you shouted and writhed, it ought at least to have been a dragon."

"It seemed more fearsome than a dragon at the time. It was the greatest wolf you can imagine. Enormous and brown, with streaks of red running through its coat like blood."

"And it wanted to harm you?"

"I'm not sure what it wanted. It was standing perfectly still, just watching me. Its eyes were black as night. No, that's not right. Black as a... I don't know, as a great, gaping nothingness."

"What a way you have with words," Violet chuckles,

handing her mistress a goblet of spiced wine and ducking a poorly aimed projectile pillow. "This ought to calm your nerves."

Aurora lets out a gentle laugh at her own foolishness, but says nothing.

"Anyway," Violet continues with a wry smile, "There aren't any wolves in the city. Excepting your dear husband of course."

"Hush!" Aurora whispers, wide-eyed. "Someone might hear you!"

She knows there is little chance of that — and she enjoys the bold irreverence with which Violet expresses her feelings about the earl, even if it does make her nervous from time to time — but welcomes the opportunity to change the subject. Violet is right that the dream doesn't sound like much cause for alarm now that she is awake and the lamps are lit, but she is unsettled all the same.

In the following weeks, the wolf and its baleful eyes revisit her in her waking hours more often than she cares to admit.

LUNA LAYS the book down on the floor beside her with a sigh of pleasure. She has read through it a dozen times already, stopping to linger over words and phrases, to turn them over in her mind again and again, drinking prose like nectar, savoring every new word.

She is lying on her back with her feet in the air, heels resting against the back of a chair – a position Falca finds comical and Nox confusing.

It has been three months since the best of all days — the day her beloved Falca presented her with the books and kitten.

The tiny, soft creature brought her so much endless delight in its first few days that she nearly forgot about the books in her fascination.

Once Falca started teaching her to read, however, it took her no time at all to remember the letters and understand how to put them together. Falca seems delighted at the speed of her progress. The real trouble now comes with *understanding* the stories, bursting as they are with the names of things she has never seen and cannot even imagine.

The story she's just finished is about a wily fox who made a bargain with the sun. The first time she read it, Luna asked Falca a great many questions afterward, many of which remained unanswered. Falca's halting description of a fox left her with only the foggiest picture of a somewhat comical creature whose tail is not at all like Nox's. The sun, on the other hand, she understands better.

"It's exactly like the lamp," Falca told her. "Perfectly round and hung overhead so that people can see what's around them."

*Why not just call it the lamp then?* Luna had thought to herself at the time. She has, however, come to understand, both from the paintings on the walls and from bits of things Falca says from time to time, that a great many people's lives are very different from her own.

*I suppose*, she tells herself now, ruminating on the story once again, *that people might have different words for the same things in different places.*

She looks at Nox and wonders if there is anywhere in the world that he might be called something other than a cat.

"It's even possible," she tells him, "that somewhere, you are a fox."

The kitten ignores this conjecture, preferring to search the thick rug for a beetle he recently found and quickly lost.

"Your tail is not very bushy," Luna observes. "And Falca said that a fox's tail is unaccountably bushy and his snout is long. But you are only a baby! Who knows whether your snout and tail will not grow as you get older. And you," she says, turning her attention toward the lamp, "Are somewhere called the sun! How do you like that?"

The lamp glows warmly, but offers no other response.

"I like it too," Luna says. "It has a nice, yellow feel to it."

She has recently begun assigning colors to things when she does not know how to say what she feels about them. It feels nice to have a word to fill in blank spaces in her mind and using colors makes her thoughts feel rich and bright, like the paintings. When she plays the harp in the corner of the room, the music is sometimes yellow too and sometimes purple and very occasionally orange. What she draws depends on whether she's feeling turquoise or deep blue.

"Are you talking to the lamp?" Falca's voice asks.

Luna squeals, startled. "You're *too* quiet Falca!" she reproaches her governess.

"Or you're too inattentive," Falca says, an unusual edge to her voice. She stands looming over Luna where she lies on the floor. "If you must talk to someone, talk to the cat. Not the lamp."

Luna can hardly see the old woman's face, silhouetted as it is in the lamp light. "Why *shouldn't* I talk to the lamp?" she demands. "You talk to your wine, you know."

This draws an astonished bark of laughter. "Of all the impertinent little wraiths," Falca says, but Luna can tell she isn't really angry.

"I was only telling it about the places in the world where it's called the sun."

Falca is quiet for a moment. Luna sits up, sensing her tension. The woman's face is creased in concern.

After a moment, she says, "Listen to me, moon sprite. You mustn't ever mention the sun, to... well, to anyone. Do you understand?"

"Why not?" Like many of Falca's commands, this one is baffling. "I only ever talk to you and Lady Watho."

"It doesn't matter why not. Don't talk about it to anyone. Not to me, not to the lamp, and most importantly *not* to my mistress. In fact, don't mention anything you read in the books, or the books themselves."

Luna has heard a hint of fear in Falca's voice once or twice before at the mention of Lady Watho. She rarely sees the lady herself – has not seen her, in fact, for nearly a year – and sometimes forgets that Falca is not the only other person in the world.

The lady's maid seems more frightened now than Luna remembers seeing her in the past, by which she guesses that Watho would not approve of the books, or of the lamp.

"Alright, Falca," she says, smiling to ease her friend's fear. "I'll tell Nox not to say anything either."

Falca still looks nervous. "Actually, love, it's best if Nox is out of sight, should her ladyship pay a visit."

Luna does not hear this last piece of advice, however.

"Falca!" she cries. "He's caught the beetle!"

# CHAPTER SIX

*A*ethon's heart is still racing when he reigns Thunderstone in, sliding easily out of the saddle before the magnificent white horse has fully stopped. Resting his hand on Thunderstone's neck, he feels the horse's excitement, the same pulsing of hot blood in its veins as in his own.

The other hunters greet him with a cheer, slapping him on the back, tousling his hair, passing him around their circle like a shared drink.

Aethon is laughing, glorying in their praise. He has just killed his first buffalo. He can still feel the surge of raw strength that welled up in him a few moments ago as he rode alongside the enormous beast, the hooves of its companions like drum beats in his ears, raised his spear over his head and thrust downward with all his might.

A clean, precise thrust. The animal's legs crumpled under it as the spear punctured its lung. The herd split and thundered on, leaving their fallen comrade and its conqueror in their wake. The other hunters' roars of approval were lost in the rush of adrenaline as he turned Thunderstone's head in a tight circle, rounding back to where his defeated foe lay in a heap of muscle and mane.

He feels Fargu's strong hand grip his shoulder warmly, though he can barely see through the sweat dripping into his eyes.

"Well done, lad!" The huntsman is shouting. "Well done indeed and two years earlier than my first."

Fargu had warned him about the strength and speed of the buffalo, the fearsome horns, and how quickly it could gore a man to death, but Aethon had felt no fear, even in the midst of the stampeding brutes. In the seconds before his victory, time had seemed to slow and a fierce, joyful calm settled on him as he picked out the bull from the herd and spurred Thunderstone toward it. He felt the breeze, the warmth of the sun on his shoulders, the rush of the herd, the tensing of his muscles, but still no fear. Certainly he recognized the danger, but could not make himself feel more than an intellectual respect for it. Either he, or his foe would win the day, he had reasoned. That he had come out the victor seemed no more or less just to him than if it had gone the other way.

It has been five years since Fiain the pony was replaced by Thunderstone, an enormous destrier, whom Aethon took much longer to master than any of his predecessors. Thunderstone is significantly larger than most of his breed and dwarfs the coursers the other hunters ride, but he is no less nimble and can match any horse for speed. Fargu chose him for his unmatched size, swiftness and spirit, seeing that no regular hunting horse would satisfy Aethon, or please his mistress. Thunderstone, for his part, does not seem to mind his new occupation, finding Aethon as capable a master as any knight and the two have become such fast friends that each seems to predict the other's movements.

Aethon extracts himself from the congratulations of the hunting party and takes the horse's face in his hands, leaning his still childish brow against Thunderstone's white forehead. The horse lowers his head, responding to his young master's touch and snorts gently.

"We did it, boy," Aethon whispers. "Well done."

The rest of the castle staff are as elated as the hunting party. Aethon is a great favorite among the servants, who always feel as though they've been knocked over by a fresh wind after encountering him, despite the turbulent rages that often come upon him.

Wagers have been placed regarding the age at which the boy will achieve his first victory on the hunting grounds, but as those who bet on an early kill far outnumbered those who guessed a later age, hardly anyone makes any money on the buffalo's death. Still, they celebrate the occasion with a lavish late afternoon feast, at which Lady Watho gives an enthusiastic toast.

As always, the white curtains are drawn across the windows and the lamps lit well before sunset. Aethon, tired as he always is from his daily exertions, drinks his evening wine with gusto and is soon afterward fast asleep in the blazing lamplight.

"Don't be irreverent, Violet," says Aurora, laughing.

"Irreverent! Hardly," Violet scoffs. "It isn't the Spirits themselves I object to, it's the ridiculous little men in their ridiculous little vestments, pretending to speak on their behalf."

Aurora looks dutifully scandalized, but more from habit than any real disagreement. The two of them have been to the temple to hear the sermon and complete the ceremonial rites and are now walking toward the city gardens, where they will spend a leisurely afternoon.

Sir Hugh rigidly insists on the household's twice weekly attendance at temple services, as do nearly all the members of the royal court and their families, but he cares little for the conversation of others and so always returns home immediately afterward. It is with some disapproval that he allows Aurora and Violet their afternoon walks when the services end, on the condition that they go only to the gardens before returning straight home — though why, Aurora cannot imagine, since he far prefers the company of other women to hers. She suspects he simply likes to remind her who she belongs to.

Aurora bristles at the fact of the limitation — even after fourteen years of marriage, she has to stifle her natural inclination to resist being told what to do — yet she would not choose to go anywhere else, were the choice hers to make.

She loves the city gardens, with their winding paths and many secluded alcoves, each harboring young lovers, philosophers, poets, and painters seated on flower-strewn benches and stretched out on grassy hills. She never feels more at home anywhere than with the garden's many strangers. She and Violet rarely speak to any of them, having been forbidden by Sir Hugh from doing so, but she feels a kinship with them all the same.

As they stroll arm in arm, Violet opines just a little too loudly that the sermon was, in her estimation, a plate of cat droppings with cream sauce.

"I know it's the orthodox position, but if you can tell me

where any of the holy texts actually *say* such things, I'll eat the earl's underthings for supper," she says.

Aurora giggles. Violet's radical theories appeal to her more than she liked to admit, but feels duty-bound to offer up resistance when Violet appears to be shrugging off time-honored doctrines like overworn tunics. "The holy sentries have preached it for thousands of years!" she protests. "Surely all the spirits haven't kept silent all that time because they were waiting for a lady's maid from Harthwaite to set them right."

She winces as soon as the words have left her mouth, but if Violet notices the unintentional jab, she gives no sign of it. She is not, so far as Aurora can tell, the least bit tempted to see her own social status as having any bearing on her right to have opinions.

"I don't know what you mean by 'kept silent'" Violet retorts. "They said what they meant to begin with, when the sacred texts were written. It's not *their* fault if people go around preaching the opposite things."

"But for centuries?"

"Why not? Isn't that how tradition works? Especially when the Sentries inherit their position by blood lineage," Violet says. "In fact I'd wager that at least half of orthodox doctrine is little more than family tradition... like... like the way my mother cooks curried lamb."

Aurora thinks she ought to look shocked again, since Violet derives a great deal of pleasure from poking at her religious sensibilities, but a movement in her peripheral vision distracts her. As she turns toward it, all thoughts of Violet's heresies vanish from her mind.

"My lady?" Violet adopts the more deferential tone she uses only in public. Aurora realizes she has stopped walking abruptly and must have forced Violet to halt too, as her hand still rests in the crook of her friend's arm. She must think the earl is somewhere around.

Aurora shakes her head, slightly, dazed.

"What is it?" Violet's voice is lower now and she is looking back and forth from Aurora's face to the empty street corner at which she is inexplicably staring.

"Nothing," Aurora says and forces a chuckle. "Nothing at all. I thought I saw someone I knew, that's all."

"Who? Was it the earl? Is he spying on us again?" Aurora should have known the other woman was not to be brushed off so easily.

"It's really nothing," she says, sincerely. "Tell me your scandalous theories. Quickly now, or the religious ladies will overhear and we'll both be excommunicated."

There is very little that Aurora does not confide in her friend and she now feels slightly guilty for the lie. She simply cannot bring herself to say out loud what would have sounded ludicrous even to her own ears — that she had glimpsed across the street, the shape of an enormous auburn wolf and it had caused her heart to go cold. Each time she's seen him in her dreams, his coat has been streaked with a more vibrant red. There's no mistaking his identity, however, for the look in his eyes — so sinister and cold — is as familiar as Violet's smile.

*Perhaps*, she thinks, *I really am losing my mind.*

LUNA PUTS her pencil down and examines her drawing with satisfaction. She has practiced drawing for nearly a year and her skill has increased considerably. Most days, she takes as much unashamed pleasure in her own artwork as in the paintings and engravings she finds in books.

Only the faces trouble her. Try as she might, Luna has never been able to draw a face she liked. They always lack some quality that she can't quite articulate. Even when drawn with perfect technical accuracy, they look to her blurry, undefined.

"As if there was no lamp inside them," she said once to Nox, but the cat did not appear to take her meaning.

As a result and nearly without realizing it, Luna has begun to draw people who nearly always face away from her, or are visible only in profile. She keeps them in a wooden box on her desk and occasionally takes them all out to look at, laid gently side by side on the floor — a hundred carefully hatched and blended women and children, their faces turned in toward the depths of their paper world.

Luna frowns slightly at her newest drawing. The woman in it has dark, flowing hair, like her own, and is glancing back toward Luna so that only her forehead, eyelashes and cheek are visible. Her face is sculpted and regal, but there is no expression in her eyes. She stands alone in a large room with heavy shadows in its corners. A globe at the top of the page appears to cast a wide, soft circle of light, into which peek bits of furniture, each half-submerged in darkness. The arm of an opulent couch, the end of a settee, one leg of a writing table. The woman herself stands on the edge of the circle, poised to step into it.

Perhaps it is this, Luna reflects, that makes her backward glance seem somehow sad.

The room, like most of the rooms her characters inhabit, bears a striking resemblance to her own. Though no two of her drawings are exactly alike, she finds that her pencil can never stray too far from some version of her own living space.

She lives in a large room that is wider than it is tall. The walls are hung with rich tapestries and curtains, but it is the vivid murals painted between these that Luna likes best — scenes of ancient battles, of prayers, of kings and queens, knights and peasants, of unknown gods — all vibrant as the day they were painted, despite their great age. She loves these and studies them intently, though they make little sense to her. They give her a gold feeling; pleasant and warm. Luna has many times tried to draw inspiration from the murals for her own drawings. She wonders from time to time, when there was ever a world so richly peopled that it could inspire such art.

*Or perhaps*, she sometimes thinks admiringly, *the artists' world was much like mine and this is only how she imagined that it could be. After all, whoever created these paintings must have lived here too.*

She thinks the artist must have been very clever to imagine so many baffling scenes, when Luna herself can only seem to produce variations of her own life. Luna has never seen any place outside her living quarters, but such places must exist. After all, Falca is not always here, nor is Watho.

It's not that she's *un*happy. She fills her time with music, poetry, and drawing. Nox, who has grown sleek and long, is a pleasant companion and he always listens to her thoughts with patience. Still, the books and the paintings fill her with a longing to know what lies beyond the walls of her little world.

"I wish," she says to Nox with a sigh, "that I had more room."

The cat looks at her inquiringly.

"What do you mean, by wondering what I mean?" she asks, casting a reproachful glance in his direction. "How should *I* know?" When he says nothing, which is his habit, she adds, "It's just that I feel sometimes there must be many more things to draw than I know about."

Nox lays his head back down on his paws, which Luna takes to mean he understands.

She places the drawing tenderly into the box with its companions, before lying down on the soft carpet to admire the lamp that hangs in the middle of the room. Nox is accustomed to this and jumps at once onto her stomach, where he curls up, waiting for her hand to rest gently on his head. Luna spends her most peaceful hours admiring the lamp, which is her chief treasure in the room.

This habit of hers worries Falca. Luna senses this, but cannot understand why. As far as she can gather, Falca harbors some fear that the lamp might abandon its station. She heard Falca say one day under her breath, "God help us if the lamp ever goes out while she's awake," a sentiment which Luna could make very little sense of.

She knows that Falca herself often goes out of the room and comes back. Did she mean that the lamp could do the same? Surely not! She eventually concluded that the lamp must leave, as Falca does, while she sleeps, being sure to return before she wakes in order to do its duty to light the room.

This thought only increases her infatuation with it.

*Where does it go? What does it do when it's out? Does it sleep, as Falca and I do?*

She has asked it these questions on more than one occasion, but the lamp silently guards its secrets. Despite her curiosity, Luna rarely mentions the lamp when Falca comes to visit. She thinks that, perhaps, the old woman dislikes the light and while the thought of being even for a moment without it grieves her, she does not wish to displease her dearest friend (excepting Nox of course).

When Falca is absent, however, as she is for long stretches of the day, Luna basks in the lamp's warm glow with unrestrained pleasure. *There must be a way*, she often thinks, *to unlock its voice and learn the many mysteries it must know. For how can the source of all light do anything but illuminate?*

CHAPTER SEVEN

*W*hen Violet enters Aurora's room, she is surprised to find her already awake. Aurora has been sleeping more since little Hugh went away and Violet often has to convince her to get out of bed.

Today, however, Violet finds her standing motionless by the window, a light blanket wrapped around her shoulders.

"Aurora?" she ventures after a pause.

As her friend turns, Violet understands. Aurora is pale and her eyes are swollen; she isn't awake early, she hasn't slept at all.

Violet sets down the breakfast tray she is carrying and goes to the other woman's side, wrapping her arms around her waist as Aurora's head comes to rest on her shoulder.

"You look absolutely awful. What's the matter?"

She half expects a joke — *I just woke up and my best friend came to tell me how terrible I look.* This is how the two of them have learned to navigate life as the property of the earl. Aurora doesn't have any humor in her today.

"I saw him again in my dreams."

"The baby?" Violet knows her mistress has dreamed of her

lost son numerous times in the last seventeen years, always just out of reach, being carried away by a faceless midwife. Not for the first time, she feels a deep swell of anger towards the servants who had not allowed her friend to say goodbye to her child. Aurora shakes her head.

"No... well, yes. The baby was there too. But I mean the wolf."

Violet searches her memories, confused. "What wolf? I don't know of any wolf."

Aurora sighs. "I didn't tell you because it sounded so... foolish. Like the ridiculous women in stories that men write, always given to fainting and imagined frights. But I've been seeing it for years. An enormous wolf, red as the setting sun."

A faint memory stirs in the back of Violet's mind — another scene from this room, only Aurora was writhing in her sleep, battling some unseen villain. "I remember you dreamed of a creature with streaks of blood in its fur once."

Aurora detaches herself from Violet's arms to pull the blanket tighter around her. She looks away, sheepish.

"That wasn't the first time and certainly not the last. He's plagued my dreams for a long time."

A pause, as she gazes out the window as if searching the horizon for unseen enemies.

"Not only my dreams, either," she adds in a low voice.

Violet studies her, looking for some clue to her meaning. "What do you mean, not only your dreams?"

Another sigh. "You'll think I'm mad if I tell you."

"I think you're mad for *not* telling me. Besides, what's a little lunacy between friends?"

Aurora finally smiles, but faintly. "I see him in my waking

hours too. At the garden gate. On a street corner. In the back of the temple. Peeking from the windows of strange houses."

"Yet I never find you like this, looking as if he'd drunk your sleep and your soul together with cream before taking his leave."

She half expects Aurora to burst into tears, but instead a look of resolve settles on her face. "You know what his color reminds me of?"

Violet nods. "Blood. Streaked through its fur, I think you said."

Aurora shakes her head. "No, that's not it. At least not just that. It's red like a woman's hair. Like Lady Watho's hair."

Violet finds herself at a loss for words; a rare condition, which she does not enjoy.

Aurora turns suddenly, as if she expects an argument. "I *know* it's mad," she begins. "That's why I've brushed it off all these years, but last night left me with a feeling I can't seem to shake. There's something to it, Violet. I went to that wretched woman's castle, I lost my son and for seventeen years, I've been haunted by a wolf with hair like hers." She begins to pace the room in her agitation. "Oh, what you must think of me! I'm raving."

"I wonder what you must think of *me* to be so afraid all this time and not tell me."

Aurora pauses in her frantic pacing and smiles tenderly at her friend. "It's not you I doubt, but myself."

It *does* sound mad, but the look in Aurora's eyes is not the look of a lunatic.

"Well," Violet says thoughtfully. "Imagine you could trust yourself fully on this point. Put aside, for the moment, any fear that you might be a mad woman. I saw your resolve a moment ago. What had you decided to do?"

"Go back to Astarsaga Castle," Aurora says without hesitation. "I don't know why. I don't know what I hope to learn. But the mistress of that place must have some answer and I intend to know what it is."

Violet nods. "Very well. How do you propose to pull it off, when his lordship scarcely allows you to take a walk in town without his leave?"

Aurora's smile has a bitter twist to it this time. "His *lordship* will be visiting his uncle the week after next. You and I can make it to Astarsaga Castle and back before he returns."

"What of Sebastian?"

They both know that while Aurora is ostensibly the earl's proxy in his absence, it is Hugh's steward, the faithful and frightening Sebastian, who truly holds the reins. He is careful to watch over his master's interests — which includes careful monitoring of the countess' movements.

"I was hoping you'd help me with that," Aurora says. "If he catches wind of our plans he'll stop us of course, but that isn't the problem. We can find a way to sneak away. The problem is keeping him from discovering our absence once we are gone."

"Erm... yes, well spotted," Violet laughs. "You have precisely identified the problem. It does seem to be of the 'impossible to solve' variety, unfortunately."

"Not impossible!" The color has returned to Aurora's face now that she has given voice to her thoughts. "It's just that everything seems impossible before breakfast and ours is getting cold."

∼

IN THE END, absconding is simple. Aurora's seventeen years of apparent submission to her husband's commands are enough, it seems, to give even the hawk-eyed steward little cause to suspect her of duplicity. When, two days after the earl's departure, Violet lets it be known among the staff that her mistress is ill, Sebastian accepts it without question, likely counting himself lucky to be relieved of one duty at least.

Violet enjoys favor among the servants that neither the master of the house nor his steward share, making it an easy task to recruit a maid or two to bring food and water to Aurora's suite, report that her condition remains unchanged, and keep the other servants away.

After that, the only trouble is getting outside the manor grounds and even that problem turns out to be easily solved. Violet has a cousin in town to whom she pays a discreet visit and returns with the news that arrangements have been made for a coach to wait for them a few blocks away and carry them to Astarsaga Castle.

As the planned escape draws near, Aurora grows, to her surprise, even more resolved. She had been afraid her nerve would break at the last moment, but now her act of rebellion has been set into motion, she feels a sense of peace that has evaded her for years.

When the night arrives, the two women wait in tense silence for the household noises to fade. It is nearly 2 in the morning before they ease the door open and tip-toe down the hall. Both their hearts nearly stop when Aurora, fumbling with the lock on the back door, knocks a pitcher over with her elbow, causing a crash that seems to reverberate for miles. They hold their breath, frozen in wide-eyed terror, but miraculously, no one stirs. Aurora closes her eyes and takes a shaky breath, willing her heartbeat to return to normal. Finally, painstakingly, they make their way out through the back gardens and find the promised coach.

Two days later they are still inside it, swiftly nearing the castle. The coach clatters over rough forest roads, jarring its occupants considerably and Aurora wonders privately how she had managed to make this journey during her pregnancy.

*Perhaps the roads have not been kept. It has been nearly two decades after all.*

The thought carries with it a pang of uncertainty. What is she hoping to find? No one at court has heard anything of Lady Watho for years. She may not even be alive. And what if she is? She had told Aurora, with kindness in her dark eyes, that the baby did not survive. There had been no reason to disbelieve her then, so why now? What does she intend to say? That she had dreamed of a wolf with red hair? She suddenly feels unspeakably foolish.

"Violet," she says, turning from the coach window to look at her friend. Despite two days of traveling, Violet looks nearly as fresh-faced and cheerful as ever. Her dark hair is arranged in a plait down her back, over a comfortable grey cloak and soft green gown. She has been silently engrossed in a book for the last few hours, but looks up now with a smile.

"Hm?"

Aurora doesn't know what to say. *I'm sorry if I'm actually insane?* "I don't know what we'll find. If anything."

Violet laughs. "You said that already. Twice."

Aurora sighs. "I know, it's just..."

Her friend's face softens. "Aurora. I've known you for nearly twenty years. You have never given me reason to doubt your sanity. I see no reason to start now."

Aurora wishes she could be as confident in herself as Violet seems to be.

As she tries to form a response in her mind, however, she becomes aware of a low rumbling sound coming from every direction. She realizes it has been swelling for the last few moments, masked partially by the rattle of the carriage and the noise of the horses.

Suddenly, it has become almost deafening, punctuated by loud cracks, as though tree trunks are beginning to fracture all around them. Aurora feels the coach sway as the horses shy and tries to brace herself against the back of her seat. Through the window she sees the earth rolling toward them like a wave on the sea, before some invisible force slams into the coach's side, nearly tipping it over.

The two passengers scream and cling to the window braces as it leans heavily to one side and then settles once more onto its four wheels.

In the few seconds of calm that follow, Aurora hears only the shouted curses of the driver and the terrified screams of the horses. She has just enough time to hope the quake has passed before a second wave speeds toward them. The earth ripples underneath the carriage and tosses it into the air, as though an invisible dog was grasping the coach in its mouth and shaking it violently. It begins to come apart at the seams, twisted by a giant unseen hand.

Her head cracks painfully against the coach's roof. It's all she can do to grasp her seat until the carriage slams back into the ground with bone-jarring force, splintering all around her.

∽

Watho and Felnys stroll through the gardens, inspecting the troops of flowers and climbing ivy as they go. Felnys has not disappeared without explanation recently, which puts Watho in such a good humor that the eye she casts on the myriad flowers is unusually forgiving. The gardeners, she knows, are watching apprehensively from various shadowed corners and must be relieved to see her in such spirits.

She examines the lumebuds closely to be sure they do not crowd one another and the morgunn to ensure the blossoms will turn their faces east at dawn and west at dusk. Touching each bud or blossom gently, she mutters spells over them in such a soft voice, that anyone watching might mistake her attentiveness for love. Most of the changes she works in the flowers are subtle, though some are more drastic. All are necessary. Everything must be made to grow exactly in accordance with its nature. Aberrations must be corrected or destroyed.

The spells leave her slightly breathless and she tries her best to ignore the whisper of alarm in the back of her mind at this. The use of magic is taking a greater toll on her than it did in her youth, the fatigue heavier after each expenditure, the recovery time longer. That even these small utterances over the flowers would thin the air in her lungs is worrisome.

"Your young man seems to be following the path you've mapped out for him precisely," Felnys remarks from where he watches her. "I hear there's no beast too mighty to be considered his prey."

She grins, glad for the distraction from her thoughts. "Are you hanging around the servant's hall listening from the shadows again? Really, I'd think chambermaids' gossip is beneath you."

When the wolf says nothing, she turns from her inspection

of the hemera blossoms and resumes walking. "Since you ask though, I'm quite pleased with his progress," she says. "The sunlight has made him strong and courageous, as I knew it would. Fargu told me recently that he bears more resemblance to a lightning bolt than a man."

She can feel the flush of pleasure as she speaks. To hear Fargu describe the boy's nearly reckless courage, a force she cultivated with her own hands, makes her uncharacteristically giddy.

Felnys chuckles, a sound that, to the uninitiated, is nearly impossible to differentiate from a growl. "And the girl? Does she progress as well?"

Watho sighs. "Do your informants not gossip about her as well, then? I suppose there's little to report."

"Ah," meaningfully says the wolf.

"She bores me," Watho says dismissively. "Dull little creature."

"Is she?" There's a note of mystery in his voice, but before she can ask what he means, he disappears ahead of her into the covered portion of the garden. A high wall surrounds this section and a makeshift roof has been fashioned from dark curtains, which will be removed in an hour or two, when night falls, to allow moonlight in. It is cool and quiet inside, the plants all sleeping, holding their breath. The scent of the various flowers mixed together in the enclosed space is cloying.

Felnys stops near the first flower bed inside to examine its inhabitants; tall stalks adorned with layer upon layer of deep purple star-shaped blossoms. Is it the light, Watho wonders, or has Felnys always had such vibrant coloring?

"Evensong, yes?"

Watho smirks. "Why the sudden interest in botany?"

"Why does it need to stay covered?" he asks, ignoring her question.

"The specimens in this section are too delicate for direct sunlight. They bloom best under the stars." She's pleased that he's taking an interest in her experiments.

The wolf makes a low guttural sound that Watho takes as acknowledgement. She turns to continue walking but he doesn't move to follow.

"This specimen specifically interests me," he says, when she turns to wait for him. "If I am correct, it was not always a night-blooming flower."

Watho hesitates, wondering where this unusual line of questioning is going. Felnys, she knows, is not prone to idle chatter and she dislikes attempts to guide her in conversation.

"It has bloomed at night for at least a thousand years," she says after a pause.

"A thousand years is significantly shorter than always."

"What of it?"

Felnys turns his enormous head slowly and gives her a significant look. "It's curious, don't you think?"

"What is?" Watho's good humor is beginning to dissipate.

"You have it planted here with the night flowers because it's too delicate to bloom during the day, but the way I understand it, evensong was once known by another name and used to grow on every hillside in the country. I find that interesting. I'm surprised you don't, as much as you enjoy understanding the way of things."

"I simply don't see any significance to the way its ancestors grew a thousand years ago. Everyone knows evensong grows best at night."

"That's just what I find curious," Felnys says, with a slightly unsettling smile. "Someone cultivated it until it could only bloom in specific circumstances, then declared that to be its natural state. I wonder why."

"Perhaps they saw what it was *meant* to be. Look at the coloring of its petals! It tells you its nature at first glance."

"One could argue that those exact colors can be better enjoyed in the light of day."

Watho turns and begins walking again, unnerved. "Say what you mean, Felnys. Your intrigues are tiresome."

"Intrigues?" he sounds amused. "I'm simply walking in the garden with my mistress."

Watho has often wondered at the way the wolf manages to sound the most threatening when his words are the most casual.

*In every pair, one of you wields all the power. Unless you are that one, you will always be under the power of another.* Her father had said it like an instruction, but it was a warning. A reminder of her role and his authority. Later, when he gave her to the Duke of Astarsaga, presenting her as a gift to a man of his choosing, the words had remained etched in her mind.

She doesn't answer Felnys. She refuses to be baited by him, as though they were equals.

After a moment of silence, the wolf stops again, this time with an unmistakable growl, hackles raised.

"Felnys? What is it?"

"I don't know, but I think you had better get to the tower, my lady."

WHEN THEY ARRIVE, the witch out of breath behind the

bounding wolf, Watho rushes to the telescope to see what threat has troubled him.

Perhaps because of his suspicious questions, she finds herself turning the dial first toward the basement rooms where Luna lives. Watho rarely visits these rooms either in person or from afar. She really has become unspeakably bored by the existence of the girl in them.

Luna is asleep already, though it's early in the evening. The time of day means less in the place she lives. Nearby on the writing table lies a paper and pencil; a half-finished drawing of a woman who bears such an uncanny resemblance to Vesper that it gives Watho a start. When did Luna develop such skill? How did her pencil reach back in time to re-cast the mother on whom she never once laid eyes with such perfect accuracy? Perhaps there is more to her than Watho has assumed.

The coiled presence of the wolf at her back prevents her from lingering too long on this scene. She turns the telescope outward toward the castle's miles of hunting ground, looking to see if some danger has befallen Aethon.

She can see him laughing with Fargu and the rest of the hunting party. Their day is drawing to a close and they are talking casually, tossing bits of meat from their latest prey to their hounds. No threat there, though they are out a little nearer sunset than she likes.

"What did you sense?" she demands.

"I don't know," the cold voice behind her says. "Something coming. Perhaps from Harthwaite."

After a moment or two more of adjusting dials and knobs, Watho finds what she is looking for. A black coach approaching and inside it a woman Watho knows all too well.

She steps back from the telescope and turns a cool gaze

toward Felnys. "Curious that Aurora would come here after all this time."

The wolf's mouth turns up in that unnerving smile again. "Strange what grief drives a mother to do."

"Felnys, what have you done?"

"I am always about my mistress' business."

"What mistress might that be? *I* certainly didn't ask you to bring that woman here and I won't thank you for it," Watho fumes. "I'll meet her and send her away."

"If it's not too late," the wolf purrs.

Watho's eyes narrow again. Peering once more through the telescope, she sees at once what he means. The hunting party is returning to the castle and the coach's trajectory seems to ensure the two will meet before either arrives.

"You know I dislike my hand being forced, Felnys," she says in a voice that would have frozen any of her human servants with fear.

The wolf appears untroubled, however. "Far be it from me to displease my mistress. I have only kept an eye on her, as I felt sure your ladyship would have wanted me to do."

"She would not have seen you had you not intended it," Watho snaps.

Felnys is quiet for a few seconds. "I think," he says at last, "that you stand always to lose him while she lives."

Rage, hot and sudden, begins to boil inside her at the wolf's hubris. He has maneuvered her into this position and worse, he is right.

She takes a deep breath and places her eye a third time to the telescope lens. With a concentrated effort, she channels her rising anger into power until she can feel the whirlwind of magic within her. She waits, allowing it to churn and build until it threatens to rip her body apart, then reaches her hand out in the direction of the forest, her arm making a motion like throwing a spear. As the power leaves her, Watho feels her body tremble and sag.

She watches through the lens as it slams into the ground in the forest, sending ripples out in all directions. Trees snap and the earth roils. The hunters' horses whinny and stamp, eyes wide with fear. Far across the hunting plains, a herd of buffalo is stirred from its grazing and stampedes to escape its unseen enemy. Inside the castle, the servants clutch tables and brace themselves against walls.

Watho is aware of all this only peripherally, her eye trained on the little black coach and its occupants, until the boiling earth reaches it, hurling it into the air and slamming it back into the earth, where it caves in on itself. The driver is thrown into a tree and lies motionless. The horses, their harnesses snapped, charge down the path, leaving the carriage to sit silent in its destruction. Watho can no longer see inside it, now that its frame has collapsed. She watches for a moment more, to be sure nothing is moving, before removing her shaking hand from the telescope and crumpling to the floor, exhausted and weak.

# CHAPTER EIGHT

$S$omething or someone is vigorously shaking the bed.

"Falca?" Luna mumbles, disoriented. The shaking intensifies. A deep rumbling noise seems to be coming from all directions. Somewhere in the room, something shatters and Luna sits up, her heart pounding.

For a few seconds, she has the unsettling feeling that she can't open her eyes. She reaches up instinctively to pry her heavy lids open, only to find that they are open already.

An old, familiar panic starts to rise.

The first time Luna remembers having this feeling, she was a child. She doesn't remember anything happening to trigger it — only the feeling itself, as though the world was suddenly constricting around her, collapsing into a space too small in which to breathe.

Her chest had tightened until her breath came in gasps. The more difficult it was to breathe, the more terrified she became, until Falca found her curled up on the floor, sobbing. After the first few times this had happened, Luna had learned to tell herself that the world was not ending, that there would be an end to the panic. She forces herself to take deep, long breaths and slowly release them.

Nox seems to know when these episodes are about to occur, for she always feels him close by, but not too close; a calming presence on which she can focus until the terror passes. He is close now, his small body pressing gently into the small of her back.

She can see nothing, even her hands moving in front of her face. Luna, who has never spent a waking moment without lamp-light, feels tears spring into her eyes. The rumbling and shaking has stopped. All is silent and dark — unspeakably, relentlessly dark.

*I am still asleep,* she tells herself. The thought eases her panic, slightly. *This is only a dream. I'm having a nightmare.*

As soon as she knows it's a dream, she knows she can control it. She needs to dream of lying down again, so that she can truly wake up to the world in which all is well and lamps shine as they ought to.

Slowly she lies down, concentrating on breathing in and out, until her breaths come more naturally, her heartbeat slows, and her eyelids grow heavy.

It is several hours before she wakes again. This time, it is Nox who wakes her, standing on her chest with his nose pressed against hers, mewing plaintively. She doesn't open her eyes right away. The visceral terror of the dream has passed and she revels in the soft warmth of the bed. She reaches a hand up to scratch the cat behind the ears, yawns, and opens her eyes.

Darkness.

This time, the panic comes swiftly, gripping her chest, the air raking at her lungs and escaping in shallow gasps. She sits bolt upright, staring wildly into the unyielding dark. Nox feels her fear and once again presses his body against hers, but this time it doesn't help.

*The lamp is really gone!*

Luna's vision is uncommonly good, according to Falca, but in this new, oppressive darkness, her eyes refuse to adjust. Strain as she might, she cannot differentiate any part of the enveloping shadow from the rest.

"Nox," she says, to break the silence and her voice comes out as a faint squeak. She clears her throat and tries again, more firmly. She has to speak, to make the world feel real. "Nox. Something has happened to the lamp. We have to think this through."

Nox, who is accustomed to being the silent audience to Luna's thoughts, waits patiently for her to continue.

The sound of her voice tamps down her fear a little. "If I can find the bell, I can ring for Falca," she says. The lady's maid doesn't always come right away when summoned, but at least Luna will have done something. "Falca will know what to do. She always knows. Oh, *what* could have happened?"

After a few minutes, when her breathing has nearly returned to normal, she begins to feel for the edge of the bed and ever so slowly to lower her feet until they touch the soft rug. She stands and reaches out with her arms instinctively to feel around her, but there is nothing near enough for her fingers to touch.

She takes a timid step forward and then another. In this manner she makes halting progress for a few more seconds until her foot jams painfully against something. Luna gasps and leans forward, feeling with her hands until she discovers the culprit; her writing table.

"Good," she says aloud, a little breathlessly, to Nox. "Now I have an idea where I am."

She closes her eyes and tries to visualize the room's various furnishings, laughing at herself for closing her eyes against the existing blackness.

Falteringly, she makes her way toward the place she hopes to find the bell connecting her room to Falca's. A good deal of the journey, however, involves walking through the open part of the room and she only makes it a few steps before she's entirely disoriented.

Something hard and sharp digs into the bottom of her foot, eliciting a cry of startled pain. She draws her foot back, searching her mental inventory of the room for what it might be. Nothing she can think of ought to be lying in the middle of the floor.

Nox winds himself around her ankle, giving her another start. She steadies herself, takes a breath and slowly kneels, groping blindly at the rug until her hands encounter the offending object. She explores its shape carefully with her fingers but it yields no clues about itself.

The object is small and gently curved, smooth on both the inner and outer surfaces, with sharp, ragged edges. Try as she might, Luna cannot associate it with anything in the furniture of her mind. Getting onto her hands and knees she runs her fingers through the rug in search of anything else that might be lying there and to her surprise finds another object, clearly made of the same material but significantly larger... then a third and a fourth.

After a moment, satisfied that she has found them all, she gathers the mysterious objects into her lap. She closes her eyes again. It feels foolish to do it, when the darkness is so thick already, but somehow it helps her concentrate. All the pieces seem to be part of the same whole, but she cannot guess what that might be.

Could Falca have come into her room while she slept? Perhaps she'd come to check on Luna and dropped something without realizing it.

"Or Watho, perhaps," Luna mutters. She hasn't seen the mistress of the house in some time and if Luna occasionally wishes for more frequent and varied company, she nonetheless finds herself more at ease in Watho's absence. Her mistress is always polite to her, if a bit stiff, but Luna finds the woman unsettling and is, if she is honest with herself, more than a little stung by her cold neglect.

The longer she considers the strange objects, the more certain Luna becomes that something terrible has happened in the room while she slept. Perhaps they had tried to wake her, to warn her. That must have been why the bed was shaken.

"No, that doesn't make sense," she answers her own thoughts. "There was no one there. I would have heard them. Falca would have said something."

While she thinks this through, she runs her fingers over the fragments in her lap, carefully, to avoid cutting herself on the sharp edges. She tries fitting the pieces together, but her fingers are maddeningly unfit to do the work of her eyes.

When at last, the broken object begins to take shape in her hands, she feels a cold dread settle in her spine. She sees at once what must have happened and feels foolish for not having understood sooner.

Something dreadful had come into her room and before leaving had killed her beloved lamp. For there is no doubt in

Luna's mind now; what lies shattered in her lap, cold and life-less, is the globe that was once full of golden light.

For a few scorching seconds, Luna feels as though all the air has been sucked from her lungs. The lamp is dead! The world, already so limited, has become smaller still; desperately, suffo-catingly small.

Luna closes her eyes again and takes a deep, careful breath. She sits perfectly still considering her predicament.

"Surely," she says after a moment, "Falca will not be able to abide this oppressive darkness any more than I can. Perhaps..." She pauses, afraid to give voice to her hope. "Perhaps, now that the lamp has gone, Falca will take me to the place she goes when she leaves me. There must be another lamp there."

As she says it, a new thought strikes her. She touches the cold shards of the broken lamp, considering.

Perhaps what she holds in her hands is only the room in which the lamp lived — like her own — and not the lamp itself. What if the lamp has gone out, as she has suspected it some-times does, while she slept? Perhaps it had not expected her to wake so soon.

"Or," she says, noticing that her voice is beginning to steady, "the shaking that woke me broke the walls of the lamp's room and it *had* to go out. It must have gone to where Falca and Watho go. Oh but doesn't it know how much I rely on it?"

As she says these last words, her voice began to shake again. Nox sidles up alongside her, offering what comfort he can and Luna strokes him absent-mindedly.

A new thought occurs to her, which fills her with equal parts trepidation and excitement. She must, she decides, go out as well. She must find where the lamp has gone and either persuade it to return, or stay with it in its new home.

Once she has settled on a course of action, she immediately begins to feel better. She carefully lays the broken pieces of the lamp's shell in a pile next to her and begins to crawl, one hand extended in front of her, until her hand makes contact with the table against which she earlier jammed her foot.

Using it to steady herself she stands, then feels her way around it, moving along its side, until her outstretched fingers touch the soft tapestry that hangs from the nearest wall.

It is in this general direction that Falca often seems to go, so Luna reasons it must provide a way for her own escape as well. Now that she has begun looking for it, she wonders why she has never done so before. After all, hasn't she been longing for her world to expand for years?

She lifts the tapestry and moves into the space it vacates, letting it settle again over the back of her head and shoulders. Her first ginger exploration of the wall behind the tapestry yields no insight into Falca's route out of the chamber. It seems to be a perfectly ordinary stone wall.

The panic returns, its claws sinking into her insides, but she forces herself to slow down. There is no doubt that Falca does in fact come and go, so there *must* be a path of some kind available to her as well. She runs her fingers along the stone again, slowly, searching for any fracture, while Nox amuses himself by batting at the tassels that hang from the tapestry at her heels.

"Not now, Nox!" she huffs, gently pushing the cat away with her foot. Not to be deterred, Nox returns immediately to toy with the tassels again. Sighing, Luna moves further into the space between the tapestry and the wall to avoid tripping over him, sliding her hands across the stone as she does.

She doesn't know exactly what she is searching for, but she knows at once when she finds it; a small seam in the stone, barely interrupting her progress as her fingers brush the wall. She quickly finds it again and follows it first downward, then up, until it makes a right angle a foot or two above her head.

A gentle press against the wall to the left of the seam is all it takes. The wall swings easily inward with a whisper and Luna feels the air shift in front of her. She is almost disappointed at how simple it is. All these years that she has longed for more room, it has never once occurred to her that she might follow her governess so easily.

Hesitantly, she steps forward into the steady darkness, holding both arms out in front of her. Nox follows with an uncertain squeak.

She shuffles along slowly at first, but after a few moments, dim outlines begin to take shape. She can see no source of light, but there must be one, for her eyes adjust to this new passageway as they refused to do in her own rooms. She moves forward with slightly more confidence for what feels like a very long time, until she comes to a long stairway. Luna has never seen stairs outside of pictures in books, but they are fairly self-explanatory. Still, the newness of it all stirs up feelings in her for which she has no words. Red feelings, shot with orange.

She climbs the stair for what seems like hours until she comes to the first landing. Here, she must make a choice; she can follow the stair, which continues to ascend before her, or turn off into one of the passages which extend in each direction.

Her first instinct is to follow the stair. She wants to be able to find her way easily back if necessary and she judges the straightest path to be the safest. When she peers down the passage to the right, however, her heart leaps. For while the stairway and the left-hand passage continue into more thick darkness, there seems to be a cool, dim light trickling into the right hand passage.

*This must be where her lamp has gone!*

Nox makes the decision for her, taking the turn without hesitation and running toward the pale light. She follows, nearly floating in her anticipation. At the end of the passage, there is another turn, and another stair, which she climbs, heart racing. By now she can see more clearly than she has ever been able to under her own sweet lamp. The light pours down the narrow stairwell from a glass pane set inside a door. Luna bounds up the stairs and has her hand to the latch in a heartbeat. To her great relief, she finds the door unlocked.

It swings open and Luna steps through it into a world like none she has ever imagined. She barely notices the feel of cool stone beneath her feet, nor the crispness of the air, full of scents both mild and sweet. There are sounds all around; gentle songs her ears cannot understand, but Luna takes none of these senses in, as her attention has been entirely arrested by what she sees. Above her, impossibly large and radiant, hangs the lamp.

For the second time that night, a cry of pain wells up in her. She had sought the lamp with the expectation of a joyous reunion but now that she sees it, she feels only grief. That the lamp had been forced for so long to contain all its glory in the cold, dead glass she held in her room seems an unspeakable injustice.

*Of course. No one killed the lamp. No one ever could. It only escaped its prison just as I have escaped mine.*

The thought startles her. She has never thought of her own room as a prison before, however much she has longed to know more of the world. Now that her mind has applied the word, however, she knows it to be true. She is and has always been a captive and so, apparently, has the lamp.

She stands still for she knows not how long, held captive by the splendor of the lamp, until her awareness begins to gradually expand, taking in the room in which it hangs. The air is colder than in her own rooms, but the coldness feels clean, alive even. In the far-off ceiling, tiny lights sparkle and wink, as though the lamp burst forth from the dark passage in such ecstasy that its light crystallized and scattered itself in sprays across the enormous roof.

Luna feels a gentle caress touch her face and bare arms, but cannot find its source. It picks up tendrils of hair and plays with them softly, lovingly. She feels no fear, only rapture. She has stumbled into the middle of a haunting song, to which her heart knows the melody.

After a few moments, Luna realizes that warm tears have been streaming down her face for some time, but cannot tell if they are tears of joy or grief. She knows the lamp can never again be imprisoned in its poor little shell in her room — cannot fathom how it was ever caught and contained to begin with. She grieves with it for all its years of captivity and rejoices to see it burning proudly with newfound freedom. It has become its true self and she will not ask it to stoop to its former beggarly service; cannot even stomach the thought.

*But what of me?* Luna thinks, feeling simultaneously selfish and aggrieved. She cannot imagine life without the lamp any more than she can imagine forcing it to return. The only solution she can think of is to escape herself, as the lamp has done.

Taking in her immediate surroundings at last, Luna sees at once that escape will not be as easy for her, not from here, at any rate. She stands on a wide stone platform, surrounded on three sides by a low wall. Beneath the wall, she sees the floor of this enormous room in the lamplight, but it is far below and looks hard and dangerous. There will be no escape from this place and she certainly cannot stay here. There is nowhere to sleep and she will have nothing to eat.

Sadly, Luna takes one last rapturous look at the lamp where it hangs.

"I will visit you again, if you'll have me," she says to it. If she can no longer live in its light, she will come as often as she can to see it. "Falca will wonder where I've gone and be alarmed."

Sighing heavily, she opens the door to begin her return journey. Nox seems as reluctant as she is to return to the dark castle and it takes a considerable amount of coaxing before he is persuaded to join her. When they come to the landing, she briefly considers following the stairs upward to see where they lead, but she feels unbearably tired and can see no purpose in exploring the darkness into which the higher stairs disappear.

Instead, she descends the long staircase she climbed before and follows the dark passage back to her own doorway, taking some comfort in the feeling of Nox weaving in and out around her ankles as she gropes in the dark.

Her room is as she left it; black and quiet. She calls for Falca, but no one answers.

With little else to do, Luna feels her way toward the bed and lies down again, the darkness lying heavy on her, folding over her like water. Drained of strength and tears alike, Luna drifts again into a troubled sleep.

∾

When she wakes the next time, it is to a sharp exclamation in Falca's voice.

"Luna!" the woman cries from somewhere in the all-consuming shadow.

Luna rubs her eyes, bleary from her sleepless night. "I'm here," she calls, though a yawn catches her voice and carries the last bit of the word away.

Falca's voice is thick with relief. "Where, child? What's happened?

Luna can hear the old woman bumping into things in her clumsy attempt to make her way across the room.

"Wait!" she cries. "The lamp has gone out and its shell is broken on the floor."

The rustle of movement ceases and Luna can feel the tension in the pause, the question mark. Falca is wondering how much she knows.

For the first time in her life, Luna feels a stab of resentment toward her guardian. Falca knows about the world outside. She knows the way out of this room, uses the secret door every day, yet she has kept Luna here, in lonely ignorance.

The resentment frightens her. Falca is her only human friend. The only being to whom she can speak and expect an answer. A kind face. If Falca is, somehow, her enemy, then she is alone.

Another, more charitable voice interrupts these fearful thoughts. Falca does not know about the lamp's true self — how it expanded, casting shards of itself across the ceiling as soon as it was given room to do so. As soon as it shed the dead glass of its own room. She doesn't know that Luna longs to do the same, should she ever find space enough. How could she? She came tonight expecting the lamp to be glowing in its usual place and is clearly terrified by its absence.

Perhaps before the shaking and the broken glass, the place outside the room was darker than the inside. Dark stairs and halls and a stone-enclosed platform under a terrible void. Maybe Falca has been keeping her safe under the lamp.

While she considers these things, Falca is making her way cautiously to where the glass lies fragmented on the rug.

Luna hears the rustle of her skirts, her feet shuffling heavily along, the muttered curse and enraged feline squeak that indicate a collision between woman and cat and finally, the dull clinking of the fragments being gathered up.

"It's alright, moon sprite," Falca's voice is soothing. Compassionate. "It must have been the earthquake. I ought to have come down here at once."

*Down here.* The phrase does not escape her. An offhand acknowledgement that Falca herself lives *up there*, that she can come at will from that other place, to which Luna is denied access.

"You must have been so frightened!" she is saying now.

Luna's shrug goes unseen. "It's alright."

She wants to reassure Falca, to explain that it was right for the lamp to escape and shine as it never can inside the glass. She wants to, but she doesn't. The splendor of that night is her own. If it is to be her last glimpse of lamplight, it must not be diluted by frail attempts at retelling. She will hold it close to herself; revisit the wondrous sensations of those few precious minutes for as long as she can.

"Luna? Do you hear me?" A touch of alarm again.

Luna shakes herself out of her reverie. "Yes, sorry, Falca. I'm here. What did you say?"

"I said, not to worry. I'm going away to speak to my mistress, but I won't be long. Will you be alright?"

Luna assures her that she will. She is glad, for the first time, to be left alone. Her feelings are too chaotic to be discussed.

"What will Watho do?" she asks Nox, who is employing a series of head-butts to communicate his desire for his ears to be scratched. "There are other lamps. Other suns. Aren't there?"

She cannot understand the way Falca and Watho and the writers of her books and the nameless painter of her wall murals, live. If she were to learn that they breathed water and ate only candle wax, their lives would not be more foreign to her than they are already.

The one thing she feels certain of is that no one can live in this unyielding darkness. There must be light in other places. Other lamps.

The thought carries with it unexpected pain. If there are other lamps, are they all like her own was? Unspeakable glory bottled up against its will?

"Perhaps that's why they are contained so cruelly," she says aloud. "There isn't room enough for them, if they get out."

Warm tears well up at the thought. All those lamps — for there must be many — struggling against their restraints; shining softly, holding back their radiance.

Whether it is these anxious thoughts, the exertion of her earlier adventures, or the warm, silent, darkness that overcomes Luna until she sleeps again, she does not know, but when her eyes open next, the lamp is shining again. Soft, warm light hangs in the air and settles gently on the rug, the furniture and Luna herself, fading gradually to shadows before it reaches the outer edges of the room. Has her lamp — so free and joyous last night — been recaptured to light this room? Is the enormous beauty she witnessed now shriveled, shoved unwillingly into a glass bowl? What did they do it to make it shrink so?

Everything is as it was before the rumbling tremors. It looks so familiar that Luna can almost believe the previous night's events were only a vivid dream, but the normalcy brings no relief. An irreversible change has taken place. Luna has stepped outside her tiny world, if only for a moment, each timid step suggesting the possibility of more. Of places where there is space enough for her to expand — where the roof extends so far that there are no corners; no boundaries.

# CHAPTER NINE

The woman in blue is laughing at a joke Sir Hugh can't hear. Her head is tilted back, face alight with mirth. His eyes glide from her smile down her neck, appraising her form with a judicious eye. Calculating, imagining, predicting.

Sir Hugh visits his uncle, Lord Alton, the Duke of Carlyle, as frequently as duty allows. He enjoys both the status by association and the robust opportunities for social connections that his connection to the duke affords.

Hugh has always preferred to be absent from his own country earldom, where little exists to interest him. He is determined to achieve the station to which he is entitled in society and the humble estate he oversees is a constant reminder that he has not yet done so.

As a young man, his path was so clear and bright with promise — he'd achieved renown as a military commander during the war, only months after marrying the beautiful Aurora, daughter of a rich and well-connected prince. He had expected to ride the swell of both these accomplishments to greater fame, higher accolades, better titles and richer lands. To his great surprise, neither of his conquests were sufficient to prevent his planned ascent from stalling within a few years.

Aurora's father has been so far uninclined to grant special favors to his son-in-law, a fact for which Hugh holds his wife personally responsible. It is quite obvious that she is working against him, planting seeds of distrust in her father's ear; there can be no other reason for the prince to keep his distance. It is true, or course, that Hugh has not allowed her to speak to any of her family outside of his presence for years, but he knows her to be conniving and deceitful.

As marvelous as his military exploits were, the kingdom has enjoyed a long peace in the intervening years that has left no opportunity for him to repeat them.

Thus he finds his only path to society's higher ranks leads through his uncle's good graces. He has faithfully attended every gathering of the duke's for years in hopes of catching the eye, or ear, of a courtier who might ferry him to a higher sphere.

There are, naturally, other reasons to be often at Lord Alton's table, frequented as it is by many female members of the court, sighing with boredom when their husbands leave for hunting expeditions, giggling coyly at his comments over dinner, soft, persuadable.

The possibility that Sir Hugh's consistent failure to ingratiate himself with the other nobles has anything to do with his penchant for dalliances with their wives has now and then been suggested to him, but he dismisses it each time with a laugh. All men are like him in this. It is expected. None of the other nobles, of course, have engaged in such behavior with *his* wife, but he has taken ample precautions to ensure Aurora does not have the opportunity. If the other nobles fail to protect their wives from temptation, they have only themselves to blame.

Tonight, he has selected a new face at the banquet table as his target; a dark-haired beauty clad in silver and blue. She is accompanied by an older man — the Duke of Loren, Lord Alton tells him, who must either be a father or uncle; certainly he is too old to be her husband. She has high cheekbones and an upward tilt to her chin that give her a mildly haughty air. Her eyes are dark and intelligent. She looks as though she is in need of taming. He tries to catch her eye, but she has yet to acknowledge him. It rankles, but this only strengthens his resolve.

"The problem," Lord Alton is saying next to him, "is that the heathens are being allowed to come over the border from Kolb unchecked. Mark my words, this poisonous increase in heresies and fables can be traced back to them entirely."

Sir Hugh turns to face his uncle. "I quite agree," he says, more loudly than necessary. He resists the urge to glance at the lady in silver and blue to see if he's drawn her attention at last. "That damned Sage Einarsson is a prime example. Look closely enough at his heritage and you'll find Kolbian blood, I'd wager."

Controversy over the border with Kolb, their closest neighbor, has been the primary topic of conversation at most dinner parties of late. Sir Hugh does not give voice to his silent hope for another war; another chance to elevate himself through military victory.

"I don't doubt it!" bellows the duke, whose loquaciousness typically reaches higher decibels when the wine has been flowing for an hour or two. "I have told the king again and again to close that border, or we'll have no hope of stemming the tide of filthy false worship."

Sir Hugh knows perfectly well that the duke is overstating

his proximity to the king's ear, but he lets it pass. If the others at the table think Lord Alton is connected to the king, they might think the same of Sir Hugh.

"Well spoken, uncle," he says. "I only wish steps had been taken sooner. It's becoming quite dangerous, in my opinion."

"Are you so uncertain, then, in your own religious beliefs, sir?" asks a raspy female voice, thick with unspoken humor. Sir Hugh turns to see the lady in blue, her eyebrows arched expectantly.

"I don't believe we've been properly introduced, Madame," he says, favoring her with a paternal smile.

"Lady Elizabeth." Her chin dips in a gentle nod. Her own smile seems amused.

"Lady Elizabeth," Sir Hugh repeats. "I'm afraid you may have misunderstood my uncle's point. There's certainly no question of his orthodoxy, nor mine."

"Did I? My mistake. I meant only that if you are confident in your own beliefs, surely you have nothing to fear from the words of pagans. If the Kolbians are such universal heathens, though I do not at all concede that they are, why not let them come freely and persuade them of your own views?"

Sir Hugh smiles again, indulgent. "It's not myself that I'm concerned for my lady, but the common people. As any educated man will tell you, the average tradesman and housewife have no inclination to understand these matters and can easily be led astray."

"I see," she nods and Sir Hugh begins to turn back to his uncle. Letting her suspect him of disinterest is a key move in this game.

"Then if only the nobles and clergy are unable to be taken in by heresy, have they not failed the people tremendously?" she presses. "A religion so tenuous that it cannot withstand the mere discussion of external ideas cannot have been very well instilled."

Sir Hugh bristles. "The nobility can hardly be blamed for the faithlessness of the masses, my lady."

"Just what I think, too," Lady Elizabeth says, looking satisfied. "And just what Sage Einarsson, whom I heard you mention, has been teaching. He contends that the individual is responsible for seeing to his own faith and as such, has the right to educate himself about it so that he can be sure of his convictions. I must say, I'm surprised to find you in agreement."

"That's not *all* he teaches," Sir Hugh corrects her. "He advocates abolishing the clergy entirely, giving commoners access to holy texts far beyond their ability to comprehend. His teachings would elevate every chambermaid and stable hand to the level of the Holy Sentries!"

"If every chambermaid could be as ready to defend her faith as you are yourself, your fears of Kolbians spreading dangerous fables could be put to rest."

Sir Hugh is quickly losing patience. *Who exactly does this woman think she is?* It seems a reminder of her role is in order. "Is your husband planning to join us tonight, my lady?" he asks after a pause. "I'd be interested to hear *his* thoughts on the subject."

To his annoyance, this only seems to amuse her more. "I'm afraid you'll have to contend with me alone sir, as my husband does not exist."

"How fortunate for him. Excuse me." He offers a stiff bow by way of dismissal and turns back to his uncle, resuming conversation at a lower volume.

A few moments later he glances back at Lady Elizabeth,

hoping she feels the sting of his disapprobation, but she is laughing again over some joke with her companion, as though she has forgotten him entirely.

Sir Hugh's thoughts return to their earlier track. He considers what it would be like to have married her instead of Aurora. This woman is arrogant. Brazen. She would likely have been more difficult to subdue, but wouldn't that only make the conquest worthier?

If she were *his* wife she would quickly learn not to speak above her station. He would not teach her through violence — such vulgar behavior is the last resort of a commoner. No, he has much more sophisticated methods of training a woman to behave in a manner becoming to her sex. He smiles again, enjoying the thought. If she belonged to him, he would soon have her pleading for his approval, as Aurora so often does.

A tap on the shoulder interrupts his imaginings.

"My lord," says a servant, bowing low and handing him a folded note.

The servant fades into the background as Sir Hugh looks at the note, written in the familiar, dignified handwriting of his steward. His lechery turns to fury in the space of a breath.

*Your presence is required*, the note reads. *Lady Aurora is missing.*

AETHON IS FUMING as he slides off Thunderstone's back and turns to Fargu, whose expression is decidedly stormy.

"Don't look at me like that!" Aethon snaps. He gestures to the sun's position. "Look, we're back in plenty of time."

Aethon knows Fargu is becoming increasingly alarmed, but

he cannot help himself. He does not understand the limitations placed on him; he knows only that they chafe.

"How can I grow as a hunter if I'm hemmed in on all sides by foolish restrictions?" he demands. "I've achieved all that I can on the plains. I'm unbearably bored."

"Be that as it may, your mistress' instructions are clear and are to be obeyed." Fargu's voice is harsher than Aethon is accustomed to. For the first time, it occurs to him that Fargu must truly fear Watho.

He looks closely at his guardian's face, searching for any sign of fear in his eyes. It must be there for Fargu to be so adamant, but Aethon cannot understand it. Fargu is brave to a fault and Watho is only a woman. What sway could she hold over him?

Aethon has, for weeks, been edging closer and closer to the forest boundaries during hunting expeditions. It was unintentional at first. He had been so focused on the pursuit of his quarry that he did not notice he was approaching forbidden grounds. Fargu had restrained him with such urgency, however, that Aethon's curiosity had been piqued.

*What dangers must lay in the forest that even Fargu dares not approach?*

Since that day, the boundaries of the hunting grounds have been drawing him irresistibly. He must know *why* these limits have been placed upon him. The thought that Watho is trying to protect him from some unspeakable danger only makes him more anxious to face it. Every day he rides farther out, pressing closer to the mysteriously dark smudge against the horizon that signifies the treelines. Every day he returns closer to sunset, though he knows the time restrictions are even firmer than the geographical boundaries.

Now, he turns away from Fargu and begins to unsaddle

Thunderstone, his movements vehement, his muscles tense with anger. Such rages have come upon him for as long as he can remember, hot and sudden and tempestuous.

Sometimes he knows why they come, but other times they seem to spark for no reason, churning in his gut, or breaking over him like the violent winds of winter beating against the castle walls. The servants lower their eyes and scuttle out of his path when he is in a fury, waiting for the heat to pass, as it usually does, leaving him broody and petulant in its wake. Only Fargu is unmoved by them.

Fargu laughs. "Ah, the brave hunter sulks like a child when his will is crossed does he? Come lad, we'll have none of that. Quit you like a man."

*Lad.* Aethon hates it when Fargu calls him that. He glowers at his guardian over the horse's back, but this only seems to amuse the older man more.

"You'd best hurry," he says, "if you expect to be served supper on time. I expect that horse to be dry as kindling before he's put up."

"I *know* that, Fargu," Aethon protests. "I don't need to be told how to brush a horse."

He barely resists the urge to hurl the saddle to the ground as he would have only a few years ago. If his outrage gets the best of him, Fargu won't allow him to ride out on the hunt tomorrow. Before this rule was in place, he had been known to give full vent to his wrath, hurling goblets and trays against walls and even beating his own head with his fists from time to time. That he has learned to throttle his passion for the sake of the hunt has not in any measure decreased its intensity. It has only increased his frustration that he cannot express it.

"My apologies, young master!" Fargu exclaims. "You

seemed to have forgotten your age for a moment, as a result of which I forgot it as well."

The storm has passed by the time dinner is finished and Aethon is soon embarrassed of his boiling anger. This is how it often goes and he has made to himself a dozen useless vows to be more reasonable in the future.

He persuades his guardian to stay and play cards with him for a while after they've eaten in a feeble attempt to restore himself to Fargu's good graces. As usual, the huntsman says he has things to attend to at home and cannot be induced to stay for more than one game.

Aethon is, by now, accustomed to the fatigue he begins to feel shortly after the evening's wine has been drunk and soon goes to bed.

In his dreams, he chases the mightiest boar that man has ever seen. It is swift and dangerous, with tusks like sharpened swords and a man-like intelligence in its eyes. It leads him on for hours until, at last, it crashes into the trees on the edge of the hunting plain.

With an ecstatic cry, Aethon spurs his horse on to follow.

When Aurora comes to, the woods are quiet. She can hear the birds asking each other the occasional tentative question in the wake of the upheaval, but all else is still.

She groans and opens her eyes. She is lying on the ground, several feet from the wreckage of her carriage. She must have been thrown from it, but she has no memory of that. Her body feels like one tender bruise and her dress is torn, but a ginger examination of herself reveals no serious damage.

Shakily, she gets to her feet and begins making her way back to the rubble, fear of the silence and all it might mean roiling in the pit of her stomach. Remarkably, the coach is not reduced entirely to kindling. The wheels still hold its frame up, though it sags a little in the middle and the roof has caved in.

The door is hanging open, dangling from a single hinge. She peers inside, expecting the worst. Violet is still in her seat, slumped over and still, but the shallow rise and fall of her breast tells Aurora what she needs to know. She forces herself to take a ragged breath. Her friend is alive.

She crawls into the wreckage and takes Violet's face in her hands, shaking her gently at first for fear of bringing the whole thing down on both their heads, then with increasing fervor as her panic grows.

Violet groans and shifts slowly. After a moment, she lifts bloodied hands to her face and leans forward to rest her head on her hands. The ache in Aurora's chest begins to subside.

"Alright, alright, I'm up," Violet mumbles, her words running together like muddy water. "A girl can't get three winks, even after she's nearly killed."

Aurora sits back and looks at her, stunned. "Has there ever been a moment you thought too weighty for a joke?" she asks at last.

"Once," her friend says, a little more clearly. Her tone is serious. Aurora waits, curious. "It was a few years ago. I remember it because the earl had just gone away that day. Cook made lamb soufflé for supper."

Aurora waits in silence to hear the rest of the story, then rolls her eyes, realizing there is no more to it.

"What?" Violet demands. "It was a truly religious experience. One should never joke about lamb soufflé."

They struggle to extract themselves from the remains of the coach and look around for the driver. The horses have long since fled, but they find the driver unconscious with his back to a tree, as though he's only had a bit too much to drink and stopped to sleep it off. They revive him with some effort, but when he tries to rise, find that his leg is broken. *If this is the worst injury any of us have sustained*, Aurora thinks, *we are lucky indeed.*

"Well," says Violet, too cheerfully, "I hope you enjoy the sound of women prattling. It looks as if we'll be carrying you out of the forest between us and the two of us never walk in silence."

The rest of that day is a strenuous one. The driver, a good-natured man called Patrick, is not small in stature. They walk slowly, each with one of his arms around her shoulder, each with an arm around his waist, supporting his weight as he limps between them.

True to her word, Violet keeps up a steady stream of conversation to distract them all from the difficulty of the journey. Aurora is surprised to find herself laughing and even Patrick cracks a pained smile from time to time.

By the time they come to the forest edge, however, Aurora can no longer ignore her aching legs and blisters on her feet. Her head is pounding and she is drenched in sweat.

It is still a long way to Harthwaite, but from here, they reason, they may be able to find transport; not to mention food and water, which they all desperately need.

With these thoughts forefront in her mind, it takes her a moment or two to understand what has happened when they stumble out of the woods and come face to face with Sir Hugh himself. He is accompanied by a handful of men — soldiers of his acquaintance, as well as Sebastian and some men she presumes to be hired mercenaries from town. They are all on horseback, having evidently discovered her absence and come in pursuit.

Sir Hugh's face is white with rage as his eyes sweep first over her, then over Patrick. Aurora is suddenly acutely aware of the man's arm, heavy on her shoulder and her own hand on his waist and hot shame rises up in her throat, bleeding onto her cheeks. It doesn't matter that the situation is obvious. To Sir Hugh, it will be a humiliation.

"My lord," she begins, but he silences her with a swift look. He will not strike her, but still, she knows another form of punishment awaits. She will feel the effects of his displeasure, one way or another.

The soldiers seize Violet and Patrick roughly, impervious to Patrick's cries of pain and bundle them onto horses for the return journey. The earl holds out a hand to Aurora without a word. Meekly, she climbs into the saddle behind him, wrapping her arms around his waist and hating the intimacy of the gesture. His body is rigid, unwelcoming.

When they arrive back at the manor, Sir Hugh takes her by the wrist and leads her like a child until they reach her chambers, whereupon he shoves her inside and closes the door behind him. She hears the click of the lock and his retreating boots in the hall.

She does not see Violet again. She knows her friend will have been dismissed but she fears worse. Sir Hugh might have accused her and perhaps the poor driver as well, of kidnapping his wife and had them prosecuted. They could even be hanged.

The worst part, for Aurora, is that there is no way to find out. The windows to her chamber, like the doors, have been locked from the outside. Her food is delivered by a servant she has never seen before; a young girl who does not make eye contact and never speaks. Aurora pleads daily for news of her friend, or any news at all, but receives no answer.

She is condemned to live in silent isolation, for how long she cannot guess.

## CHAPTER TEN

For the week that follows her brief escape, Luna cannot shake her listlessness. The room in which she has spent every hour of her life but two seems to have shrunk. Books and poetry hold no pleasure. Her food seems tasteless; the music she plays, flat; the vibrant murals muted and grey. The worst part is the lamp. Once her primary source of warmth and joy, it now appears so small and lackluster.

It is not, she concludes after some self-examination, that she was once content and now is not. Rather the discontent has always been there, hiding in the shadowed corners and under the bed. She has always had reason to suspect that there are larger and greater things outside her tiny world than she has yet experienced, but that suspicion had been akin to being told that somewhere in the world water is green and tastes like milk; the idea has always been too foreign to take any real shape in her mind.

Now it's different. Now she has tasted the purple and silver of the air outside her room; has seen the great lamp embedded in its vast roof. Now that she knows what she saw on that momentous night is only a fraction of what there is to see, she can no longer be satisfied to pace her own worn rug every day.

She has begun to study the murals on the walls with new interest. She understands that they depict the lives of people, real or imaginary, in a manner that the viewer is meant to identify with. If everything in them is alien to her, then it must be because her own education is lacking.

One painting in particular stands out to her. The hours in which she feels the most at peace are spent studying it, sometimes in silent contemplation, other times running through her thoughts out loud, asking Nox for his opinions.

It is one of the simpler paintings. It depicts two people, one in a long, red gown, not unlike some of Luna's own, the other wearing clothing she cannot identify — wrapped around the legs and with shoes that come up nearly to the knees.

The woman in red is holding a baby and the other in the strange clothing is holding her hand. Above their heads hangs a bright orange ball, with spears of orange that extend out from itself — a lamp. Luna used to think that it was exactly like her own lamp, but now she realizes it isn't the same at all. It is much more like the lamp she saw on her adventure the night of the earthquake. The people with the baby are standing near a low, stone wall — not unlike the one she saw that same night.

"Who are the people in this painting?" she asks Falca one day, attempting nonchalance.

Falca glances up from the book she is reading to see where Luna is pointing. She offers a disinterested shrug, but not before Luna sees a flash of unease cross her features.

"They aren't real people," Falca says. "Just a scene from an old ballad."

"A ballad?"

"It's a type of song that tells a story. Like the fables in your book. No one really remembers them anymore. How about a game of buncles? You have a record to defend."

She is already moving to retrieve the bag of polished stones she keeps on hand for this purpose. Luna notes the deft change of subject, but says nothing.

It cannot be a coincidence, she decides. The painting must depict other people who have stood, at some time or other, just where she stood the other night, under the same blazing light. She is astonished at first that the people in the painting are looking away from the lamp. That their attention can be anything but transfixed by it is not credible.

It is as a result of this study and from looking again and again at her own lamp's depleted brilliance, that she has decided her initial conclusions about the lamp must have been wrong. This lamp and the one she saw when she went in search of it cannot be the same one. It is not possible, she now knows, for the enormous glory that shone on the balcony (for that is what Falca says the people in the painting are standing on) to be taken captive and contained in so weak a vessel. Perhaps her lamp is one of the tinier fragments that were scattered about so haphazardly.

The conclusion has brought a measure of relief, as well as an increased sense of longing. What she saw from the balcony was not a lamp, then, but the great light from which all smaller lamps descend. It must be, she realizes one evening with great wonder, the sun of which she's read in books. How foolish she once was to think "sun" was only another word to describe her little orb of captive light!

With the relief of knowing the sun has not been captured after all comes a fresh bereavement at having been barred from knowing of its existence for so long and at being denied further access to it.

The painting shows her another possibility; that of a life spent in communion with other people under the glorious sun. Sometimes, if she looks at it for *too* long, the old panic begins to rear its head and she has to turn away while she can still breathe.

Falca has been present much more frequently since the earthquake, which prevents Luna from repeating her escape attempt. The woman never seems to be gone long enough that Luna can feel confident she will not be caught. Perhaps she senses Luna's restlessness, or perhaps she feels guilty for having left her alone in the dark for so long. Luna tries not to be impatient with her guardian, but she can't help feeling anxious.

She is certain of only one thing: there is no satisfaction to be found in this lonesome, dark room. She will have to see the sun again.

IT IS NEARLY fourteen days before she has another chance. Falca has taken to staying to talk, or read, or play games long after the evening meal. Often she is still reading quietly in the room when Luna falls asleep. By the time she wakes up each day, breakfast is arriving and it is too late to attempt another journey.

What has brought on this capricious change, Luna cannot divine. She must have said or done something, for the woman to become so relentlessly attentive. The more desperate Luna becomes, the harder she tries to appear content. If she behaves well enough for long enough, surely Falca's suspicion will eventually dissipate. She has all but given it up as a lost cause when, one evening just after supper, Falca stands with a pained expression.

"What's the matter, Falca?" Luna asks, her genuine concern and a sudden flare of hope warring within her.

"It's only gout," Falca says. "It happens more and more these days. But I'm afraid I had better go and put my feet up, moon sprite."

It is all Luna can do to make herself sit still after Falca departs. She knows she cannot venture out until the time for sleep has passed. She is a little unsure about how people other than herself live and spend their days, or where, but she knows that meals are prepared and linens are changed by *someone*. It stands to reason that the someone — as well as Watho herself — are nearby and might catch her if she goes out too soon.

She leaves her wine untouched, knowing that it will make her too sleepy. She tries to pet Nox, but he senses her nervous energy and dislikes it.

When she feels sure that enough time has passed, she forces herself to wait longer still.

Finally, exultantly, she makes her way to the tapestry behind which Falca disappeared and gently presses the door open. All is as it was before — dark and still. The only difference is that this time, a little light from her own room spills out into the passage.

Carefully, she closes the door behind her and creeps up the stairs until she comes to the landing, turns into the passage and ascends the second set of stairs. Until now, a tiny part of her has begun to think her previous outing had been only a dream. To be out of her room a second time fills her with a hope for which all words seem inadequate. At last, she finds herself on the platform with its low walls, in the place where the air feels and smells and sounds so different.

She has been steeling herself against the possibility that the wondrous mother of lamps may not be there. Perhaps all her conclusions had been wrong. She knows more than ever that her understanding of the world is more limited than she had ever previously imagined. She hopes to see its dazzling luminescence above her, but tells herself to expect only darkness.

She is entirely unprepared for what she sees.

The silvery lamp is still there, but it is not the same. It looks as though it has been eaten away by a wasting disease. So diminished is it, that only a sliver remains. It still gleams, far more brightly than her own little lamp, but it has been drained of its vitality and become a weak and shriveled thing.

For the second time on that little balcony Luna feels hot tears on her face. The sun is dying. She has seen it only once and it is only days — maybe hours — from being reduced to nothing. Panic clenches her stomach with its clawed fists and her breaths come sharp and shallow.

Luna searches the far-off ceiling for some sign of what could have brought on the change. Are there more of the tiny, sparkling fragments than before? Has the sun been dissipating into a shining mist this entire time? She can make no sense of what she sees.

She closes her eyes until her breathing steadies. If the sun is on the verge of death, Luna resolves, she will not leave it to die unloved.

She stands there for as long as she dares, taking in nothing — not the air that moves around her, nor the strange, chirping songs that ride on its wings. She has eyes only for the dying lamp. The thought of this gift, so recently bestowed, being snatched away so soon fills her with resentment.

She doesn't know how long she stays; it might be hours. Eventually she becomes aware of her aching legs and the coolness of her skin. She has been gone too long. With an aching heart, Luna returns to her own room, to mourn the passing of the sun alone.

WATHO ARRANGES her face into its most gracious smile to greet her young ward as he enters her office.

At seventeen, Aethon has become more robust and vibrant than she had ever hoped. Fargu enters behind the young man, wearing the vaguely shipwrecked expression which has taken up permanent residence on his face over the course of the last two years.

The beleaguered huntsman had come to her yesterday afternoon with a request for her intervention.

"My Lady," he had pleaded, "I can no more make the young man do my bidding than I can persuade the thunder to stay silent or lightning to retreat. The boy does not know the taste of fear."

This was not the first time Fargu had compared Aethon to a thunderbolt and Watho suspects that he knows how the comparison pleases her.

"If you wish him to obey your rules, I beg you to lay the charge on him yourself and relieve me of the burden. Should the mood strike him to venture out beyond the bounds laid out for him, he'll heed not a word of mine on the matter."

Watho had favored him with a magnanimous smile, which she very nearly meant. She was not, after all, a cruel woman.

"Very well, Fargu. You have carried out your duty admirably. Bring the boy to see me tomorrow and henceforth you will not be held responsible for his obedience."

Fargu had looked as though he had been carrying a buffalo around on his shoulders and had finally been granted permission to lay it down.

Today, she examines her creation with satisfaction. The sun-soaked lad is the very picture of courage and youthful vigor. He returns her smile politely, as he always does.

"You wanted to see me?"

"You look well!" Watho says warmly. "I'm pleased to see it. Will you have some wine?"

Aethon takes this as an invitation to sit down and does so.

"How goes the hunt?" she asks.

While he answers, speaking enthusiastically and with broad gestures about the daily thrills of stalking and conquering his prey, Watho's eyes are drawn to the long scar across his jawline, stretching from his right ear to the corner of his mouth.

She remembers the injury that caused it. She had overheard the kitchen staff recounting how Aethon had burst into the kitchen, laughing and clutching a blood-soaked cloth to his face. A boar had been the culprit. Aethon had struck the beast directly in the breast with a spear, but this had only angered the creature, which had charged up the length of the spear until it reached Aethon, twisting its head and slicing open Aethon's cheek with its razored tusk. The enraged animal would have killed the boy, had Fargu not been near enough to rescue him with another well-aimed spear.

"It was my fault," Aethon had said with a careless laugh,

when Watho questioned him about the incident. "I knew better than to go after a boar with the wrong spear, but I couldn't resist. Once he saw me, I would have been forever a coward had I let him go."

Far from being chastened, the lad had seemed to enjoy his brush with death.

*If he knows no fear, as Fargu says, it is not because he has been given no cause.*

She nods patiently as he concludes his account of recent adventures.

"Your guardian tells me," she says at length, "that your curiosity draws you more often toward the forest and keeps you out later each day."

"Oh yes," Aethon admits readily. "There is so much I have yet to see and so many creatures that remain unchallenged." His eyes sparkle with the suggestion of these new adventures.

Watho adopts her sternest expression, one she knows can reduce the strongest man to a mere shell of himself. Aethon meets her eye with a defiant uptilt of his chin.

"Be that as it may," she tells him, "you must understand that there is a very good reason for the limitations placed upon you. As your guardian, it is my duty to protect you. Fargu's requirements of you are not his own, but mine. Do you understand?"

Aethon nods, but his eyes are hard, his lips pinched tightly together.

"What are the limitations I just spoke of?" she demands.

"I'm not to go near the forest and I'm to return home before supper," Aethon recites, his voice insolent, eyes glittering with unspoken anger.

Watho sighs a little ruefully. She's heard tell of the boy's fits of rage. Perhaps it is inadvisable to challenge him head-on. If he will not bend before intimidation, an appeal to affection might do the trick instead.

"Aethon," she says, more gently now. "Do you understand that my dearest desire is to keep you safe? I have loved you like a mother and I could not bear to see you harmed by the fearful creatures that lurk in the dark."

It is a mistake. She sees this at once.

Aethon nods gravely and assures her he understands, but as the flash of anger subsides, a gleaming curiosity takes its place. She does not miss how his eyes light up at the mention of fearful creatures.

She will have to think of some other way to restrain him. She can use magic, of course, but she will avoid the use of force for as long as possible. She wants to know that her power over him is real. For now, she hopes that loyalty to her will act on his conscience until a better solution presents itself.

"Thank you Aethon." She smiles to dismiss him and the pair turn quickly to depart.

As their echoing footsteps retreat, Watho turns to Felnys, who has been watching the encounter from his place across the room, unobserved by the visitors.

"I seem to have created an even wilder man than I could have hoped," she laughs.

"Are you pleased with your success, then?" asks the wolf.

"Excessively."

She thinks she sees a predatory smile cross his face, but then again, he is a wolf. All his smiles are bound to be predatory.

"And what of the girl?" he asks. "Does she still bore you?"

"She has given me no reason to take interest," Watho replies.

"Perhaps I may be of service in that arena."

"Oh?" Despite the tenuous nature of her success with Aethon, Watho is feeling buoyant and ready to have her interest piqued.

"I have heard," says the wolf, "that the female creature's drawings have taken a surprising turn of late. Falca is very uneasy about them. She told Fargu, where she thought they could not be overheard, that the girl has been drawing the moon."

Watho gives him a sharp look. "Are you certain? Not merely the lamp? Perhaps she's reproducing the paintings from the walls."

The wolf slowly shakes his enormous head. "I advise looking at the drawings yourself," he says. "Falca had one with her. It did not look like the paintings on her wall, it was far too striking a reproduction to be taken from that. It looked, in fact, exactly like a tower balcony."

Watho arches her eyebrows. "If that is the case, Falca has very good cause to be alarmed. For if the girl has been out of her room, Falca will have to answer for it."

"I can see to that, if you like," he says, his voice low and hungry.

"Not yet," Watho says. "There is something else you may do instead."

## CHAPTER ELEVEN

*S*urely the sun is gone. Luna keeps telling herself that it must be gone. If it dwindled so quickly in the days between her first visit and her second, surely there can be nothing left of it now that another fortnight has passed. Still, she needs to be sure. She will have to risk the corridor again.

She had tried to do it a week ago. Just as she had done the previous time, Luna had waited until she was sure the castle slept before creeping silently into the corridor. When she reached the landing, however, she could go no further. An enormous beast was stretched out across the passageway, apparently asleep.

Luna could not put a name to the creature from any of the descriptions or pictures in her book. It may have been a fox, for she could see even in the pale light from the window that its fur was deep red, but Falca had described the fox as though it were a small animal, like Nox. Surely the colossal creature in the corridor could never have matched that description even in its youth.

She stared at it, frozen in surprise and curiosity, watching its massive back heave and settle with its breath. After a few cautious moments, she began looking for ways around or over it. It was, after all, sleeping. It seemed like an act of cowardice to turn away and slink back to her rooms simply because an animal was asleep in her path.

While she considered this, however, the creature had lifted its head slowly to look at her. Luna realized instantly that its relaxed pose had been a ruse; even while it feigned sleep, its muscles had been coiled, ready to spring. The beast gazed at her with black, inhuman eyes, waiting to see what she would do.

A dull sense of unease blossomed in her stomach and began to wend upward, waking her nerves as it went. She and the creature watched each other silently, neither moving a muscle. The creature was not, she decided, like Nox. There was an intelligence in its eyes that was not at all friendly.

Unsure what else to do, Luna cleared her throat and spoke. "May I pass?"

The beast looked at her in silence for another moment, then answered. "And go where, little one?"

She felt that she should be surprised when it spoke, but she wasn't. "I only wanted to go to the balcony and see the sun."

The creature said nothing, but rose to its feet, hackles raised.

Luna took an involuntary step back. She half expected the panic and shortness of breath to come, but it didn't. What rose up instead was a new feeling: anger at the implicit threat in the creature's presence and movements. How dare he try to take away the tiny shred of freedom she had only just grasped?

"Let me pass," she said, heartened to hear the resolve in her own voice.

The creature bared its teeth. There was now no mistaking

the malevolence in its gaze, as a low growl echoed off the passage walls.

"Go back to your room while you still can."

Luna's first instinct was to obey, as she had obeyed every command since birth, but another, stronger instinct kept her feet rooted in place.

She lifted her chin defiantly. "I will go back to my room when I've seen the sun."

She moved to squeeze past the creature, but in the space of an instant, it was upon her. Her head struck the stone floor with a loud crack, her vision blurring instantly with pain. She felt its enormous paws pressing into her, the pointed claws piercing her shoulders.

She stared up at its snarling face, wide-eyed. No one had ever intentionally hurt her before. Even in her shock, she knew the beast was holding back, giving her just a taste of the punishment further defiance would bring.

Even as she lay there under the weight of her assailant, she felt the walls of her rooms contracting yet again. There was to be no liberation for her after all; no extension of the limits imposed on her. They would not yield.

"Go back to your room," the creature repeated slowly, its glistening teeth only inches from her face.

"Yes," she wheezed.

The beast withdrew, satisfied.

Shakily, she regained her feet. After a few hesitant backward steps to be sure he would not leap again, she turned and ran back to her chamber.

Since that night, she has told herself to accept that there will be no further reprieve. She dares not venture into the passage again. Luna has tried to overcome her fear, telling herself that the creature considers her duly warned and will not return. Every time she presses her hand against the door, however, she is unable to go any farther. The panic rises, a green, suffocating feeling. The air thins in her lungs and her hands grow clammy and begin to tremble. She feels the creature's hot breath on her face and the gashes in her skin from its sharp claws.

Still, she feels the call of the sun from beyond her prison walls. She can't stop thinking of it — how it became only a shred of its former self in such a short time. She feels, with increasing conviction as the days pass, that if she does not know for certain the sun's fate, she will go mad.

Luna eyes Falca with suspicion now. She doesn't want to, but she can hardly help it. Now that she knows from whence Falca comes and goes, she realizes her governess must know about the beast in the corridor, yet she is allowed to pass.

Falca seems to sense the shift and has become increasingly solicitous — bringing with her new games and books, apparently hoping to ease Luna's boredom and restore her spirits. Despite her best intentions, however, Falca's gout flare-ups are becoming more frequent and she is forced to withdraw earlier in the evenings, though still always taking care to wait until Luna is asleep.

It is Nox who comes at last to Luna's rescue.

As she does most nights now, Luna feigns sleep until Falca leaves, then rises and takes out her drawings. If she cannot see the sun again, she will have to settle for her own recreation. She has applied all her skill and patience to the task of recreating the beautiful balcony scene of her first expedition. When her heart aches the most, she likes to study the drawings, holding them up to the lamplight to mimic the sun's glow.

Nox is not at all interested in the drawings. He is chasing a beetle with great enthusiasm — a habit that Luna found endearing as a child, but is not much amused by tonight. She wants stillness, in which to remember the gentle caress of the cool air on her skin and the glow of the faraway mother of lamps. Instead, she has only a pale rendition on paper, while the cat rockets back and forth across the room in the ecstasy of his tiny hunt, weaving between her legs and leaping over furniture. Eventually, he seems to have cornered his prey across the room and begins batting at it with his paws. Luna thinks the hunt must be nearly over.

She is, therefore, annoyed to realize several minutes later that the cat is still toying with the thing — darting at the wall every few seconds and bouncing off it in a frenzy.

Huffing in exasperation, she marches over to him, intending to scoop him up and let him know her feelings on the matter. She plans to remove the beetle — and with it the cat's temptation — but when she finds the spot on which Nox is focusing his efforts, there is no beetle to be found.

She kneels, feeling about with her hands and peering under the couch.

"*What* can have enthralled you so, you tiny monster?" she mutters.

Suddenly she freezes, on her hands and knees with her face pressed to the ground. Something brushes her cheek. It is not the beetle, nor its feline tormentor.

It is cold air.

Moving air. Air that feels alive, like the air on the balcony. The thought that strikes her then feels so momentous that it is several seconds before she can move or blink. It has never crossed her mind that there might be more than one exit to her chambers. Falca always appears from the same place, after all.

From where she crouches she can see a small gap between wall and floor through which the beetle must have made its escape. Slowly, she rises and moves aside the tapestry that hangs there. There is no need to feel for a crack in the stone as she did on the night the lamp went out. It is there, easily visible; another door.

Luna reaches forward, then pauses just before pushing it open.

What if there is a beast outside this one as well? Have sentries been stationed at all the doors? Are her captors — for that is how she has begun to think of both Watho and Falca, almost without realizing it — waiting to catch her? She steels herself, feeling the same resolve that got her knocked down in the corridor surging within her again.

"I won't know if I don't look," she says aloud and pushes the door open. The hinges creak loudly as it swings slowly outward, as though from long disuse. This, Luna thinks, is a hopeful sign. She steps lightly into the corridor upon which the door opens and her hope grows. In the light from the room behind her, she can see thick dust, crumbling stone and cobwebs. No one has trespassed this place in a very long time.

Luna lets go of the door, which settles slowly back into place behind her, leaving her in thick darkness. She reaches out a hand and shudders slightly when it comes in contact with the grimy wall.

As she walks, she tries to prepare herself for what she will find at the end. Should she make it somehow to the place where the sun once was, she knows it might be there no longer. After all, she reminds herself, two weeks ago it was emaciated almost beyond recognition.

Still, it is better to be sure.

The corridor is long, but there are no stairs to climb and no turns to take. After a few minutes, it simply ends in a heavy door.

Luna feels around until her hand finds the latch. This door is difficult to open — it seems there is something pressing hard against it from the other side. She pushes until the crack is wide enough to slip through and finds herself behind what she assumes is another tapestry. It is much wilder than her own tapestries, made of thick, tangled, fibers with little bits sticking off of them in various places. She moves sideways behind it and sure enough, finds she is able to emerge from underneath it after a few feet into the room beyond.

As soon as she does, her heart gives a tremendous leap.

The sun is back! No longer the pale fragment of a few weeks ago, it is restored to its former glory — perfectly round, enormous and bursting with silver light. Luna feels as though her heart will break for joy. Whatever illness the poor sun endured, it has conquered.

*Oh bless you,* she prays silently. *You gentle, glorious, creature, I ought to have known you could not be so easily destroyed.*

She stands in silence, basking in the sun's splendor for a long time. Eventually, however, she begins to notice other things about the room into which she has stumbled. It is nothing like the stone platform from her previous ventures. Like her own room, the floor is lined with a thick rug, but it does not feel like the rug in her room. Its fur is much longer and coarser, but it is cool and soothing beneath her bare feet. The room is vast — Luna can see no walls, excepting the one from which she just emerged — and full of foreign shapes and subtle sounds. Invisible voices chirp and whistle from all directions, punctuated occasionally by louder sounds, like strange creatures calling to one another. Beneath it all runs a low, musical hum, adorned with little splashes and burbles.

It sounds like laughter. Like a song.

Some distance away, dark silhouettes spring up from the floor to what seem to be great heights, tall and narrow, throwing their many arms upward as though in worship. As though they want to touch the sun. She feels a swell of kinship toward them. They, too, wish to be as close to the beloved light as they can.

She is walking before she realizes it. The air is still tonight, not toying with her hair or clothes, but still it feels more alive than the stale air in her room. Sometimes she catches a hint of some sweet scent on the air as she walks. Luna feels that she could easily live in this place, drinking in the sweetness of the air and the glory of the sun forever.

As she walks, the humming sound grows nearer and the splashes and gurgles become more frequent. The floor is uneven, rising and falling in little hills and valleys, so that she cannot see clearly where the sound is coming from until she is almost upon it.

A silvery ribbon of water cuts into the floor and runs past her, leaping and tumbling over itself as it goes, like Nox when he is feeling playful. Instinctively, Luna steps into it and laughs as it surges around her ankles and splashes her legs.

Suddenly, a terrible thought comes to her. This water is alive, laughing and playing and singing. The water in her own rooms, that comes in drinking cups and wash basins and heated for her baths is still and lifeless. It reminds her of the feeling of the dead glass in her hand the night the lamp went out. Is this water killed for her use, she wonders? Or is it like the lamp; only a pale copy of the living version?

She hopes it is the second. Perhaps everything in her room is a copy of something in this larger room. Watho may be trying to recreate this room, with its rugs and light and water, but hasn't yet learned the trick of it.

She sits down next to the ribbon of living water, letting it run around her feet while she thinks. The strange rug is littered with other objects, colorful and delicate on slender stalks that come up from the floor. She tugs gently on one, but cannot pick it up. Leaning down to examine it more closely, she breathes in its sweet, pungent scent. It is so soft and seems so frail, that Luna feels a little afraid on its behalf. How can something so small and vulnerable live in the open like this?

She wants to cover it in glass to protect it, but as soon as she has the thought she knows it is wrong. That would only suffocate it. It would be a captive, as she herself is and would not get to feel the sweet air on its face and listen to the laughing water. It is braver, she realizes, to live as it does — exposed and vulnerable, gracing the air with its pleasant scents, enjoying the world around it.

"Hello, little one," she whispers to it. "What can I call you?"

She knows it will not answer and it doesn't, but she feels she must learn the names of all the things in this wondrous world, just as she knows the names of the furniture in her own room.

She revels in her new discoveries for hours, her heart sinking at the thought of returning to her dim chamber. When at last, wisdom bids her take leave, she says farewell to each new acquaintance and promises to visit again.

CHAPTER TWELVE

*a*ethon has heeded his mistress' instructions for months. Despite his insistence that he has outgrown them, he has found plenty of mighty enemies to conquer on the moors and sunlit plains, and miles of land to enjoy without ever coming near the forest.

Even when he isn't hunting, the plains allow him ample room to give Thunderstone his head, and enjoy the sunlight and wind flowing over his shoulders, through his hair, stinging his eyes and whipping his tunic. He feels, on these occasions, as though he and Thunderstone are part of a vast, rushing river, swept along by an unseen current. With so much to revel in, he sees no need to transgress Watho's orders without reason.

Until today.

Aethon reigns Thunderstone in as they approach the gory mound of animal flesh in their path: a half-decimated boar, torn to shreds but not by human blades. It looks as though it was killed some time ago; perhaps long before he awoke, though not as long ago as yesterday.

Earlier in the morning, Aethon had spotted, far off in the

distance, a flash of gold — the coat of some animal he has not yet met on the plains. Through the spyglass, he saw it more clearly, albeit only for a few seconds – a great, golden cat, with a burst of wild mane around its head. As Aethon watched, the beast slunk behind the far-off treeline, though he had the impression it lay quietly and watched the hunting grounds from its hiding place for some time.

"What is it?" he asked Fargu, after describing the creature.

"It's a lion," Fargu said. "King of beasts."

"King?" Aethon scoffed. "It's hiding in the trees like a coward!"

Fargu laughed. "You wouldn't think it such a coward if you met it after dark," he said. "It's as mighty a predator as you are yourself."

Aethon looked at him with new interest. Fargu may have read his thoughts, for the man looked as though he would gladly have swallowed the words he had just spoken. Aethon shrugged, pretending for his mentor's sake to think nothing more on the matter. They rode out with the rest of the hunting party as planned, without another word about the lion.

By midday, however, Aethon knew he was not fooling anyone. He was distracted, his thoughts always wandering back to the cat in the trees, and his participation in the hunt lacked its usual vigor. He knew his companions noticed his uncharacteristic quiet and tried to shake himself out of the strange mood, but still, he could not get the lion out of his mind. It prowled in the shadows, peering out at him, taunting him.

*What difference does it make whether it's night or day?* he asked himself again and again. *If he can only hunt and kill in the dark, then surely he is a coward, as I said. And yet... Fargu ought to think so too and didn't.*

He cannot express, even now, why this bothers him so deeply, but his curiosity, once awakened, is not easily put to rest. What if there are other wild beasts prowling in the woods, waiting for nightfall before they strike? What if there are mighty combats he will never have the chance to fight from within the boundaries of daylight?

Almost unintentionally, he has been guiding the party closer and closer to the edge of the forest, which is how they have come upon the decimated corpse of the boar.

"What creature is responsible for this?" he asks, watching Fargu's expression carefully from beneath his mask of nonchalance.

Fargu's eyes are no less sharp than his own. The man appears to struggle with himself for a second or two. "The lion you spotted this morning, most likely. He or some other like him."

Aethon nods. His curiosity about the golden creature, which cowers in the shadows during the day but kills so brutally at night, is increasing by the moment.

Fargu looks at the sky, as though he expects foul weather, though it is clear and nearly cloudless. Aethon smirks; he is not the only person who isn't fooling anyone.

"Might be advisable to make our way back early today," Fargu says, though he has found no excuse in the heavens to justify the sentiment. He looks already resigned to protest, so when Aethon shrugs and says, "As you like. The buffalo are long gone by now," Fargu's expression changes quickly, first to surprise, then abject relief.

Aethon feels a stab of guilt for taking advantage of this, but dismisses it at once.

"I had better give Thunderstone his head and let him spend

his energy, else he'll be restless," he says, and without waiting for a response, wheels the horse around and thunders ahead of his companions back toward the castle.

He glances over his shoulder once or twice and sees that the rest of the party have accepted this reasoning. They are following, but at a more leisurely pace.

When he arrives at the stables, Aethon forces himself to take his time attending to Thunderstone, brushing him thoroughly and cleaning his hooves. Fargu strictly forbids his turning the horse over to the stable boys and Aethon himself is loath to let anyone else touch the animal.

He is anxious to be done before Fargu and the rest find him there, but he needn't have worried. Despite Fargu's suggestion, he is not eager, Aethon realizes, to return too early and be called to account for laziness by his mistress.

When at last the horse is brushed, stabled, and fed, Aethon seeks out the stable boy.

"When my master returns with the men, tell him that I've gone to bed early with a headache," he says, not waiting for the boy's response before marching toward the castle's main entrance.

As soon as he is out of the boy's line of sight, he changes direction, skirting the edifice. He will hide behind the castle until nightfall, Aethon decides, then return to the forest and see what he finds there.

To that end, he runs along the side of the castle until he finds a place near the hillside from which he cannot be seen and settles down to wait. On this side of the castle, he is closer to the edge of the forest than he's ever been. His mind is racing, but the exertion of the hunt and the warm sun on the grass work together to lull him into a comfortable sleep.

AETHON WAKES an hour or two later. It is still daylight, probably only a little later than he normally would have been returning to the castle.

For a moment he does not understand where he is, but as he remembers he feels a wonderful anticipation take hold of him.

"Only another hour or two," he tells himself, "and I will go to meet the lion, or find out what other great beasts linger in the woods."

His stomach growls, but he ignores it. When a man is hunting, he cannot think of things so trivial as supper.

Aethon has never seen the sun set, but understands the basic mechanism from his time with Master Cardaisseau. He imagines he is prepared to recognize and accept its occurrence.

He is not.

As the time wears on and the light grows dim, he begins to feel a sensation that is entirely unfamiliar to him. The world around him seems to be slowly drained of color, the vivid hues of green and blue and gold growing dull and running together. At the same time, the sun turns a frightening shade, like a fire about to go out. It must have suffered some fatal injury, for it begins to sink, bleeding across the sky in violent shades of red and orange. The warmth of the day seeps out of the air until Aethon finds himself shivering, as though his own blood is being sucked out of his veins.

The darker it becomes, the more Aethon's terror increases. Never before, even indoors, has he experienced real darkness, but now it descends on him like a swarm of flies on the rotting corpse of a buffalo, wrapping him in itself from all sides.

Aethon stands and begins to run.

He intends to go back to the castle — to safety and warmth and blazing light — but the darkness disorients him. He can no longer tell where one thing ends and the next begins, everything a dismal gray, quickly fading to black.

He runs wildly, crying out in terror, until he steps into a stream and shrieks. He has seen the stream before — has dipped his feet in it on hot days — but in the darkness, it no longer feels like a happily bubbling brook; it is an enemy, creeping up on him from behind, cold hands slithering around his ankles to pull him under.

He can hear his own heartbeat pounding dangerously. He can hear other sounds as well; each one more alarming than the next. Creatures in the shadows screech and hoot and call to one another like malevolent spirits. Whatever makes those sounds is hidden in the dark, shielded from sight so that he does not know from which direction each new terror comes.

Aethon hears a terrible, strangled cry which fills him with unspeakable dread, though a part of him whispers that it is coming from his own mouth. He falls to his knees on the bank of the stream, crawling desperately to escape its clutches and finally throws himself headlong onto the grassy hill, rolling onto his back and covering his face with his arms. A moment later, relief descends on the wings of unconsciousness.

Watho watches Felnys where he is sleeping in his usual place by the fire and tries to remember when she first met him. Has he always been with her?

There must have been a beginning to him, but she has no memory of it. Perhaps, however, there ought to be an ending.

She's thought it before, but she can never bring herself to dismiss him. She wants to understand him first; why his power has such a familiar scent.

Watho wonders, not for the first time, whether she's really the one in control of their association. She thinks back to her father's lessons on the rules of power. She recalls his hands gripping her small wrists and the marks that remained long after he let go, how he mocked her tears and scorned her plaintive cries. She remembers her mother – meek, subservient, eager to please. She despised her mother's weakness, as her father despised hers. Her mother had allowed herself to be dominated. Watho has sworn she never will.

When the Duke of Astarsaga died, she promised herself that she would never be in anyone else's control. The only person free from the dominion of the powerful is the *more* powerful. Of this she is certain. Being Felnys' mistress has always meant having his considerable power at her command.

Only, it's beginning to seem that any control she has over him is tenuous at best — at worst, an illusion.

It's not that the wolf has ever directly disobeyed her orders. On the contrary, he is the picture of submission. He does everything that is asked of him and more. It's the *more* with which she is chiefly concerned. He does, Watho suspects, exactly as he pleases. Serving her just happens to be what currently pleases him.

*Why?*

She cannot fathom putting herself in the service of another without necessity. What does he get out of it? She hates the way he toys with her, exposing the parts of her she'd rather leave unexamined, making her schemes and machinations feel childish and small without ever saying so directly. He doesn't do this out of any love or loyalty for her, but simply for his own amusement.

She is to him, she realizes with dawning anger, just what the day boy and the night girl are to her: an experiment in what he can make her do.

She knows her thoughts will only be clear while he is asleep; further evidence of his unnatural grip on her. She can even imagine herself sending him away, being free of his influence and truly back in control of her own realm, but this lucid moment won't last.

Even when he leaves, he's not *really* gone. She feels her own helplessness as much in his absence as in his presence. How has she allowed a mere brute beast to hold so much sway over her?

Felnys stirs and Watho's shoulders sag. She will send him away for good. She must do it now, while she has the will. She opens her mouth to tell him he's dismissed and hears her own voice say, "What do you think about the girl?"

The wolf's eyes glint with laughter. *He knows,* she thinks, raging internally.

"I suspect," he says, "that she has begun to wake up. It's a process that, once begun, will not be easily stalled."

"But you told me she hasn't tried for the balcony again, since your encounter with her." This isn't the first time they've had this conversation. She despises herself for needing reassurance, for seeking it from him of all people, knowing he will offer only the semblance of it; just enough to make sure she always needs it again.

"She hasn't," he agrees. "But I don't believe it's fear that restrains her. She showed none when she looked into my eyes. It felt strange, to be viewed without fear by a human."

It's an intentional barb. She won't rise to it.

"That's hardly surprising. She has lived a sheltered life, with no cause for fear," she says. "But what makes you think she is, as you say, waking up? You yourself admit it's not fear keeping her in her room."

"It's just a feeling, I suppose. It's one you must share, or you would not be asking."

This much is true. She cannot put a name to the change she sees in Luna when she looks in on her through the telescope, the girl just looks more alive somehow. Her features, though always intelligent, now seem as though they've been lit from the inside. *Surely,* Watho thinks, *if it were simply the memory of standing on the balcony that invigorated her, it would have worn off by now.*

"Thank the spirits the boy has no similar inclination," she says at length.

The wolf smiles. "What motivation would he have to awaken from such a pleasant dream as the one you've given him? So full of pleasure and the favor of all he meets?"

"What motivation has *she?*" Watho fires back. "She lives a life of luxury and comfort, attended by food and wine and music, and nothing is asked of her to earn it! What more could she want?"

"I suppose that depends on what kind of person she is."

"She's the kind of person I designed her to be," Watho snaps. "What else *can* she be?" After a pause, she adds, "perhaps it is time to acquaint the girl with fear."

# CHAPTER THIRTEEN

*A*fter discovering the second door, Luna would not have attempted the first again, even if she dared. The world at the end of the second passage is so much more beautiful than the first that, had it not been the site of her first blessed glimpse of the sun, she may have forgotten the stone balcony entirely.

Her guardians have apparently forgotten the second door — perhaps never knew it existed to begin with — for the only footprints to disturb its dust over the following months have been her own and the tiny paw prints left by Nox.

Luna makes the trip down the crumbling corridor at every opportunity, until the wonders of the outside world have become her most familiar friends.

At first, each trip had exposed her to some new, startling event. The second time she wriggled out from behind the wild tapestry of vines the air had been moving again, but not as it had on the balcony. It didn't caress her skin, or toy with her hair. It howled and pushed at her and shrieked in rage. It bent the backs of the trees (for she now understood that this was the name for the tall shapes with their many outstretched arms) and tore the heads off of some of the flowers.

She thought she must have done something to make the sun angry. Had she transgressed somehow when last she visited? She looked up to search its face for comfort and saw that the sun was even more beleaguered than she. Dark shapes raced across the sky — whether they were driven by the air or drove it themselves she could not tell — swallowing the sun bit by bit until Luna could hardly see it. They had swallowed all the tiny lamp shards already. Luna was tempted to run back to her room in case whatever spirits had flown into such a rage tried to consume her too, but she could not bring herself to leave. The sun was being devoured. Its children were gone. What if she never saw it again?

She watched until the sun was absorbed into the inky shapes, clutching her arms to herself as her nightgown whipped furiously around her ankles. Invisible hands pulled at her hair, throwing it wildly in every direction. The sun roared, deafening in her death throes, and began to hurl herself to the earth in spears, piercing the darkness with flashes of anguished brilliance. Water drops landed on Luna's face and arms, soaking her and everything around her. The floor softened and squelched beneath her feet. The sun was weeping, as she herself had been.

When Luna returned the next day, however, anxious and heartsick, all had been restored to peace. The earth was still damp from tears, but the sun herself beamed as though the previous night's violence had never occurred.

In the intervening months, Luna has learned as much as she can about this new, marvelous world. She cannot ask Falca any questions without giving herself away — and she cannot risk being found out again. The thought of one day opening the secret door and finding the red beast in the corridor turns her blood cold.

Instead, she pores over her few books and poems, looking at familiar stories in a new light, revisiting even the childish fables which taught her to read. From these, she begins to understand more clearly. She sees that the lamp is not in a room, like her own, but outside and over all rooms. She has learned the names of some of her new companions — the trees, the stream and the flowers can all be found in poems and paintings. Despite her delight at every new discovery, it is frustrating to know that there must be so much more to be understood than can be found in the meager materials to which she has access.

She has become accustomed to the changes in the sky. Sometimes the sun is distant, so small she can hide it with her thumb. Sometimes it is so large she imagines she can touch it. It shines in varying shades of silver, red, and orange. She has learned that it will wither every month, as it did the first time, but that it always begins to swell again before it is too late and will soon be restored to health.

She has considered escaping for good from time to time, but has never been able to bring herself to do it. The outside world is still too strange and unfamiliar.

*Where would I go?* she asks herself, each time the thought occurs to her. *I don't know how to survive away from here. Anyway, I'd miss Falca and Nox.*

She draws pictures of her new friends often. Her world has expanded beyond what she could have imagined and, while confined to her room, she examines it as best she can through her fingers. She sketches everything — the sun, the vines, the hills and the stream, Nox frolicking in the grass — but her chief delight is in the flowers. She lovingly attends to each delicate petal. She loves the way the blossoms wrap their gentle cloaks around themselves. On one occasion she cautiously peeled apart their petals to see what their hearts looked like, but it felt like a violation. She doesn't do it again.

She no longer keeps the drawings in the little box with the others, but instead keeps them in the hidden corridor itself, nestled down in a crack between the stones. It is vital now to make sure Falca never stumbles across them, or, heaven forbid, shows them to Watho. Luna's friendship with her guardian has not been the same since she began venturing outside. The woman is just as affectionate and kind as ever, but Luna cannot help but see her as a co-conspirator with her captor, though she tries to be understanding, knowing Falca is only afraid.

She might have continued on in this way, sneaking out periodically, returning to the safety of her room and recording what she had seen in drawings for some time, had Watho not come to see her.

The visit is unexpected. Watho had come to see Luna often when she was a child. She would ask polite questions, to which Luna always had the vague feeling there was a correct answer, but she could never guess what it was.

After a while, these visits became more perfunctory, until they tapered off almost entirely. When Watho did appear, she performed a cursory examination of Luna's quarters, scowled at the lamp and looked Luna up and down with vague disinterest before disappearing. This happened so rarely as Luna grew, that she sometimes only remembered the existence of her mistress when Falca invoked her name to encourage obedience.

For all these reasons, Luna finds herself nonplussed when Watho makes an appearance in the middle of the day only a few months after the incident of the Creature in the Corridor (as she has come to think of it).

Watho sails in boldly through the door that leads to the stair, sweeping the tapestry aside with her arm. This confirms what Luna already knew; Watho is aware of her escape to the balcony and no longer sees a need to keep the door a secret.

She had forgotten how beautiful and stately her mistress is. She looks like a gracious deity, standing there with her shoulders pulled back in a regal blue gown. Her imperious eyes sweep the room, seeming to mark all its shortcomings, of which Luna does not doubt she is one.

When Watho is near, Luna always feels small and contemptuous by comparison. She wonders if Watho has come to punish her for her escape. She wonders, for the first time, what possible punishment the woman could inflict. She is already kept in isolation, forbidden from seeing even the light of the sun.

Luna has always been an obedient child. She has accepted the restraints placed upon her without complaint and submitted cheerfully to Falca's every command. To do otherwise had never occurred to her until the night the lamp went out.

"Good afternoon, Luna," Watho says, in her silky voice. "I hope you are well, my dear."

"Very well, my lady," she replies guardedly.

She feels that Watho is waiting for her to say more, to ask about the occasion for the visit. Instead, Luna says nothing, revelling in the tiny rebellion that has sprung up within her.

*Let her be the one to squirm.*

Watho smiles placidly, as though she can read all these thoughts clearly and is untroubled by them. "It has come recently to my attention, that you may have become dissatisfied with your accommodations here. I am told you recently snuck out and climbed one of the towers."

*Snuck out.* The words somehow make her feel ashamed. "I only went in search of the lamp," she explains. "It had gone out and I was left alone in the dark."

Watho tilts her head sympathetically. "Oh dear. That must have been very frightening."

It *had* been frightening, but suddenly Luna does not want to admit it. "I only wanted to see where it had gone."

"Yes, of course. Just as anyone would. And what did you find, my dear?"

Luna suspects it will do no good to lie. "A dark passage, some stairs and a little platform from which I could see the sun."

Watho's eyebrows arch. "The sun," she repeats, but as it seems this remark is not directed at her, Luna stays silent.

"How did you learn about the sun, Luna?" This time there is a faint warning beneath the tranquil surface of her voice.

However upset Luna is with her governess, she does not wish to betray her to Watho. She points at the painting on the wall, depicting the two people with the baby.

"I saw it there," she says. "Falca told me it was only a painting. She said there was nothing real in it. But after I saw it with my own eyes, I *knew* it was real."

Watho looks where she is pointing, then slowly rises and walks over to the wall. She examines all the murals carefully. Luna holds her breath, lest the examination reveal the other door — the one she suspects Watho knows nothing about.

After a moment, Watho returns to where Luna sits and looks down on her again.

What is that behind her eyes? Admiration? Curiosity? Luna has the sneaking feeling that she has piqued her mistress' interest for the first time in her life. She wants to keep it. She wants to impress Watho. This annoys her.

*You're not Nox,* she chides herself furiously. *You needn't lap up your master's attention, or beg to be petted.*

"Are you unhappy, here?" Watho asks.

"I don't know," Luna says honestly.

Watho nods, the picture of maternal sympathy. "I came to talk to you," she says, "because I feel you are now old enough to understand why you are here."

Luna waits, hating the desperation she feels. She will grasp at any reasonable explanation and Watho knows it.

"Do you remember," the woman says, after an excruciating pause, "some months ago — the night the lamp went out, in fact — when there was a mighty earthquake?"

Luna nods.

"That was a sign of the times. The unfortunate truth is that the world has become exceedingly dangerous in recent years. There have been earthquakes and wars and murders. Your own father was murdered before you were born."

Luna gives an involuntary start. She has heard of fathers and mothers in some of the fables, but it has never occurred to her that she might have ones of her own.

"My... my father?"

"Yes dear. That is how dangerous the world has become. A man can be poisoned to death in his own home. Your mother came here after his death to protect herself. And you."

"I don't understand," Luna says.

"I know dear," Watho says, patting her hand. "There is much that you don't understand. That is why I keep you here, for your own safety. Your mother wanted me to protect you and I have done my best." She looks a little sorrowful. "Perhaps my best was not enough, though, if you have felt that you need to escape. Have I not given you every comfort and met every need?"

"I only went to search for the lamp," Luna says, eyes downcast.

"That's not true, though, is it dear?" Watho chides.

"It is true! The lamp went out and I didn't know what to do!" Luna exclaims. She means it to be forceful, but it comes out sounding petulant.

"Ah, but the lamp was replaced that same night, wasn't it? Yet you went out again."

Luna hangs her head, hating how Watho can so easily reduce her to a child.

"Tell me, have I failed you in some way, that you find my accommodations so unbearable? Have you not had the best food and wine, a lamp to light your rooms, the company of your governess and sweet music? Have you lacked any of these things?"

Luna shakes her head. "No, my lady."

Watho looks at her with such deep sorrow that Luna cannot meet her eyes.

"It's... I only wanted to see the sun again. It was so beautiful," she says weakly.

"It may seem beautiful at times," Watho concedes. "But the sun has burned strong men. Its moods cannot be controlled."

*This is true*, Luna thinks, remembering the violent tears and the way the sun had hurled spears of sharp light toward the earth.

"Your mother wanted to shelter you from it. She was content to live in this gentler light." Watho's voice is now reproachful. "I have tried to do as she asked and keep you safe, even at great expense to myself. I have come to ask that you help me in that regard. Promise me that you will not use that door again." She takes Luna's hand in both her own and looks into her eyes. Her hands are beautiful, but cold. Luna wonders if her mother's hands had been cold.

"I promise," she says.

Watho nods, satisfied. "Very well."

She turns to leave. Luna watches her, noticing how the lamplight gleams on her sleek, red hair. That hair reminds her of something; sharp claws digging into her skin, her head smacking the stone floor. The memory sweeps over her, leaving raw anger in its wake.

"Is that why you sent the beast to attack me in the corridor?" she asks. "To protect me?"

Watho turns to look at her again and this time her eyes are hard.

Luna ignores the warning she sees in them. "What would it have done to me, then, had I continued to resist?"

"You misunderstand. The beast was not there to harm you, but to guard you from the other creatures outside that wish to do you harm."

The words are reasonable, but Watho's voice is cold.

"Then I thank you for your protection, my lady," Luna says, keeping her own tone as chilly as her mistress'.

Watho turns without a word and sweeps out of the room as imperiously as she had entered. Neither of them are under any illusion, Luna thinks, that the matter has been resolved. Watho had successfully made her feel ashamed for a few moments, but as soon as she is gone, this fact only spurs Luna's budding defiance.

She might have been content with her little acts of rebellion before the visit. Afterward, however, she comes to a new conclusion: she must find a way to escape permanently.

Perhaps her mother *had* brought her here to keep her safe. After all, Luna has seen the violence of the outside world first-hand, when the sun had wept and roared and fought off the devouring shadows. But how her heart had beat in those moments! Everything in her had felt alive; even her skin had responded to the air.

It is better, she decides after Watho's visit, not to live in safety. Not in Watho's brand of safety, anyway. She would rather live like the flower.

In that moment, she decides to leave.

WHEN LUNA next wriggles out from behind the vines, she is no longer thinking about how to recreate the flowers and trees in drawings. She wants to understand the grounds around the castle better. She decides she will venture farther out each time she goes outside, until she knows which direction to go. One night, very soon, she and Nox will leave through the forgotten door and not return.

Tonight will be her first real examination of the castle grounds. There is real determination in her step as she sets out toward the stream.

So lost in thought on this topic is she, that she nearly doesn't notice the shape of something long and pale stretched out on the grass by the stream. As soon as she sees it, she changes course and runs to investigate. Luna has not yet learned to truly fear any object in her new, gentle world and feels only curiosity toward the new thing.

It takes her a moment to recognize the object, but when she does, she gasps.

"It's a girl!" she exclaims aloud.

The girl is lying on her back, with her arms flung over her face; asleep, Luna guesses. She has pale skin that reflects the sunlight so that she seems nearly translucent, and long, yellow hair.

Gently, Luna lifts the girl's hands and places them at her side. The face beneath them is peaceful and beautiful, though a long scar mars one cheek. *She looks*, Luna thinks, *like an artist's rendering of the sun with her hair spread out around her face that way.*

The girl moans and begins to stir.

# CHAPTER FOURTEEN

*A*ethon feels gentle hands caressing his face, but does not open his eyes right away. He remembers the terrible darkness in which he has trapped himself and he can still hear the shrill, menacing calls of whatever creatures inhabit such a place. He remembers the baleful moon shining above him; a sickly, mutant version of his beloved sun, leaking feeble light.

The hands on his face must be Watho's, he thinks. She must have come to find him and is here to bring him back inside where all is safe and bright.

Slowly, he opens his eyes, crying out involuntarily as he does so. The eyes that look back at him are decidedly not Watho's, but that is not the cause of his alarm. Aethon, imagining himself more prepared to face it a second time, had half-forgotten already the fearsome darkness. He was not prepared. The night assails him, coating the world like oil, pressing in from all sides.

An unfamiliar girl looms over him as he lays on his back in the damp grass. She has dark skin and hair, and blue eyes that seem too large for her face. She is smiling at him and saying something in a soothing voice. In his panic, it takes him a moment to focus on her.

"It's alright," she is saying. "There's nothing to be afraid of. It's alright."

*Her eyes are the color of daylight,* he thinks. He wants to swim into them and be free. He sits up suddenly and looks around wildly, another anguished cry escaping his lips before he can stop it.

Startled, the girl looks around as well. "What is it?" she asks.

Aethon looks at her, amazed and inexplicably angry at her apparent obtuseness. "Can you not see it? We are trapped in the night! Out in the open like prey in this abominable, inescapable dark."

The girl looks at him as though he's just suggested the sky might be made of oranges. She looks around again slowly before turning back to him with growing concern in her expression.

"I see you are not well," she says at last. "Perhaps you had better lie back down."

"It's no use!" Aethon cries. "If I lie down, the dark will swallow me. Oh, let the day come!"

Despite his protest, he throws himself down again, covering his face with his hands. He feels the girl lift him gently by the shoulders and place his head on her lap. Her cool fingers once again touch his brow, gently brushing his sweat-soaked hair off his forehead.

"Shh," she says. "Poor girl. It's alright."

Aethon can hardly believe his ears. This affront to his dignity stokes a rage which momentarily dwarfs his terror. He jumps up a second time, this time to his knees.

"I am *not* a girl!" he shouts. "How *dare* you?"

She looks mystified but not afraid. "I'm sorry. I didn't know. What can I call you?"

He barely hears her. He is doubled over again, his hands at the sides of his head, clutching his hair in desperation. The darkness is like a living thing, crawling all over him. Aethon can feel it seeping into his skin, a poison in his veins, siphoning the strength from him. His inability to dispel his own fear causes a desperate anger to rise in him, and with nothing on which to vent it, he begins to beat his fists against his skull, a furious scream escaping his lips.

"Stop!" the girl cries in alarm as her hands take hold of his, pulling them away from his face. He resists her for a moment, then allows her to guide his hands back down to his lap where she holds them firmly.

"I'm sorry," she says, and there is real remorse in her voice. "I see that you're not a girl after all, or you would not be so frightened, when there is nothing to fear."

This insult ought to kindle his outrage again, he thinks, but the terror is all consuming now.

"I might as *well* be a girl," Aethon moans. "This darkness reduces me to nothing."

The stranger, to his consternation, laughs. It is a beautiful laugh that makes him think of the wind in Thunderstone's mane. The sound of it calms him, if only a little.

"*What* darkness?" she asks, incredulous. "Poor thing. You aren't in your right mind."

He lets her hands guide him until he is returned to his previous position, with his head in her lap. From there, he can bear to open his eyes, since her face looms over him, blocking the terrible sky. Her hair falls down on either side of her face and surrounds his as well, like a cocoon to shield them from the night air.

*What kind of creature is she*, he wonders, *to be so impervious to the toxic night?* She must be one of the fabled beings from the stories Lucy read to him as a child.

"It's all very well for you," he says. "I suppose a dryad doesn't mind the dark. The moon doesn't burn your skin."

The girl looks bemused.

"Hush, dear," she says softly. "You're quite mad."

"Can't you see it?" he wails, gesturing wildly. "Does it not make your very soul ache? What I wouldn't give for the sun on my face!"

"Oh!" says the girl. "I'm sorry," and she moves her head, which has been blocking the moon from view.

"No!" he clutches his eyes again. "Cover it again! Wretched, malevolent moon!"

"How sensitive you must be!" she laughs. "I think I see why. Your eyes are black, like the night the lamp went out. They can't let the light in, poor creature."

She sounds genuinely pained. *Like someone who knows what it is to be without light*, he thinks. His own misery, however, drives the thought from his mind. No one can understand his current suffering, least of all a creature who seems so much at home in the night.

"I love the daylight too," the girl is saying. "I sometimes think I might die if I have to go another second without it."

Her words make no sense, but her voice steadies him. He knows he is delirious, but he is suddenly convinced that the dark girl with daylight in her eyes is his own courage, which fled his body when the sun set. She has been pulled from his veins by the dark, but stands by him now to give him strength.

"Keep talking," he pleads. "It helps keep the awful night at bay."

~

LUNA KEEPS TALKING.

"In my room," she tells the one who is not a girl, "there are pictures on the walls, painted in splendid colors. There are animals and people in them doing all kinds of things, and sometimes I like to imagine I am one of the painted people. One of the pictures is the coronation of a queen — that's what Falca told me, though I don't know exactly what that means.

"The queen is high up above the rest of the people, with a shining crown, and all the people are looking up at her. I sometimes pretend that I am one of the people looking up. I wonder what it feels like to stand in a crowd, with so many others around me. I wonder how their shoulders feel and what thoughts are behind their eyes."

She goes on telling the poor, frightened creature about the paintings, until she has described them all. The other drifts in and out of sleep while she talks, sometimes moaning as though in pain, though what causes this distress Luna cannot tell.

When she has finished detailing the paintings, she tells the not-girl about the day she got Nox. Then about the night the lamp went out and her first time standing on the balcony beneath the blessed sun. She describes her own drawings and recites the fables from her youth.

She talks and talks until her throat is sore, in a low steady voice so as not to alarm the not-girl. It doesn't ask any questions, or interrupt. She suspects it doesn't hear anything she is saying, but the talking keeps it calm. On the few occasions that the creature's black eyes open, they dart all around in wild terror, until they connect with her own. Then, the other takes a ragged breath and she feels its body begin to relax infinitesimally.

Finally, after more hours than she can count, she begins to notice changes in the air around her. *The sun*, she thinks, *has begun to get brighter.*

Looking around for it, she is startled to see it has sunk in the sky so drastically that it is nearly touching the earth. Luna has learned by now not to let the fluctuations of the mother of all lamps frighten her, but this is unlike anything she has yet seen. She feels her heartbeat quicken. For a few moments it seems that all the light bound up within the sun has begun to seep out, slowly filling the sky.

The colors of all the things she's come to love are changing; becoming garish in this new, strange light.

Luna's lungs tighten and she struggles to gulp in air. She looks down at the face in her lap and sees that its deathly pallor is gone. The anguish has subsided and a new vigor is settling on the not-girl's features like a fine coat of dust on the furniture in her room.

Whatever assault is being carried out on her beloved sun is filling the sky now with violence, changing its gentle blues and blacks to gaudy shades of orange and red.

Shadows begin to crawl from under every rock and tree, stretching out long and dark, fleeing for their lives from the coming light. Luna jumps to her feet and whirls to see what they are running from. The sky near the horizon has been torn open by unfeeling hands and through the injury there bleeds a terrible, blazing light. This is not like the gentle, silver light of her own sun.

It is a ripping, savage light. It will burn all that it touches,

Luna is certain of that. Already it is burning her eyes. She cries out and covers them with her hands, just as the poor not-girl did under the light of the sun.

*If that light had frightened the other, this new light may kill it*, Luna thinks, and turns again to look for the not-girl who has been her ward for these past hours.

The other is not afraid, however. It has leapt to its feet and is facing the terrible light joyfully. Strength and vigor shines on its countenance.

Luna finds she is on her knees, crawling toward the other, or rather crawling away from the piercing glare behind her. She can feel it increasing with every moment; can feel its heat and see the way it lays bare the landscape. It is a ruthless, exposing light, and Luna feels sure she will shrivel up and die under its touch.

The other one who is not a girl turns its face toward the sky and laughs loudly. Jubilant, it turns back to Luna to find her kneeling, her hands over her face in a pathetic mimicry of its previous posture. The not-girl laughs again, unable to contain its elation.

"Oh help," Luna pleads weakly. "It's too terrible! Take me back inside."

"What? Now, when the sun is finally up and there is no longer anything to fear? What a silly girl you must be!"

"I can't stand it!" She is frantic now. This monstrous light is growing, and will keep on growing until it has burned up the whole world.

The other sounds incredulous. "Don't be foolish! Can you not see that the danger is past? The darkness is gone, child! All is well!" It laughs again as it says this last part, not cruelly, but as one whose joy has spilled over.

"Don't leave me," she says. She knows she is pitiable and hates it, but the light is too much to bear. "Please don't leave me exposed like this, to die!"

"I feel the plains calling," the not-girl says, as though she hadn't spoken at all. "I hear the thundering hooves of the beasts. Thanks ever so much for keeping me company. If you ever need anything, I'm at your service."

She hears its footsteps splash in the stream as it charges away and she knows she is alone.

*I'll die,* she thinks. If even the sun is overpowered by this brutal new light, how can she escape the same fate?

She wonders if Falca has discovered her absence yet. Perhaps she will come looking and rescue her. Or perhaps she will be burned up alongside her.

Instinctively, she begins to crawl toward the castle. There may yet be time to escape. Even if there isn't, she has to try. She inches her way forward, trembling. The grass beneath her fingers and knees no longer feels friendly, but sharp and piercing.

The journey is interminable. With every inch of progress, the brightness all around increases. She is afraid to look at her skin, for fear of what it has done to her.

Somehow, she finds the tapestry of vines and manages to wriggle behind it. The blazing luminescence has not yet devoured the tapestry, and it provides just enough shelter to revive her a little. Gathering herself, Luna pushes herself to her feet and, facing the wall, feels her way along it with her eyes closed until she finds the door and stumbles through it into the cool, dark corridor.

CHAPTER FIFTEEN

*A*urora's months of isolation have taught her a lesson, if not quite the one Sir Hugh intended.

She had been full of hope entering into her marriage to the earl. It was an arranged marriage, as she had always known any union would be, but she was beautiful and the daughter of a prince, and he was charming and well regarded. It had the potential to be a mutually satisfying match.

Though it had become apparent early on that the marriage would never be a loving one, the thought of leaving had never crossed her mind. She did not wish to bring such disgrace on her father, herself, or even the earl.

When her husband's career had begun to falter, she had even sought her father's favor on his behalf, but found him reluctant.

"Truthfully, I did have high hopes for the young man, but he's turned out to be a disappointment," the prince had told her. He'd refused to give a reason for his failing faith in Sir Hugh, but the sorrowful look he'd given his daughter told her what his words could not: the earl had fallen out of favor with the other nobles due in large part to his unseemly behavior with many of their wives.

Aurora turned to her mother for advice, but the princess had only admonished her to try to be more pleasing to her husband.

"The duty lies on us, my dear, to ensure our husbands are happy in their homes," she had said. "If he has no complaint, he has no need to wander."

Even at the time, Aurora had found the word *wander* ludicrous. As though a man could simply miss a turn on the way home and find himself in the bed of a strange woman. Still, she had tried her best during the initial years to follow this advice. She had paid attention to Sir Hugh's preferences in food, fashion and conversation, and adapted every aspect of their home to bring him satisfaction, but to no avail.

Eventually, she had resigned herself to finding fulfillment from other sources; first, little Hugh, then when he had been taken away, her charity work and her friendship with Violet.

Now, even that is gone, and in its wake, Aurora is beginning to wonder if societal disgrace is not an easier burden to bear than this. It does not seem that escape is possible — Sir Hugh has effectively cut her off from any help — but escape she must. She becomes more convinced of this every day.

She has been watching, waiting and preparing for months. She has a small valise packed and stowed under the bed. When the opportunity comes, she will be ready.

Aurora has considered all the possibilities. Escape through a window isn't possible. Even if she could fashion a long enough rope to climb down, the locks are sturdy. She could slip out when the chambermaids come to change the linens and clean, but it would be only seconds before she was caught. The chambermaids always come in pairs, to ensure that neither one will speak to her and she can hardly incapacitate both. Only the servant who brings food comes alone, since she only needs to leave a tray at the door.

Aurora has tried unsuccessfully to draw this servant into conversation many times, but the girl never makes eye contact as she nervously deposits the meal and locks the door again, looking over her shoulder as though the walls had eyes. Aurora is convinced this servant is her best chance, so she has focused her efforts on wearing the girl down. So far, however, her efforts have been fruitless.

If she can find a way out, she has decided she will go to her parents' house. They will not approve, but neither will they turn her out into the streets. Her father may even insist that she return to the earl, but in the safety of his castle she will have time to think of a new plan and will not be kept in a room with bars.

Perhaps she can find Violet and the two of them can escape together. In her most elated moments, Aurora imagines finding young Hugh and leaving the country with him, though her more rational self knows that her son would never betray his father. On most days, the thought of little Hugh is too painful to bear at all.

She spends the bulk of her time writing in her journal, or reading; Sir Hugh, probably fancying himself merciful, allows books to be brought to her only after he personally approves them. She has learned not to request specific books, since these are likely to be dismissed on principle.

A few books have slipped through that she thoroughly enjoyed, including one or two of the more scandalous theology books of which Violet is so fond. Aurora suspects that her husband has either not read these or not understood them. She doesn't agree with everything she finds in these volumes, but they inspire new ways of thinking and they remind her of Violet, so she loves them.

So pervasive is Violet's presence when she is reading some of them that Aurora nearly forgets to be surprised when she turns a page one day and a slip of paper bearing her friend's handwriting falls out. Aurora smiles. Violet must have read this book herself before she was dismissed. She picks up the note, wondering what Violet had found so interesting about the passage that she needed to write her thoughts down.

*A — News of your son. You're going to want to hear this.*
*Find a way out. Now.*
*—V*

Aurora stares, aghast. This was not written when Violet lived here. This note is for her *now*. How can that be? Violet must have some contacts still among the servants, which means that her friend is alive.

She reads and re-reads the note. News of Hugh? Has something happened to the boy? Her heart beats like war drums; whether from fear or hope she cannot tell.

Quickly she scrawls her own note, not to Violet, but to the servant. She prays that whoever put the note in the book will be the same person who returns it to the library shelves.

*Need help,* she writes. *Come as soon as possible.*

~

THE TELESCOPE HAS ITS DOWNFALLS. When adjusted

correctly, it can see anything inside or outside the castle for miles around, but in order to truly see everything Watho would need to be looking into it all the time.

More and more she has the feeling that things are going on in her own domain, right under her nose, that she knows nothing about. She has tried varying the timing of her trips to the top of the tower, but to little avail.

Luna, in particular, is causing her concern.

Once she had imagined that the girl would never be of interest at all, but now she feels as though the two are locked in constant battle, the rules of which are unclear.

After Felnys confirmed that the girl had made a second attempt at the balcony, Watho had begun paying more attention to her. Watching her through the telescope had, however, revealed very little.

She draws often and plays the harp with apparent skill. The girl appears to have a pet cat, which Watho is quite certain she has never been asked about. *Still*, the witch thinks, *it was a judicious decision on Falca's part, to give the child a distraction.*

She will have to see to it that Falca is punished for making unsanctioned decisions, but not too severely. The old woman is valuable to her and it is a small infraction.

It strikes her as strange that Luna, having once discovered the outdoors, seems to be content to remain in her quarters, but Felnys stationed himself in the corridor for weeks after his encounter with her and reported no further escape attempts by the girl.

Watho's visit to Luna failed to ease her mind. The girl had a new defiance in her eyes, which Watho had not seen during previous interactions. Against all odds, the child seemed to have developed a mind of her own.

It amuses Watho to think that the girl mistook the moon for the sun, but it also alarms her that Luna is not afraid of the moon. She has been raised in near darkness for 18 years, yet she seems to love the moonlight.

Aethon has adapted so well to his sunlit life — why does the girl not respond the same way? She ought to love the darkness as much as Aethon loves the light. The two are designed to be opposite creatures, after all.

Watho makes her way up to the telescope tower with these thoughts on her mind. It is early morning and her sleep the previous night was troubled. Her head aches, as it often does after such nights, making her irritable. The telescope is already trained on Luna's rooms, so Watho does not have to make adjustments.

Luna is nowhere to be seen.

Watho swings the telescope from side to side, searching every part of the room, but the girl is not there. Watho quickly adjusts so that she can see the passage outside Luna's door and the stairs which lead to Watho's own room, if followed straight, or to the balcony, if one turns right at the landing. The passages and stairwells are empty, the balcony likewise.

Watho's eye returns to Luna's rooms, just in time to see the girl fall into bed looking weak and exhausted.

A white hot rage descends on Watho. *Where has she been?*

There is no other way to leave Luna's rooms. Watho is certain of it. Just as certain as she is that the girl was not in the room when she first looked.

She watches Luna for a moment more. The girl is curled up on her side, sound asleep, though a haunted expression lingers on her features.

Watho tears down the stairs to her office and rings the bell for Falca before she is fully in the room herself.

To be left unsupervised, she fumes, is a privilege. If Luna cannot be trusted with that privilege, it can be revoked.

AETHON LOOKS up at the sky and closes his eyes, enjoying warmth on his face, letting his skin soak in the golden incandescence of the sun. He feels like a man who has drunk from a fountain of vitality. Strength courses through his veins, hot and bright.

The hunting party had that morning encountered the king of boars; an enormous beast with whom they have been performing a respectful dance for weeks, both parties the hunter, both parties the prey, drawing ever nearer and waiting to see who would strike the first blow.

Resplendent with new vigor, Aethon had charged so recklessly and joyously into battle with the beast that even Fargu was taken aback when he felled the brute with a single strike and a fierce cry.

It's now amid-afternoon, however, and Aethon's mood has been rapidly deteriorating. His victory over the boar is tainted by the memory of last night's events; chiefly, his own cowardice when darkness fell.

What does it matter how gloriously he performs or how mighty his foe in the sunlight if his courage flees the instant the sun goes down? He is furious with himself, with his companions, with the world that has hobbled him thus.

He feels as though he watched a different boy than himself endure that long night. In his current mood and ensconced in sunlight, Aethon can find no common ground with the whimpering creature he was in the darkness. Only the tender ministrations of the mysterious night girl — a nymph or perhaps a dryad — had carried him through those hours of torment. The more he remembers his debasement, curled up like a child in the lap of a girl, the more viciously he condemns himself.

With his thoughts darkened thus, gloom descends heavily as the day progresses. He finds himself sulking as his companions celebrate all around him. He simply cannot reconcile the man he knows himself to be with the frightened child he became last night. There must, he reasons, be an explanation outside himself.

As soon as this thought crops up, he nurses it with desperation until it flourishes, eclipsing all other possibilities. Has he not, after all, acquitted himself admirably before every foe he's ever faced? Why, then, would he be reduced to nothing by something so small as a change in the atmosphere? The only possible answer is that he was struck down by a powerful spell of some kind, or perhaps poisoned by the water he drank from the girl's hands.

*The girl*, he thinks with sudden distrust. Could it be that she was not his savior but his enemy, having first caught him unawares by some mystical power and then reveled in his humiliation? Not only is it possible, he tells himself, it is the likeliest thing in the world. He cannot be blamed for having succumbed to the curse. After all, he had been unprepared; a disadvantage at which he will not be found again. He was not a coward! He had only been waylaid, as any honest man might be, by a cunning enemy who worked by intrigue because she could not face him courageously in battle.

Now, however, he knows the signs. Now he can face the

night, and any enemy therein undaunted, and redeem himself.

These thoughts cheer him considerably. He ignores the nervous glances exchanged by his companions as they watch his fluctuating humor.

For the second time, he takes his leave of them early. He whistles a tune out of key while he puts Thunderstone away and follows the same path he took last evening, around to the side of the castle, where he settles down to wait for sunset.

This time he will not fall asleep. He cannot risk being found unconscious by the dryad, should she return to do him harm a second time. Tonight, he will meet whatever the darkness hides with courage.

Thus fortified in his confidence, he sits on the banks of the stream and removes his boots, letting the cool water wash over his feet and refresh him while he waits.

True to the promise he made himself, Aethon does not fall asleep. He is fully alert as the sun begins to sink and the colors of the world begin to fade. When his heart starts to race and his stomach churns, he feels every pounding pulse.

The darkness descends upon him like an army, shouting its haunting war cries. Malevolent eyes gleam from the shadows, then wink out and reappear in new places. Nameless things move with the cracking of twigs and fearsome whooshing sounds. A cold wind picks up, prickling his skin and making his head ache. The water no longer feels sweet and cool, but slimy. He withdraws his feet so quickly that he nearly falls over backward. The hair on the back of his neck stands on end, as if in response to the breath of some silent, watching being, creeping up on him from behind.

Unable to restrain himself any longer, Aethon jumps to his

feet and begins to run headlong into the darkness; from what he cannot say, and toward what, he knows even less.

Only a moment later, his bare foot strikes something — a rock, or a tree root, or a trap left there by demons — and he pitches forward, landing hard on the grass.

Unable to get up again, he curls up on his side, clasping his hands to his eyes just he did before, whimpering for some reprieve.

He repents of his suspicions about the dryad and prays she will come to care for him again. Every moment he hopes to feel her touch, brushing his hair off his forehead again. All night he lies there, eyes clenched tight, terrified to move lest he draw the eye of those mysterious enemies that hoot and caw from the poisonous blackness. He beseeches the spirits for comfort, but none comes.

# CHAPTER SIXTEEN

*A*urora tells herself that no one is coming. Her message has been missed, or intercepted, or perhaps there was no messenger after all.

She tries again to get some response from the servant who takes the empty trays and finished books, even a glance, but the girl never looks at her.

*Not her, then. So who?*

She knows that if there is a response to her message, it may not come right away. It could be days — weeks even — before the person responsible for slipping her the note finds her reply.

Still, she doesn't change for bed. When supper is taken away and she can be certain of no further visitors for the evening, she checks and checks again to be sure that her valise is ready for traveling. Aurora hears the house settle into silence as its occupants finish their daily tasks and take themselves off to bed. Putting the lights out in her own room, she paces restlessly in the dark, pausing to listen at every creak or whisper of movement outside her door.

By 2 o'clock, she is certain that there will be no response to her note tonight, but she cannot bear the thought of giving up and going to sleep.

*What does it matter, anyway?* she thinks. It's not as though she has pressing appointments tomorrow. If she sleeps through the day, no one will notice or care.

She stops pacing by the window, staring out through the bars at the moonlit gardens, where she and Violet used to walk arm in arm — where she caught her first glance of the wolf.

*I thought I was unhappy then.* Aurora feels her mouth twist in a bitter smile. *If only my sons had been the only thing he took from me.* She no longer blames herself for the loss of the first child. These last months have taught her better. It was her fear of her new husband, after all, that drove her to seek the help of a witch to begin with.

The sliding of a key in the lock behind her is so quiet that it barely pierces her consciousness. Not so, when the door creaks open and she hears soft footsteps behind her.

Aurora holds her breath, her heart tightening within her chest. She has been waiting so long for that door to open, but now that it has, how can she be sure the visitor is a friend? She knows all too well how few of those she has. It may even be Sir Hugh, come to pay one of his loathsome midnight visits. He does this, occasionally, when there are no other women to satisfy him.

Suddenly, Aurora finds that she is tired of being afraid. There is nothing, after all, left to lose. She no longer has to fear that her husband will never love her; that much is certain. Her children have been stolen, her only friend banished, and even her limited freedom to choose where she spends her days is gone. Everything she feared has already come to pass. She turns, calmly, to face the silent presence in the room and comes face to face with a young woman. Not the servant girl who brings the food and books, but one just like her. Timid, trembling. A mere child.

Aurora wonders how long the woman has been in her employ. Does she know any of the servants anymore? Has the earl cleansed the entire house of familiar faces? She wonders if the cooks and footmen have been dismissed as well, and why she never considered the possibility until now. It makes sense that after her flight, the earl would trust no one in the house except Sebastian. At once she feels a pang of guilt, realizing how many people have been turned out, certainly without reference, on her account.

The woman says nothing, but her expression betrays her terror. She has come at Aurora's bidding, but she would rather be anywhere than here. Aurora suddenly feels enormous affection for the poor brave girl.

"It's alright," she says softly. "Was it you who slipped the note into my book?"

A quick, sharp nod. The girl's eyes dart around the room as though she thinks someone is listening.

"Why?" Aurora asks. She knows she ought to get on with the business of escape but she wants to understand why this clearly petrified young woman, who has no duty or loyalty toward her, would take such a risk.

The woman's eyes mist, but she draws her shoulders back slightly, shaking her head. "It weren't right, m'lady. What the earl has done to you. Forgive my saying so, m'lady, I mean no disrespect. Only I couldn't bear to see anyone be held prisoner in her own home."

Aurora wonders if this trembling woman has some experience of her own on which to draw. She suspects that she does.

For a moment she doesn't see a frightened servant speaking to a countess, only a fellow woman acquainted with tyranny. At this moment, Aurora would gladly crown the girl queen of the five realms and swear fealty forever.

"I am in your debt." She hopes the servant can hear her sincerity. "If you leave the door unlocked behind you when you leave, is there any reason for someone to guess it was you who did so?"

The woman nods again and Aurora's heart sinks. If her escape means her punishment is passed down to this stranger — and it will be no doubt worse for a servant than for the lady of the house — she cannot in good conscience take the risk.

"The others suspect me of bein' sympathetic," the woman says, "and report back to his lordship everything they see. Begging your pardon m'lady, I don't wish to impose, but it's best if I go with you."

She looks apologetic, but Aurora's heart leaps. "Of course," she says. "Are you ready now? Or shall I wait for another night?"

A sharp shake of the woman's head. "No m'lady! Now. There won't be another chance."

Relief, hot and sweet, floods Aurora. "Good." She reaches underneath the bed and retrieves her valise. The girl tries to take it, but Aurora shakes her head.

"What's your name?" she whispers.

"Sarah," she says, motioning frantically toward the door.

Aurora holds up a hand to stay her. "Just one moment."

She retrieves a soft, blue traveling cloak and throws it around Sarah's shoulders. It will cover her white chambermaid's gown and keep them better hidden in the dark.

"I'm not your lady," Aurora whispers. "I'm Aurora. As you

are my only friend in the world you may as well call me by my name."

Sarah shakes her head, astonished — not, Aurora realizes, because she's been graced with the privilege of using the countess' name, but because Aurora would choose now of all times to pause for introductions.

"Sorry," she mutters, with a sheepish grimace.

Silently, Sarah tip toes out the door, with Aurora in her wake, clutching her valise with white knuckles.

The journey through the manor takes so long that Aurora wonders if her home has expanded during her captivity. She hears every creak and shudder, and the squeak of every door resounds like temple bells in her ears.

At last, however, she finds herself in the cool night air, waiting impatiently while Sarah's trembling fingers turn the key to open the garden gate.

As she closes it behind her, Aurora casts one dismissive glance back toward her home of nearly 18 years. Twice, now, she has left it under cover of darkness. This time, she vows, she will not return.

She tries to take the lead, heading toward her father's house. It's a long trip, but she may be able to find a cab and promise payment from her father's hand when she's delivered to his door.

Sarah catches her wrist and shakes her head.

"This way," she whispers. Aurora is tempted to argue, but she won't do it standing outside the manor's gates. Sebastian may be upon them at any moment. Sarah turns in the opposite direction, and Aurora follows.

By the time they reach the temple, Aurora understands it is the better choice. Sir Hugh will look for her first at her father's, who will be honor-bound to produce her. There can be no safety there. At least at the temple, she can claim sanctuary for a while. The Holy Sentries will not help her; they will try to appease the earl by finding ways around the law of sanctuary. Still, their political maneuvering will take time, and that is what she needs.

They slip in by a side door and Aurora looks around in wonder at the massive room, seeing it empty for the first time.

*What now?*

Sarah touches her elbow and motions to the long rows of brocaded cushions on the polished floor. Aurora lowers herself gratefully onto one, expecting Sarah to do the same, but the girl surprises her again.

"Wait here," she whispers. "I won't be long."

She moves with purpose and disappears through a door at the back of the room, behind the altar. Cold fear seizes Aurora by the throat. She has trusted this stranger, she realizes, followed her blindly and allowed herself to be left alone and exposed. She forces herself to calm her breathing, but her body remains tense, ready to run should the need arise.

After what feels like hours, she hears the gentle click of the latch and the door opens again. Sarah reappears, with another woman in her wake.

Aurora jumps to her feet, forgetting caution in her elation.

"Violet!" she cries. "Thank the spirits."

Violet looks as radiant as Aurora feels. For once she doesn't have a joke.

"You're safe now," she says, and Aurora finally allows her body to relax into her friend's arms, blinking hot tears away.

After a moment she draws back from Violet's embrace, wiping her nose with the back of her hand.

"Your note said you had word about little Hugh." The child is 17 by now, but to his mother he will always be *little Hugh*, as he was when she saw him last. "What's happened to him? Is he alright?"

Violet is shaking her head. "Not Hugh. I have news of your other son."

The earth seems to stop spinning. She feels as though she can hear it grinding to a halt on its axis, time sharpening to crystals, suspended in the air around her.

She tries to speak, but her voice doesn't come.

"Come on," Violet says. "I want you to meet my cousin, Alyvia."

~

"MY LORD."

Sir Hugh looks up from his breakfast to see his steward standing respectfully in the doorway.

"What is it Sebastian?"

"It's her ladyship, I am told she absconded with a chambermaid during the night."

The earl nods. He has been expecting this visit for some time. Aurora has never known what's good for her. Although he has suspected she will try to leave him again, the reality of her rebellion is no less an outrage.

*How dare she?*

He is *entitled* to her obedience. He is already devising new punishments before Sebastian has finished his account.

"They were seen heading toward the temple," he is saying. Sebastian has a network of sources to whom he appeals when necessary. Sir Hugh does not doubt that his information is reliable.

*Clever. They can seek sanctuary in the temple.*

He continues sawing at a congealing slab of ham with a knife and fork while he considers. When he found Aurora the last time, she had been going to Astarsaga Castle. He never asked her why; he needed no explanation. The failed delivery of his first son had taken place there. No doubt some feminine hysteria had driven her back to the scene of her crime.

He doesn't know what happened in the forest, or why his wife and her companions came limping out of it with no coach and no horses, but he knows she never made it.

"Are you not concerned that she will obtain sanctuary from the Holy Sentries?" Sebastian asked, perturbed, no doubt by his lack of consternation.

The earl shakes his head, talking around a mouthful of ham. "She won't stay at the temple. I know where to find her."

AETHON OPENS his eyes to see Fargu's concerned face looming over his own, silhouetted by sunlight. He's lying on his back in tall grass, Thunderstone standing placidly beside him. He doesn't need to move to know his tailbone is badly bruised.

"What happened?" he mumbles.

"You fell off your horse," Fargu says. "I should think that much would be obvious."

With Fargu's help, Aethon sits up. His head is pounding, his body feels weak, and his eyes burn with exhaustion. He barely remembers the morning. He must have saddled Thunderstone and gone out with the hunters as he always does, but it seems like a memory from long ago.

"Come on," Fargu says, extending a hand to help him stand. "You've been wandering around in a daze all morning. You aren't well."

Aethon shakes his head. "I'm fine. I only need some water,"

Fargu laughs. "I think not, lad. Back to the castle with you. I'll not have my mistress finding out you were sick and I didn't see to you."

His words fall around Aethon in a jumbled heap which he cannot begin to untangle. He stares hard at Fargu, willing his mind to work — to coherently interpret his surroundings — but his thoughts are sluggish and unresponsive.

The last thing he remembers clearly is the moon. It burns through his consciousness like a brand, though it long ago gave way to daylight. He remembers curling up under it like a child, begging it to leave him be. Again.

For seven days he has told himself that *this* time, he'll be prepared to face the night. For seven nights he has ventured out, fortified by the strength of the day, to redeem himself, lest he be forever a coward in his own eyes.

Every night he waits for the dryad but she never comes. Perhaps, he tells himself, she only came the first time to lull him into peace so she could cast her spell, and now she has no need to torment him further.

He is convinced, now more than ever, that some pernicious spell gains power over him when the sun sets. For each morning when it rises, his courage returns and he is himself again.

His strength, however, has begun to flag even during the day as a result of his nightly exertions. Two days ago he realized that his body was becoming weaker and reassured himself that *tonight* he would find the key to the spell and conquer the night.

Now, the moonlight runs together with the sunlight in his mind, like poison in wine. The night has caught up to him, followed him into the sun, it seems, for he can barely think and his body no longer responds to his commands.

Fargu is helping him onto his horse now and speaking again, but Aethon has stopped trying to understand. Thunderstone follows the huntsman as Aethon lolls in his saddle, trying to remain conscious.

When they reach the castle, Fargu helps him down and convinces him to leave Thunderstone's care to the stable master. The huntsman supports his weight until they reach Aethon's room and ushers him to bed. He feels his guardian removing his boots, with an almost motherly care. He is asleep before Fargu has left the room, but it is a troubled, restless sleep.

He tosses and turns, waking frequently. Sometimes he thinks he sees things lurking in the room. Once, he sees an enormous red wolf, watching him with sharp eyes, black as his own.

*I could not hunt, so the hunt has come to me,* he thinks incoherently.

Another time he sees Watho herself. She has come to see him, but the look she gives him when their eyes meet is so full of contempt that his stomach turns.

He watches her, unsure of himself, until he is confident that it really *is* her, not some hallucination, in the room with him.

He tries to speak, but the words whither on his tongue. She whirls and walks to the windows. One at a time, she draws the curtains, usually only drawn at night when the lamps are lit.

Aethon feels the now familiar terror begin to rise in his belly as she moves from one window to the next, until the room is filled with shadow. Only one lamp is lit. Aethon has never seen his own room in this dim light before.

Watho turns to him again, a scornful smile on her lips, and extinguishes the lamp with a flick of her wrist. She leaves him then, in a darkness with no moon or stars to punctuate it. He turns to bury his face in the pillow and for the first time since childhood, begins to weep.

WATHO IS THERE AGAIN when Aethon wakes up. The room is still drenched in shadows, the curtains still drawn, but he can just make out her shape by the bedside. She's sitting perfectly still, watching him.

He can't discern her expression in the dark, but he feels her contempt all the same; his own disdain for himself reflected back at him. He wants to jump to his feet — to face her. To cast off the restraints of oppressive darkness and show her his strength.

He knows he can do no such thing. The darkness pins him down, robs him of valor.

"Ah, the mighty hunter awakes," she says from the gloom, scorn thickening her voice.

"Please," he rasps, "light the lamp. Have mercy. I'm not well."

"No," she laughs. "You are not well. Why do you think that is, Aethon?"

He casts around for the answer she is looking for, but the darkness clouds his mind. He cannot think clearly without light.

"Is it perhaps," she says, not waiting for a response, "because you repeatedly violated my commands? Did you think I had no purpose in issuing them?"

"I wanted to hunt the lion," he mumbles.

"And why should the lion want to be hunted by you?" she asks. "You yourself told me there's nothing to be gained from combat with a coward. What merit have you that the lion should deign to engage you? Curled up like a weakling, afraid of the dark."

"I... I didn't know," he pleads. "There is some magic in the darkness. Some spell that overtakes me. Please Watho! It's not my fault."

"No," she says mournfully. "It's not your fault, is it? You are not strong enough to withstand the darkness. That is why I have always tried to protect you from it."

"I'm sorry," he whimpers. "I'm so sorry. Only please light the lamp."

He hears the chair crash to the floor as she leaps to her feet and he cowers, unable to see what she will do.

She crosses the room now and Aethon hears a familiar sound that takes him a moment to place. She's withdrawing arrows from their quiver, where Fargu must have left it. He can almost feel the heat of her fury as she bounds across the room again and he feels one of the razor-sharp arrowheads sink into his arm.

Then another jab, this time in his shoulder. The cuts are quick and shallow. She strikes him again and again, while he throws his arms over his face protectively. He cries out, more in fear than pain. She is like a wild animal in her anger, taunting him.

"What is it you say about a worthy opponent?" she laughs as she hurls his youthful boasts back at him. "Am I not worthy?

Can you not disarm me? Or are you such a pathetic creature that you cannot overpower a woman?"

*She wants me to fight back*, he thinks, but he cannot. The darkness is too heavy, the assault too frantic.

She is holding the arrow by its shaft, lunging as she speaks. He barely hears her movements, the whispers of her gown as she dances like a swordsman in the dark. The sharp point pierces his ribs, the tender skin under his arms, his thigh, his shoulder. He tries to believe it's chivalry, rather than terror, that prevents his returning her attacks. She is like a demon, hiding in the darkness, leaping at him from the shadows.

He begs her to stop, pleading like a child. Eventually she does. He hears her sigh of disgust as the arrow clatters to the floor. Without another word she leaves him to wallow in his fear and shame.

## CHAPTER SEVENTEEN

$\mathcal{L}$una makes it back to her own familiar room, tired and shaken. She climbs into bed, whispering a prayer of thanks for its softness and safety. Watho was right; it's far too dangerous outside.

Falca is in her room when she wakes up. She is watching Luna with an expression Luna has never seen — something between anger and apprehension.

"What have you done, child?" she says softly, when Luna is fully awake.

So she knows then. The thought brings some relief. Falca has been, for most of Luna's life, the source of all knowledge. Being unable to appeal to her for answers to her many questions has been almost unbearable over the past few months, when she has been learning so much but so slowly.

On the heels of this bright thought, a darker one follows. If Falca knows, that means Luna's excursions are over. In this moment, at least, Luna doesn't mind. If what she faced this morning is any indication of what she can expect outside the castle walls, she wants no part of it.

"I'm sorry, Falca," she says. "I ought to have told you. I won't sneak out again."

"You certainly won't," Falca says ruefully. "Nor will you have the opportunity. Our mistress has determined that as you cannot be left alone, you shall not be."

Luna winces. So Falca will pay for her disobedience. "Do you mean you can't leave at all?"

"Couldn't if I wanted to. The doors are locked from the outside."

*Doors, not door.*

Instinctively, Luna casts a glance toward the secret door, but Falca's already shaking her head.

"That one will be no use to you," she says. "Our mistress inspected your quarters thoroughly. *All* the doors are locked."

Luna looks at her governess with dawning horror. She has accepted, at least for now, her own fate. She knows she won't survive if she leaves, but surely Falca should not be condemned to share her prison forever. How selfish she has been.

"Oh Falca, forgive me. Tell Watho I won't try to leave again. I know better now! I understand what she wanted to protect me from."

"I imagine you'll have the chance to tell her yourself," Falca says. "But what's all this? What do you mean you know what she's protecting you from?"

Luna shudders. "It's a long story."

Falca's laugh is a touch bitter, and Luna cannot help but wince again.

"If there's anything we have, child, it's time," Falca says.

So Luna recounts her adventures from the previous night. She tells her of her plan to leave and how she encountered the one who was not a girl lying terrified by the stream, and how, when the light began to change, the other was filled with new strength and abandoned her to the terrible, murderous light. She's surprised how much it stings to recall the stranger's unkindness, the careless, merry laugh as their footsteps retreated.

Falca listens, eyes wide, to this tale. When it's over, she doesn't speak for a few moments. She looks decidedly nervous.

"I'm glad to be able to tell you," Luna says at last. "I have had so many questions for you, these past weeks."

Before she finishes speaking, however, Falca is shaking her head. "You've learned enough, I think," she says.

There is something else behind her eyes. *Fear*, Luna thinks, but she can't be sure.

"My head is aching," says Falca. "Would you play a little music, Luna? That always helps."

"Of course." Luna is glad for an opportunity to do her guardian a favor after her disobedience.

She goes to the harp that stands at the foot of her bed, leans it gently against her shoulder and begins to move her fingers across the strings. The melody is the color of amethyst, sweet and sad. Luna closes her eyes and lets herself sink into the music. She replays the encounter with the stranger and the fearful light in her mind, trying vainly to understand.

"Don't stop playing and don't look up," Falca says in a low voice from nearby. Luna glances at her, startled, but looks immediately back down. Falca has moved her chair close to the harp and appears to be focused on a piece of embroidery. When she speaks again, Luna has to strain to hear her over the music.

"Watho can see and hear everything we do," Falca says. "Don't ask me how, I don't know. It's how she knew you'd been gone. She saw you come back."

Luna closes her eyes, heart sinking, but her fingers continue their work, not missing a note.

"Our mistress has given strict orders about your education," Falca continues, "which she must not know I have broken. I will answer your questions, but we must be careful."

"But surely she can't see us all the time," Luna says, keeping her own voice low. "After all, your teaching me to read was against the rules."

"I never would have done so had I known," Falca says. Luna can hear the fear in her guardian's voice, even over the mournful tune. "However, I think you are right. She must have some way of looking in on us, but only when she chooses. Still, we have no way of knowing when that is, only that it is bound to be more often, now that you've drawn her attention to you."

Luna's stomach drops as the implications of this news settle on her.

"Be that as it may," Falca continues, "it's not right to keep you here in ignorance against your will. My mistress will kill me if she hears me say so, but I have wrestled with my conscience long enough. I think it's time to tell you about the world. Tell me what you wish to know and I'll do my best."

Luna can hardly believe her ears. How Falca can feel she owes her anything, when the woman has been condemned to imprisonment on her account, is beyond her. Still, she is not going to pass up the chance to get answers to her many burning questions.

"Tell me about the stranger," she says. "The one who was afraid of the sun."

"I think I had better tell you first about the sun."

Thus, Luna's education begins.

Over the next seven days, Luna's universe expands yet again. Her education unfolds at a painstaking pace, some of it mumbled under the music of the harp, much more if whispered under the blankets as she and Falca pretend to sleep.

Falca has begun turning off the lamp at night, proclaiming loudly that she may be locked in this tomb with her ward, but she will not be able to get a wink of sleep with the light on.

Luna hates to be without the lamp for even a moment, but now that she understands, she can bear it better. Falca tells her that the weight of darkness may be enough to dampen Watho's interest in watching them.

It seems to work, as their isolation remains undisturbed even after several nights of lying in the dark, while Falca illuminates the world in whispered revelations.

Luna learns first about the real sun, and the moon. This knowledge floats at the top of the great reservoir of new things she is coming to understand. The other bits of knowledge are sometimes jumbled, tumbling over each other like water in the stream. The fact of the moon, however, stands on its own, shining and soft.

This word is better suited to the gentle beauty of the moon than the word *sun* was. She knew it as soon as she heard the boy curse it in his terror. Now that she understands what the sun really is, she regrets her ignorance. She hopes the moon will forgive her for calling it by such a harsh name. She hopes she'll have the chance to ask.

She learns also about the boy, whom Falca says is called Aethon, who has been raised in only sunlight, never allowed to see the moon.

"He is raised to be your opposite in all things," Falca whispers. "He has received a varied education, while you know only music and art. He knows only light, while you know only darkness. He's been raised to be strong and brave, while you've been taught meekness and obedience."

Luna turns these things over and over in her mind while Falca teaches her about crowded towns where people live side by side, the nobles and kings who rule them and Holy Sentries who see to their souls. Beneath this rushing current of understanding, the sun and moon circle in her mind's eye, regarding one another from afar, like enemies, or dancers, or lovers.

"I do not think we are opposites," she says abruptly one night.

"What?" Falca, who has been telling her about the tavern in Harthwaite and its proprietor, the giver of kittens, pauses in confusion.

"Aethon and me," Luna says. "I don't think we are opposites, as you said. We are the same."

There is a tense pause. Falca thinks she will have to explain it all again, Luna realizes.

"He is as much a prisoner of Watho's as I am," she says.

She has adopted new positions a dozen times in the past few days, repented of a hundred thoughts. She has vacillated wildly between her conclusion that Watho has only been trying to protect her, and her previous belief that she must escape at all costs. More and more, it seems that she is a captive, rather than a ward, but each time she has this thought, the terrible implications crowd her mind and she hurriedly pushes the thought away.

If she is a captive, then Watho is wicked and she ought to escape. If she escapes, she must face the sunlight again.

*I will think about that later,* she always tells herself. The more Falca talks, however, the more frequently her thoughts turn in this direction.

"I suppose so," Falca allows. "But you live in opposite worlds."

"Do we? You say that he knows only light and I only darkness, but that isn't true. We both love the light and hate the darkness. It is neither of our faults that we have a different understanding of them both."

"But he spends his days in freedom, while you are confined to this room," Falca points out.

Luna has been considering this too. "Perhaps," she says slowly, "it only looks like freedom. He has wider spaces and more company, but he is restrained, just as I am. He is only allowed the strength to kill and conquer, and is denied the pleasures of music and art and gentle conversation."

"I doubt he much regrets their absence," Falca says wryly.

"Perhaps not, but only because he doesn't know any better," Luna replies. "Neither he nor I can leave of our own choosing, or live in the whole world — both the night and the day, under sun and moon — as we are meant to. Of the two of us, I have the advantage, at least now, of knowing what's been taken from me."

"I still say you are not the same," says Falca, her voice taking on a hard edge. "For when you found him crippled by the dark, you ministered to him and kept him safe, if only from his own fears. A mercy he did not return when the situation was reversed."

"Yes," Luna says quietly. "That much is true."

She thinks the memory should not sting as it does. After all, he is a stranger, from whom she has no reason to expect any kind of behavior, good or bad. Still, he's a stranger whose head she held in her own lap, who has seen her crawling in terror and simply turned away.

In that, she agrees, they are not alike.

WATHO HAS RETURNED AGAIN and again during Aethon's sickness. Sometimes she only looks at him and leaves. Other times she taunts him as she did the first time.

He's tried to get up and turn on the lamps himself, but each time he feels feverish and weak as soon as his feet touch the floor. He begins to suspect that his illness is more magical than physical in nature, to keep him so effectively bound to his bed.

He vacillates between bouts of exhaustion and brief spurts of fury. His fists are bruised and bloodied from beating them against the wall in his helpless rage. He finds himself even more depleted than usual each time one of these spells has passed.

He has, however, slowly grown more accustomed to the darkness of his room. He no longer feels panic when he opens his eyes, only sadness. He misses the light, but his eyes have adjusted to the dimness enough now that he can make out the furniture, and can see Watho and the servants when they come and go.

The wounds she inflicted with the tip of his arrow on her first visit have begun to itch as they heal, but new injuries have been sustained in their place during subsequent encounters. No one has changed his bed linens and they are smeared with dried blood from the attacks.

Though the fever persists, his thoughts have begun to flow more coherently. He is sorting through them slowly, attempting to make sense of the drastic change that has been wrought in his life. He has replayed the night of the dryad time and time again. He has considered how he must have looked to the strange girl's eyes, curled up on the ground and moaning in terror when there was no threat. Each time Aethon remembers that night, he feels the heat of Watho's contempt rise up in himself.

As he has nothing but time in which to consider these things, however, his thoughts on the matter have begun to shift. He remembers seeing the lion for the first time and hears Fargu's voice in his head; *you wouldn't think it such a coward if you met him at night. He's as mighty a predator as you are yourself.*

He had been so quick to charge the lion with cowardice for skulking in the shadows during the day, but only that night that he found himself doing just the same, or worse.

Could it be, then, that there are creatures who are just like him — whose bravery waxes and wanes with the turning of the earth? Perhaps the lion is his counterpart in courage; occupying the opposite space in the same circle of the sun's rising and setting.

*If that is the case*, he thinks, grudgingly at first, *what is to prevent the girl from being the same as the lion? After all, she was as much braver than me in the moonlight as I was braver than the lion in the sun.*

He thinks of Watho — of her sneering disdain for his weakness. *Isn't it she*, he thinks, *who orchestrated it? Isn't it she who kept me from ever touching a shadow for long enough to understand it?*

Once he has begun to think in this direction, the thoughts carry him along almost against his will until he feels as though a different kind of sunlight has burst on him, illuminating dark corners of himself that he never wished to see.

He remembers the girl, cowering at his feet as he stood exultant in the light of the breaking dawn and feels that his guilt will suffocate him. It is this view of him, he realizes, that must condemn him in her sight, not his whimpering fear during the night. For her ministry to him was entirely without censure or contempt when he thought he might die from the oppressive darkness.

Yet when the sun had risen and restored his strength, and she like the lion had shrunk from it, he had left her alone in her misery. He remembers with painful clarity how he felt when he caught his first glimpse of the moon — how certain he had been that no one had endured such suffering as his.

He knows now, and the knowledge is like a sharp blade sliding between his ribs, that the strange girl has endured far more with no one to wipe her brow and murmur comfort in her ear.

The shame these thoughts bring is not like the shame he felt before. He aches to find her again, if only to see if she's alright. He has ceased to think of her as a dryad, though he cannot say when the change occurred. He supposes, in his most honest moments, that he had only ever wanted to believe her a supernatural creature in order to excuse his behavior.

The longer he lies in the darkened room, sweating out the toxins of his mistress' wrath, the less inclined he is to deal so dishonestly with himself. By the time he has been bedridden for five days, he has come to see his illness as a mercy, which may have struck in time to spare his soul from something far worse.

# CHAPTER EIGHTEEN

"*I*'m sorry Falca," Luna says under her breath. The old woman looks up at her, questioning.

It's the middle of the day and she is not playing the harp. The two of them have been sitting in silence, Falca reading a book and Luna drawing. During the first few days of their captivity, they tried to fill the daylight hours with manufactured conversation about mundane topics for the sake of their listener, but this quickly became burdensome. Now, they talk very little, especially during the day.

Now that the initial trauma of sunrise has faded, Luna's resolve has returned. She still shudders at the thought of being ever again exposed to the brazen daylight, but she no longer believes there is anything of protection in Watho's motives for keeping her here. She's more determined to escape now than she was before, for Falca's imprisonment weighs heavy on her conscience. Long after her guardian falls asleep each night, Luna lies awake turning their situation over and over in her mind.

There's no way to sneak out, that much is clear. She's tried the doors, late at night when the lamp is out. She's felt every inch of the walls for other forgotten seams, hunting until the inevitable panic rises, clamping down on her lungs, turning her breaths shallow and frantic. There is no way out. They may as well be buried alive.

The doors never open, even for the delivery of meals. Watho apparently wishes to spare Luna any temptation to either overpower or persuade the servants. Instead, food arrives and is taken away by magic. The table is laid out when Luna wakes up most mornings and is cleared after each meal.

Luna had wondered aloud one night why, if Watho could do such a thing, she bothered to employ servants at all, but Falca explained that using her power too often left Watho fatigued.

"She prefers not to waste magic on mundane tasks. She stores it up so that when she does want to use it, it's a spectacular display of power, " she had said.

Luna mulled over these things night after night, until, at long last, she had an idea. It was a feeble, tenuous thing, as ideas went, but as it was the only one to have presented itself, she clung to it with all her might.

It took her a day or two to work up the courage to execute it. She had cast around for other possibilities — any option that wouldn't result in her escaping from the dark tomb only to find herself defenseless under the burning sun.

She had nearly talked herself out of it.

Then she saw Falca, squinting at her book beneath the dim lamplight. The old woman's eyes were weak and straining, but she had not complained once. Luna realized at once that the longer she waits, the less likely she is to act at all. Before she could stop herself, she whispered her apology.

"Sorry for what, child?" Falca asks.

"For betraying your trust. For sneaking out and for not telling you. It's all my fault that you're locked up in this place."

Falca looks stricken. Luna's words have evidently caused the old woman pain.

*She does hold it against me,* Luna thinks. *She's tried not to say anything, the noble thing, but how can she help it?*

Falca's eyes are misty and Luna opens her mouth to speak again, searching for any words that will bring comfort, but the old woman holds up a hand to stop her.

"You don't know what you're saying, child." Her voice cracks and she looks back down at her book to hide her tears. "Don't say anything more, we'll talk tonight."

For a moment Luna considers obeying. She wants to give Falca the chance to say her piece, to express whatever pain and betrayal she feels, but a voice inside her tells her not to wait. If she doesn't do what she must right now, she may find a reason to put off the moment forever.

"I've been thinking about our mistress," she says in a louder voice than either of them have used in days. Falca's head snaps up, her eyes wide and fearful.

"Hush!" she hisses.

Luna ignores her, looking back down at her drawing so she doesn't have to meet Falca's eyes. The hand holding the pencil is trembling, but she keeps her back straight. It probably doesn't matter. The odds that Watho is looking in on them at this precise moment seem low.

"I think I understand her better now," she continues. "I thought she must hate me, to keep me confined in this place, to prevent me from ever seeing the moon, to make me terrified of the sun. But how could she? What have I ever done to give her cause to hate me so much?"

Falca stares, her face a mask of speechless dread.

"I see now," Luna says, struggling to keep her voice even, "that it isn't me she despises, but herself."

She hears Falca gasp. "What are you doing? Do you want to die?" she whispers.

Luna dares not look too long at her friend, for fear of losing heart. Oh how she wishes there were any other way. All she wants is to gather Falca and Nox into her arms and steal away into the gentle night.

"She must see something of herself in me. I represent to her some weakness that she wishes to trample. So she tells herself that she is only keeping me in my natural state. Perhaps she even thinks she's allowing me to flourish, by robbing me as she has."

"Luna, stop! What are you saying?" Falca demands, her voice rising in her panic.

*Thank the spirits for that,* thinks Luna. It's essential that Falca contends with her loudly enough to be heard. Luna's rebellion must not roll down on another's shoulders again.

She keeps speaking, her voice gaining confidence now that she's committed to this course. "She is mistaken, though, to think me weak. She mistakes violence for strength. But I have seen a different kind of courage.

"I see it in the way the stream keeps laughing, even when the sun drives the moon away, and in the way the flowers, which are so delicate and so easily destroyed, choose to live exposed to wind and rain instead of cowering in safety. I even see it in you, Falca."

She looks up at last and sees that tears are running down the old woman's wrinkled cheeks.

"I see it in your kindness and lack of complaint, even when

you've been banished from the life you knew and condemned to stay here with me forever."

Falca looks as though these last few words pierce her like knives, though Luna meant them as a balm.

"No, Luna," Falca protests. "You're wrong. You have it entirely backward."

Before she can say anything else, the door crashes open behind them. Luna twists, to see Watho standing in the doorway, fury wrapped around her like a cloak, eyes blazing.

*She looks like an avenging spirit*, Luna thinks. Her crimson hair is worn down today, a wild mane of curls that makes her look even more fierce than usual. For a moment, she wants to swallow all her words. Watho is right, she thinks, to despise her. To treat her as too mean and simple to face the world outside this cavern. The witch has done her a kindness by keeping her here, fed and warm and comfortable.

She swallows these thoughts and they go down like fire, burning inside her. She stands to face her mistress, staring her coldly in the eye as though they were equals.

For a moment, she thinks Watho's fury is fading, for the witch begins to smile. It's a calculating, unpleasant thing.

"Very well," Watho says, in a carefully controlled voice. "If you tire of my hospitality, you are free to see how you fare without it."

She lunges forward to take hold of Luna's wrist and there is nothing of the quiet restraint of her voice in her grip. She turns toward the second door and Luna feels her arm wrench painfully as she's dragged along behind the witch.

"No!" Falca shouts, reaching for Luna's other arm.

*Oh please don't, Falca*, Luna pleads silently, willing the old woman not to interfere. *Let her think you're on her side.*

Watho's pauses long enough to take Falca by the throat with her free hand, never loosening her grip on Luna's wrist, and hurls the old woman across the room where she lands with a terrible crunch and crumples to the floor.

A scream tears through Luna's lungs. *It wasn't supposed to happen this way.* She feels another painful jolt in her shoulder as Watho turns again toward the door, pulling her helplessly along.

The witch gestures with her free hand and the door flies open, the tapestry dropping from the wall and puddling in front of the opening. Luna is dimly aware of being dragged into the dark corridor, of her bare feet scraping against the rough stone, but she can think of nothing but Falca in a heap on the floor.

She remembers the passage being long, but it seems that only seconds pass before the door at the end of the passage bursts open and the searing light pours in.

Luna has been steeling herself to face the light all day, but the reality of it is nothing like the memory.

Watho charges into the sunlight, pulling Luna with her. It is so much worse than she remembers. It is unbearable. The sun is higher now in the sky, the whole world enveloped in its scorching glare.

Luna cries out involuntarily, covering her eyes with her free hand, but Watho isn't finished. She marches on for what feels like miles, her fingers digging painfully into Luna's wrist as Luna stumbles blindly in her wake.

Once or twice she trips over a boulder and falls to her knees but Watho never breaks her stride. She simply drags Luna on her side as though she were already dead, until she regains her feet. The sun beats down on them relentlessly, burning Luna's eyes and skin.

At last, with a vicious jerk, Watho hurls Luna down in front of her. Luna doesn't dare look up at her tormentor, though it's not the witch she fears but the sun. She stays on her knees with her face buried in her hands, hating the pathetic figure she must appear in Watho's eyes.

"We shall see which one of us is weak," Watho spits.

The witch turns on her heel and is gone, leaving Luna alone under the cloudless sky and brutal sun.

Luna can no longer think of Falca, or of Nox, or of her own future, or of Watho. The only thing that matters is to find relief. She must find some corner of kind shadow or she will die here. She is certain of it.

Taking a ragged breath, she pushes herself up to her feet and begins to run blindly.

Aurora is in the last place her husband would think to look for her; a comfortable tavern.

Across the table from her sit Violet, Sarah, and Violet's cousin, Alyvia, who apparently owns the tavern.

She's been given lamb curry, spiced wine and news that turned her whole world on its head.

Her son, whose loss she has grieved for so long, may be alive.

Alyvia told them all the story of her acquaintance with Falca and Fargu. She recounted their first whispered conversation, at the very table where they now sit, of which she had been able to make nothing at the time.

Then, nine years later, Falca had revealed the existence of a child — a girl — at the castle, who was assigned to her care. It wasn't until later that Alyvia pieced things together, remembering brief snatches of Fargu's words: *I wouldn't trade yours for mine,* and *he's too fearless.*

"It can't be any other," Violet says, her eyes alight. "How can it be? The timing lines up perfectly."

Aurora nods. Her heart responds as soon as she hears the tavern mistress' words; she knows in the way that only a mother can know. When Alyvia recounts the words of the strange huntsman who frequented her tavern, speaking of her own son as though he belonged to him, she feels a hot hatred bubble in her gut.

"What about the girl?" Sarah asks. "If the boy child is Lady Aurora's, where did that one come from?"

Violet shrugs. "It could be anyone. What I want to know is, *why?*"

"It *could* be anyone, but I think I know who," Alyvia says. "Do you remember the Duke and Duchess of Petrich?"

"I think so," Violet says. "There was some talk of the duke being poisoned, wasn't there?"

"Aye," Sarah rejoins. "And then the duchess up and disappeared. They say she went blind when the duke died. Silly of her if you ask me. I don't know a man worth going blind for."

"That's right," Aurora says, her interest piqued despite her tumultuous feelings. "I remember now. She went blind, then simply vanished. But what makes you think she was with child?"

"She was!" exclaims Violet. "I knew her lady's maid, Fina. No one else knew at the time."

Aurora's heart is racing now. She looks around at her unlikely companions and tries to organize her chaotic thoughts.

"That would mean," she says, after a moment, "that the

duchess of Petrich was staying with Lady Watho at the same time that I was. But I never saw her, nor heard a whisper of her presence."

"Would you have?" Violet asks. "After all, if kidnapping was Lady Watho's intention, she would have kept you both from each other, wouldn't she? Do you remember anything strange at all, from your time there?"

This is the first time Violet has ever inquired about Astarsaga Castle, Aurora realizes. She has until now, avoided the subject with the utmost delicacy.

She nods. "It *was* a little strange. I stayed in my quarters most of the time. They were beautiful. They had enormous windows and were absolutely drenched in sunlight all the time."

Sarah shudders. "Can't say I would enjoy sunlight *all* the time."

"I'm sure she doesn't mean it literally," Alyvia says. "After all the sun goes down at night."

Aurora shakes her head. "I never saw it go down. Not once. Watho gave me a sleeping draught at supper every evening. At the time, I thought she was doing me a kindness. Now..." she stops. Now, everything about Astarsaga Castle feels pernicious.

Violet turns to her cousin. "When was the last time you saw this Falca woman? Or Fargu? Have you any reason to think either of the babies are not still there?"

"Only a few months ago," Alyvia says. "Of course they never tell me anything about Watho, or the castle, or the children, but they seemed perfectly normal, as they always are."

"We have to go back," says Aurora. "At once. We have to find out."

"Yes..." Violet says, dragging the word out as if she needs to consider how to say the words that come after. "But I do feel duty-bound to remind you of what happened last time we tried. There was nothing natural about that earthquake, mark my words."

"I know," Aurora agrees. "But I have to go, even if I have to walk. None of you are obliged to join me. I mean that sincerely. It's my son, after all."

"Oh thank the spirits for that, at least," says Violet, rolling her eyes. "Best of luck to you then." But she smiles and places her hand over Aurora's. Aurora offers a grateful smile in return. Of course her friend won't leave her to do this alone.

"Begging your pardon, m'lady," says Sarah, "but I've recently lost my position. If it's all the same to you, I'd like to come as well."

Aurora feels she should refuse; how can she justify exposing Sarah to danger, after all she's done? Before she can respond, however, Alyvia speaks up.

"Actually, I was about to suggest I come as well. I know Fargu and Falca, after all. Who knows but that may get us somewhere?"

Aurora studies her in silence for a moment before responding. Her feelings about Alyvia are too complicated to unravel at the moment.

"Thank you, but no," she says at last. "I'm grateful for what you've told me. Truly I am. But if you'd told someone sooner, my son might be with me now."

Alyvia winces.

"Aurora..." Violet says, placing a steadying hand on her arm. "I know you're upset but it isn't her fault."

"She *knew*." Her words are fierce now, all the rage and frustration of the previous months boiling over. "She didn't know it was *my* child but she knew it was *someone's* and she made friends with the captors and never breathed a word."

"That isn't fair," Violet begins, but her cousin stops her.

"Of course it is," Alyvia says without a hint of self-pity. "If it were my child I would feel exactly the same."

Aurora wants to say something to ease the burden she has placed on the shoulders of a stranger — the first person to bring her any hopeful news in years — but the words of some unknown man speaking of her son still ring in her ears. She looks down, unwilling to meet the other woman's eyes.

"I am sorry, Lady Aurora," Alyvia says. When Aurora says nothing, the other woman pushes her chair back. "I had better see to the dishes."

In the uncomfortable silence that follows, Aurora glances up at Violet, afraid of what she may see in her friend's eyes.

"Well!" Violet says, a little too brightly, "If nothing else, we'll take the witch by surprise. I'll wager her castle has never been stormed by a posse of countesses and lady's maids before."

## CHAPTER NINETEEN

*L*una is dying. It won't be long.

The violent heat will overcome her; she can feel it tearing at her shoulders, pressing on the back of her head. She cannot withstand the assault. Her body will whither, and her limbs grow heavy. The grass stabs her bare feet as she stumbles blindly, hands clamped over her eyes to shield them from the terrible light.

*There must be some reprieve. Some dark cavern in which to seek refuge.*

Only days ago she was longing for freedom, dreaming of escape. How foolish she was!

Now, there is little she wouldn't give to return to her prison cell; to feel the whisper of silk sheets against her skin, the cool touch of stone walls, the soft glow of lamplight. To hear the friendly voice of her warden and drift off to sleep on the wings of spiced wine.

This is not freedom. This is death.

*Is Watho watching?* Luna wonders. It seems likely. She can

feel the laughing eyes of her mistress, tracking her movements as she falls to her knees and crawls desperately from the raging heat, eyes squeezed shut. She can almost see the witch's triumphant smile.

She takes a deep breath.

*If I die I will not die like an animal. I will not let her enjoy my torment.*

The hot earth has been rising steadily beneath her feet for a few moments, but now it flattens out again. She must have crested a small hill.

Already on her knees, Luna does not try to rise. She knows her limits. Neither, she thinks, will she continue to crawl like a beast. Instead, she stretches herself out on her stomach, laying her face against the hot grass. Her dark hair pools around her head and falls over her face, creating a blessed shield against the searing light of the sun.

She takes another deep breath and relaxes her body.

*Let death find me here, at peace.*

She closes her eyes and thinks only about the next breath, and the next, until her thoughts at last grow dim.

"Feeling better?"

Aethon feels himself begin to smile even before his eyes open to see the huntsman watching from his bedside.

He *is* feeling better. The room is still dark, but he no longer writhes under its influence. The colds sweats and fevered dreams have subsided and his mind feels clear for the first time in days. Watho's daily visits have likewise ceased and the wounds from the arrow tip have scabbed over.

Now, Fargu holds the arrow, but there's no threat in his posture or gaze.

"You came," Aethon says. "I didn't think she'd let you."

"She didn't," says Fargu. He's tapping the arrow absent-mindedly against his palm as he studies Aethon, his eyes dark with worry. "I'm sorry lad. I tried to come sooner but there was magic sealing the doors."

"How did you get past it?"

He shrugs. "It's gone now. It seems she may be done with you."

Aethon surprises them both by laughing. The anger seems to have been drained from his blood, leaving only relief in its place. He pulls himself into a sitting position with a groan, swings his legs over the side of the bed and leans forward to rest his arms on his knees. He feels new strength in his mind and spirit but his body has never felt so weak.

"I've had my fill of her as well, if I'm honest. Will you open the curtains?"

"Aye," Fargu says. "I thought as much. That's why I've come. It's time you leave here while you still can."

He rises and draws the curtains one at a time as he speaks. Aethon closes his eyes and breathes in the light that spills into the room. Sunlight brushes his skin like a familiar kiss.

"Why not come with me?" he asks.

Fargu smiles ruefully. "It seems she still has some use for me; the spells that bind me here are as strong as ever. Anyway, there's Lucy to think of."

The name splits the air like a slap.

*How long has it been since he heard that name?*

"Lucy?"

"My wife."

"Your *wife?*"

"You knew I had one," Fargu says.

"I didn't know it was *Lucy*. How is it you never mentioned her name?"

"I was forbidden to do so." His face is tight with regret. "So you remember her then."

"Of *course* I remember her. I cried every night for weeks when she went away." The words tumble out before he can stop them; the confession bitter as it slides off his tongue. The heat rises to his cheeks. Since his first foolish taste of moonlight, it seems there has been no end to his mortifications.

"You hid it well. I never knew."

"Men don't cry." Even as he repeats Watho's admonition — words that have hung around his neck like a stone for nearly a decade — the rising emotion makes his voice tremble. It sounds small in his own ears. Childish. He hangs his head, furious with himself.

"They *do*," Fargu says, so vehemently that Aethon looks up sharply and is surprised to see the other man's eyes shining with sadness. "They do, and you'll do well to forget all such useless lies you've learned from my mistress' poisoned tongue."

Aethon looks away again. Fargu has never spoken to him in this manner before. He wants to wriggle away from the words; to return to more comfortable terrain.

When he looks up again. Fargu is examining the tip of the arrow with interest.

"Tell me lad," he says, "When did you start to improve, do you know?"

Aethon shrugs. "A day or two ago, I suppose. It's hard to keep track."

Fargu nods. "And when was the last time Watho came to see you?"

His mind shies from the memory. It's not her barbed words, nor even the tormenting arrow's edge that makes him shudder, but the memory of his own response. Each time she had come it had been the same. She taunted and railed, and he lay helpless on the bed, cowering beneath her blows. He knows he could have disarmed her — after all, she's only a woman with a stick — but he never has. He's never even tried. It is this impotence that has filled Aethon with rage so many times in her absence.

"About the same time," he says, after some thought.

"Just what I thought. There's some poisonous magic on this arrowhead. I felt it a moment ago when my fingers brushed the edge. She's been keeping you ill."

Relief floods him like lamplight driving away the shadows in his soul. He is *not* a coward. She really did cast a spell on him. A moment later, Aethon is deflated again.

Watho may very well have weakened him with magic, but the dryad never did. He knows this with the same certainty with which he understands precisely when to drive a spear into a boar's heart.

*The dryad.* In his relief at seeing his guardian, he had forgotten his shameful behavior toward her. Though he now knows she is no dryad, he doesn't know how else to think of her.

"Fargu, have you ever seen a girl around the castle grounds?"

"A what?"

"A girl. A delicate, dark girl with daylight in her eyes."

Fargu stares at him, dumbfounded.

"I thought not," sighs Aethon.

"It's not that." Now it is Fargu's turn to sound uncertain. "There *is* a girl. The same age as yourself and raised here just as you were. Only I don't know how you could have seen her. She's never seen the light of day."

This draws a sharp laugh from Aethon. "I did get that impression."

He recounts his story, leaving nothing out, though he feels his face turn warm again when he tells Fargu of his dread in the darkness. He cannot meet the other man's eyes when he describes how he bounded into the daylight, leaving the girl alone in her terror.

"So you see," he says when the story is done, "I have to find her before I leave and beg her forgiveness If I ever wish to face myself again."

There is something indefinable in Fargu's smirk when he asks, "And what does *she* stand to gain from this encounter?"

"What?"

"You say you want to beg her for forgiveness so that you can be absolved. Is that the only reason?"

"I... I suppose not?"

"I should hope not. If so, it's nearly as selfish as what you need forgiving for."

Comprehension comes slowly, creeping like honey across a table top. His shoulders slump.

In all his shame and grief, his eye has still been turned constantly inward, his chief desire to liberate himself from guilt. Until this moment, it has never occurred to him to apologize to the dryad simply to lessen the pain he's caused her.

Suddenly, he laughs. "Fargu, it appears there are many layers to my self-regard. I peel one away and find another beneath it."

"Don't despair lad. For I see that you can laugh at yourself and there's no better start than that." His expression suddenly clouds. "But I don't think there's much chance of your seeing the lass. The servants whisper that our lady has tired of her as well and turned her out this very day."

Aethon jumps to his feet in alarm. He looks out the now undressed windows as though he expects to see her just outside. It's late in the day, but the sun is still shining.

"The sunlight will kill her!" he cries.

"If it will, it has already. But why should it? The moonlight didn't kill you."

"She's weaker than I am. I must find her!"

To his astonishment, Fargu guffaws uproariously at this. "I wonder if she says the same of you. By your own account it was she who was strong when you met."

Aethon winces, but doesn't argue. "All the more reason for me to find her now and repay her kindness. If she feels the sun as I do the moon, she is suffering terribly... and alone."

"We've talked too long at any rate," Fargu agrees. "There can be no good left for you in this place."

He is still holding Watho's arrow. Now he places the offending item in the quiver with its companions and holds the quiver and bow out to Aethon.

"You won't want to carry much. There's a little food and water in a satchel I've prepared for you. You'll want these as well."

"Thunderstone?" Aethon asks hopefully, though he knows the answer.

Fargu shakes his head. "Bound here just as I am. Just as all the witch's servants are."

This is the first time Aethon has heard anyone, other than

Watho herself, openly refer to the woman as a witch. It gives him a start. When Watho described herself thus it had a noble ring to it. In Fargu's mouth, it's suddenly a hateful thing.

Now that he knows the dryad is alone in the sun, there's no time to waste. Fargu accompanies him downstairs and through the kitchen. The cook is there, but they see no other servants, to his relief. She looks teary-eyed, but she doesn't stop them, even to say goodbye.

Fargu surprises Aethon again, by grasping his shoulders and kissing his cheek.

"I'm sorry lad," he says.

"What for?" Aethon searches the older man's face. Has he betrayed him after all? Is Watho around the corner, waiting to catch him in his escape?

Fargu looks as though he is searching for a difficult answer. "For your childhood," he says at last. Aethon tries to protest but Fargu holds up a hand to stop him. "You'll understand someday, lad. Off you go. No time for chatter."

"I'll find a way to free you if I can," Aethon promises, then turns and begins to run.

THE SUN HAS NOT RELENTED, but Luna has not yet died.

The torrid heat seeps into her body, rising in waves from the ground beneath her. She is lying stretched out on the warm grass, arms flung over her head as though to protect it from some attack.

Something, she realizes, is moving nearby. Something large. *The wolf?*

No, it can't be the witch's messenger. She remembers his voice like velvet and his deep, rumbling growl. That voice was nothing like the bestial grunts she now hears coming from somewhere near her head.

She wants to look up at it, but forces herself to stay still. The sounds are not pleasant, but neither do they seem directly threatening. If the creature has not noticed her, she ought not to do anything to draw its attention. Perhaps it will think she belongs here, like the flowers and trees.

A panicked voice inside reminds her that an open hillside under the cursed sun is the last place she belongs. Any natural inhabitant of such a scorched place will surely recognize her as an imposter.

Still, the beast hasn't threatened her. Its movements sound like those of a wanderer. There's no hint of purpose in its steps.

She listens, barely daring to breathe, as the animal moves closer. Something rough and damp touches her hand; sniffing her, she thinks. She tries to imagine what it might be, flipping through images from her books and murals in her mind, but she doesn't have enough information to draw a conclusion. It could be any one of a hundred unknown inhabitants of this strange world to which she has banished herself.

*It may be like Nox and mean me no harm.*

She may even be able to befriend it. Ever so slowly, she lifts her head, peering through the folds of her dark hair to catch a glimpse of the creature.

A burly animal with a rough hide stands over her, its sharp gleaming tusks only inches from her face. A boar, most likely. It's one of the more popular subjects of paintings, though why she can't imagine. To her it seems a strange, ugly creature. From here she is painfully aware of her own defenseless position beneath its tusks. If the boar chooses to attack, she'll be dead before she has a chance to move, much less run.

After a few, heart-stopping moments, the boar seems to lose interest. It must find nothing to threaten or entice in her scent, for it wanders away slowly, stopping now and then to root in the earth. She lies still for a long time more, her body tense.

When several more minutes have passed, she cautiously removes her arms from her head and lifts herself up onto her elbows. It's a relief to lift her face, which has begun to itch unbearably from being pressed into the grass for so long.

She doesn't look up. Her hair hangs down around her face, creating a tiny shelter in which she can hide to keep the unholy sunlight off her skin. To her delight, she finds she is not alone in her tiny shelter. Just next to her wrist is a small flower.

Its delicate white petals look familiar, but there's something wrong with it. She remembers the night she peeled back the petals of a similar flower to see what was inside and how those petals rushed back into place when she let go, folding protectively around itself, shielding its golden heart from sight. This flower is like that one, but someone has pried its petals so far back that they cannot close. Its heart lies exposed, just as she herself is.

Gently, Luna cups her hands around it and tries to help it cover itself again, but the damage does not seem reversible. The petals fall back open as soon her fingers move away.

*Is it already dead?*

She wonders who could do such violence to such a vulnerable creature. The flower's little yellow heart, she muses, brushing it with a fingertip, looks a little like the sun itself, if the sun were not so unkind.

As soon as she thinks this, she begins to see the flower differently. She remembers how Aethon transformed, when the terrible dawn broke. How he expanded and grew in response to the burning light. It was not unlike the feeling she had when she stood under the moon for the first time, which made her feel as though she could stretch to fill all of the new space she had been given.

*I wonder,* she thinks, *if it's not the same with the flower.* Perhaps the flower, like Aethon, curled up to protect itself from the darkness and joyously bared its face to the sun when daylight came. Could this open and exposed condition be the flower's preferred state? Had the flowers she'd come to love always been asleep?

This thought introduces new possibilities. Falca *did* tell her that most people not only tolerate but prefer the daylight, but she finds that she never quite believed it. Now, as she looks at the little white and yellow flower, she wonders. If such a fragile thing can not only survive the day but welcome it with joy, then perhaps the sun is not as cruel as it seems.

After all, for all its brutality, it has not done her any *real* harm yet. She is not dead or withered to a husk, as she imagined she would be by now. She's unbearably hot and frightened, but that's a far cry from burned to death. Perhaps there is some possibility of reconciliation between the sun and herself after all.

At the moment, it doesn't feel likely. She can feel sweat dripping down her back, and her face is slick with it. Only her hair shields her eyes from the blinding glare, but she is not dead, and if she is not dead, she may perhaps survive until nightfall.

"Who knows," she says aloud, though her mouth is dry and

her voice cracks, "if the sun has not killed me by the time it sets, then my strength may yet be restored before it rises again."

AETHON DOESN'T RUN for long.

The castle grounds are enormous and he has no way of knowing which direction the dryad has gone. He searches first the place by the stream where they met, but he knows he will not find her there. After all, if she's been turned out by the witch, she won't be hanging around the castle doors.

Slowly, he expands his search farther out, but by the time the sun begins to set he has still found no trace of her.

At the first sign of creeping darkness, the now familiar panic begins to twist his insides. It's not like the darkness he's grown accustomed to in his room. That was at least safe. Contained. There were rooms outside his own, only a doorway away, where the lamps were lit. That truth was always at the back of his mind. *This,* though... this is all encompassing, stretching itself across the whole world. There's no escape from it.

When it becomes too heavy, he stops walking. He knows he won't be able to see her in the darkness anyway. It's a cloudy night, with hardly any moon to speak of and no stars. He sits on a grassy hillside, pulls his knees up to his chest and bows his head, but he doesn't curl up on his side, as he did that first night, nor explode in anger as he has been so often wont to do. His illness and imprisonment have taught him how to better tolerate the gloom.

Instead he turns his attention to his own breathing.

*Deep breath in.*

He thinks about the calm that comes over him in the middle of a stampeding buffalo herd.

*Exhale slowly.*

The patience and focus he has when stalking a hart.

*Deep breath in.*

The soothing voice of the dryad, telling him about the painted crowds gathered to crown the queen.

*Exhale slowly.*

Her hand gently touching his shoulder, comforting him in the dark.

He takes a few more breaths before he becomes fully aware that the hand is truly there. The tension drains from his back and shoulders as he relaxes into her presence.

"You're really here," he says, without looking up. "I found you."

"Did you?" her voice is tired, but there's laughter in it. "I thought I found you."

Now he looks up. She's there, sitting next to him, her knees drawn up to her chest, her posture mirroring his own except for the arm that's extended to rest her hand on his shoulder. The weariness in her voice is nothing compared with the exhaustion on her face. The day has been difficult for her.

"I was afraid the sunlight would kill you," he says.

"So was I," she admits.

"I didn't know." He's still looking for absolution but he can't help himself. "Before, when we met. I didn't know it was the same for you in the sun as it was for me under the moon."

"I tried to tell you." There's no bitterness in her words. She forgave him before he ever asked it, he realizes, and this too stings.

"Yes. I should have listened."

The words hang between them in the silence for a while. He wonders if he'll be able to persuade her to leave with him. If she can trust him not to abandon her again.

At length, she says, "Watho thought I would die of fright. When she discovers I haven't, she'll be angry. I need to be far away, by then. Will you come with me?"

*Thank the spirits.*

"Yes," he says quickly. "We'll go at dawn. I won't leave you again, I swear it."

"At dawn? No, we have to go now."

"That's not possible. We're both tired already and I cannot travel without light. There are wild animals everywhere. We will get some rest and leave as soon as the morning comes."

She is shaking her head before he finishes. "I can see the animals long before they see me. There's no time to rest. We're still so close to the castle."

He looks around, considering. He can't make out the shapes of the hillsides. Every rock and tree takes on a new and threatening appearance under the cloak of night, and once they make it to the forest, it will be darker still. He glimpses a flash of green in the distance; the eyes of some creature, watching.

He looks back at her, tries to make his voice sound steady and commanding, but he's pleading with his eyes. "Trust me, we'll have time. We can be out of sight before the witch knows we're gone."

She's silent for so long that he begins to hope she has relented. At last she sighs and it's full of regret. "Aethon," she says quietly. He wonders how she knows his name and realizes he doesn't know hers. "I am leaving. Now. I hope you'll come with me, but I will not stay here."

As she begins to get to her feet, his panic returns, threatening to snatch the breath from his lungs, and with it his anger.

"Why can't you just *trust* me?" he demands. "Do you think me so incapable of protecting you?"

She only gives him a sad smile and turns to walk away.

*How quickly my repentance proves false*, he thinks.

He takes a moment to steady himself, then runs to catch up to her.

# CHAPTER TWENTY

*W*atho has been using much more magic than she would like to these past weeks and it's making her irritable. The constant pull of tiny streams of power leaves her depleted.

It wasn't always like this. There was a time the use of magic didn't empty her out, but in recent years it had begun to cost her so much more.

*Damn those children,* she fumes. *Why couldn't they just do as they were told? I've given them both a comfortable enough life, haven't I?*

The experiment, then, has failed.

She's climbing the tower stairs, listening to the familiar click clack of the wolf's claws as he climbs behind her.

One more look to be sure that the girl is dead and then she'll see to the boy. And she had been so *hopeful* for him! If only that wretched Luna had not led the boy astray, he would still be thriving; her sunlit child, her glorious day boy.

The telescope is still trained on the place she saw the girl collapse yesterday, but today there's no sign of her. Watho silently curses.

*She must have had some life in her after all.*

She makes a few adjustments and scans the surrounding areas. The pitiful creature was barely stumbling along last time she saw her. She can't have gone much farther in such a state.

"Is all well?" Felnys must be able to sense her tension.

"Fine." The word is more brittle on her tongue than she intended it to be. "She's moved." Or she's been carried off by a wild animal after dying of fright. The thought reassures her, but she can't bring herself to turn away from the telescope. Something is not right.

She widens the range again, scanning slowly. Nothing is out of the ordinary. The hunters are on the plains, without Aethon of course, pursuing the dogs that bound ahead of them. On the moors and beyond the forest edges, hart and buffalo and boar are going about their usual business. It's as though the girl vanished, burned to cinder by the sunlight she feared so much.

Watho's brow creases. Perhaps Luna survived til sunset and miraculously avoided being set upon by a wild animal. If so, she may have regained her strength after dark and left on foot. Where would she go? Through the forest, or over the plains?

*Through the forest.* She would naturally gravitate toward the cover the trees afford. Watho expands the range of the telescope's view again, looking deep into the wood. The crumpled remains of Aurora's coach are still there, undisturbed, though the expected corpses are gone. Escaped, or devoured by wildlife?

The girl could not have gone much farther than that. Watho is about to give up when a movement on the murky edges of her field of vision draws her attention. Her fingers deftly find the right knobs, turning until the telescope is focused sharply on the spot.

It's a small clearing into which the sunlight filters through the trees, settling like a dappled cloak over the figures that stand in its center.

*Two figures.*

In the gentle blend of light and shadow, they almost look like one person for a moment. They are leaning against each other, arms wrapped loosely around one another's waists. Luna's head rests on Aethon's chest, his head bent forward so that his golden mane mixes with her black curls.

Watho steps back from the telescope, her back rigid. *How can this be possible? How did they even find one another?*

She feels for the thread of magic that bonds Fargu to her, for it must have been he who helped them. Aethon could not have found it in himself to orchestrate this betrayal. Her fingers tense, as she considers. One sharp pull and Fargu will be painfully reminded of his duty to her.

That will have to wait. If the children make good on their escape, who knows what they will do. Aethon's father is still alive. Maybe his mother too. Perhaps she will be found out and the king will come for her. Perhaps she will have to fight. She can deal with that when the time comes. Her blood is not boiling for fear of the king, however. It's the rebellion of her own subjects that is responsible for the rising heat.

*How dare they think they can defy you? Falca, Fargu, the children... how long have they conspired together against you in your own house, while availing themselves of the generosity of your table?*

It's not her own voice posing these questions in her mind.

It is the wolf's.

She whirls to face him. Felnys' spine is rigid, muscles taught. His black eyes connect with hers and seem to lock into place. She cannot break away from his gaze.

Suddenly, she understands why the power emanating from him has always felt so familiar. It isn't his power at all; it's hers. It's no wonder she's felt as if her well of magic is running dry. How long has Felnys been slowly drawing his power from it, draining her day by day? Decades, at least.

The wolf is smiling now. He sees that she knows.

Watho begins to gather up her power, as she did the day of the earthquake. She will pull her magic back from Felnys by force. Let *him* feel the emptiness of its absence for once.

*You could do that,* the wolf says, *or you can let me help you.*

He's speaking in her mind again, though he could say it out loud. Dimly, she understands why. The words have more power coming from inside herself. Why throw them at her openly when he can mix them with her own thoughts?

She doesn't answer, doesn't want his help. Whatever he thinks he has to offer, she's had enough of his machinations.

He doesn't speak again. At least not with words. Instead, she sees a picture in her head, as clearly as if it had already taken place.

A wolf is laying on his side atop the tower. He looks withered without his magic, no more dangerous than a large dog, his coat restored to its original drab brown. Watho herself lies near him, likewise depleted though her fatigue is of a different kind. She's pulled all her magic out of him and back to herself. She is spent from the effort, but when her strength returns it will return to her alone. There will be no doubt, when the weakness has worn off, who is the more powerful of the two.

She smiles, feeling the flush of victory not yet achieved. The vision is so sharp, she doesn't doubt it for a second. It's as good as a promise. Then the picture changes.

Luna and Aethon are sitting together at a richly appointed table, surrounded by glittering nobles. Falca is there, dressed ridiculously, in expensive gowns, as though she were a dowager princess. Fargu, likewise ornamented in clothes above his station, has a fatherly hand on Aethon's shoulder. They're laughing, telling the story of how they outwitted the witch and escaped Astarsaga Castle.

Watho, who has already begun to reach for the wolf's magic, pauses at the last second. She can deal with Felnys' mutiny later. Why not use him to her own ends first? A small voice inside her suggests that this is his idea, not her own, but she waves it away. There's no reason the first vision can't still come true now that she knows what Felnys has been doing.

She's no longer pulling the magic out of the wolf and into herself. Now she's pulling the wolf himself, magic and all. He's standing close to her now. She reaches out, wraps a hand in his thick coat and feels the force of their magic, sparking and burning on her palm.

She can see the magic now, strands of power the color of her hair and his whipping themselves into a frenzy, now separating, now combining, swirling around them both until she can no longer differentiate between herself and the wolf and the magic itself. It's growing dark inside the tunnel their power is forming. Images leap out from the swirling energy and fade away, one after another. They're muddled, indistinct. She feels rather than sees them. A torrent of memories, only some of which belong to her.

A sharp pain, like unforgiving fingers digging into the tender shoulder of a child. A father's revulsion at the child's tears. At her weakness. The desperation of a frail woman looking anywhere but toward the violence in her home. A surge of pride and accomplishment as a young lord greets his new bride for the first time. Twisting resentment in the gut of a bride compelled to accept her father's choice. A flutter of excitement at the first stirring of magic. Cold victory as the young lord takes his final breath.

Felnys, she understands too, was born of all these things; pulled from the cauldron of her own fear and wrath. She wants to turn back — to reverse this disastrous melding of her ideal self and her most brutish parts — but it's too late.

The images move faster and faster until they are all one writhing mass of memory-infused magic. Then, suddenly, Watho feels searing pain, like needles of ice puncturing muscles and nerves. She writhes, but finds she cannot cry out. The needles travel in waves, starting in her toes and rushing up her legs, spiraling around her belly and wrapping around her chest and arms. When they reach her throat, the pain becomes so intense she stops breathing.

Then, with a tingle like falling asleep, it's gone.

She can no longer feel her fingers curled around the wolf's silky fur. She can no longer feel her fingers at all. She feels what the wolf feels. The raw power wound up in the muscles of his hind legs. The strength of his neck and shoulders. *Her* neck. *Her* shoulders.

The spell is complete.

She waits for the fatigue that should follow on the heels of such a powerful working, but it doesn't come. She feels nothing but the wolf's hot blood and pounding heart. The throaty growl she hears is, she understands belatedly, coming from her own mouth. Their mouth. Their powerful jaw is clenched, teeth bared.

Beneath the animal power, Watho is aware of a vast, gaping terror. She has capitulated to the beast with whom she has been at war all these years. There is no question anymore about who is in control. She is the wolf's passenger now; nothing more.

Before she has time to consider her next move, the wolf has made it. They whirl around toward the tower door and bound down the stairs. In what seems like seconds, they emerge onto the castle grounds.

Watho feels the sun and wind ruffling their fur as they move, impossibly fast, their limbs lithe and graceful. They tear across the earth toward the forest. Toward their wayward children.

Every part of Luna's body aches. Her optimism of a few hours ago feels foolish now, as stones jab into the tender flesh of her bare feet, and the muscles in her calves scream their protest with every step. Her right arm is wrapped tightly around Aethon's waist and he leans heavily on her as he stumbles at her side.

Under the added weight, a deep, throbbing pain radiates from her shoulders down her back. She knows he's carrying as much of his own weight as he can and makes no attempt to dislodge him. She remembers her own weakness in the burning sunlight; how it drained the vitality from her bones. Still, she is beginning to wonder how much further she can realistically walk. They have not made nearly enough progress to be safe from the witch's wrath, but her steps are becoming unsteady as the pain in her legs increases.

The scent of something wild drifts toward them on the breeze. It's not the first time she's sensed the presence of a predator lurking in the darkness. The gleam of feral eyes and soft swish of stealthy movement has punctuated the stillness at various times throughout the night. As with the previous times, she recognizes the creature before it senses her and moves in a wide circle, gently maneuvering Aethon out of its path. She says nothing about it to her flagging companion, seeing no need to stoke his fear.

*How many hours have we been walking?* Luna wonders. She never thought she would find herself longing for morning, but her enemy the sun has become an ally during the course of this arduous night. Its daily victory over the moon will herald the return of Aethon's strength, and only then will she be allowed to rest.

When it comes, however, she finds for the second time that the memory of the sun pales in comparison to the reality. The relief she hoped to feel at having her burden eased is eclipsed by its fiery gaze, which finds them even among the trees. It weaves in and out of the comforting shadows, permeating the forest like water, making the colors harsh and unwelcoming.

It takes Luna a few moments to realize that she has stopped moving. The weight of her companion has lessened by degrees throughout the terrible dawn, until Aethon at last lifts his arm from her shoulders. She turns to look at him, shielding her eyes from the glare. He stands in a gap between trees, face turned upward, drinking the morning sunlight into his skin. It's not the fierce, joyful look that was on his face that first morning they spent together, but is full of glad relief and gathering strength.

She can almost believe he's drawing it directly from her, so quickly is her own strength ebbing. Her legs give out at last and she collapses with a whimper that is part pain, part relief, but her body never touches the ground. Aethon catches her in the crook of his arm, then places the other arm under her knees and scoops her up.

She rests her head against his chest with a weary sigh. The nearness of him, feeling the expansion of his lungs against her cheek, helps dispel a little of the sun's terror.

He says nothing, but starts walking. They will make much faster progress this way, for as long as his arms can hold her. Luna closes her eyes and the gentle rhythm of his stride becomes a lullaby, singing her to sleep. For the first time, she allows herself to be comforted by the warmth of sun on her cheek. With her eyes closed and Aethon's steady heartbeat beneath her ear, it's easier to imagine a day when she and the sun might lay aside their enmity.

When she opens her eyes again, the light has changed significantly. Aethon's steps have slowed and the sag of his shoulders reflects his exhaustion. It's been only a few hours, but after their strenuous night, even the sun's power is not enough to restore him completely.

When she shifts, he glances down at her and offers a weary smile.

"We should stop," Luna suggests. "If only for a few minutes."

Aethon nods, but walks on. "The underbrush is too dense here," he explains. A moment later, they emerge into a small clearing. As the shadows fall away, Luna shrinks from the unfiltered light, but she's no longer the Luna of yesterday, convinced of her impending death.

Aethon sets her down cautiously, as though she might crumble when her feet touch the ground. She smiles at this, but she doesn't want to move away from him, with the sunlight pooling around them and pain coursing through her legs. She leans into him at the same moment he wraps his arms around her waist, leaning toward her, so that they find themselves holding one another upright.

She doesn't know how long they stay like this, swaying, eyes closed against the heat and light as they each bear the weight of the other; it feels like an hour, but may only be minutes.

Eventually, Aethon guides her to a place where the shadows are thick, and they both lie down to rest. She can tell by his uneven breath that his sleep is as fitful as her own.

She's about to suggest that they keep moving, although the very thought of it makes her bones ache, when the quiet of the forest is suddenly broken.

Something is moving toward them. Something enormous. Something *fast*.

One of the wild animals must have caught their scent. Aethon's body tenses as he hears it too. They both jump to their feet, looking around for the sound. When at last she spots it through the trees, Luna's body goes rigid, her blood turning cold. The creature gaining on them at an impossible speed is one she's seen before and the sight of it dwarfs her fear of the sun.

Thundering toward them is a massive red wolf with black burning eyes.

There's no time to run. There's nowhere to run *to*. They are in the wolf's sights, and in their weakened state they stand no chance of escape. The wolf will hunt them down where they cower and tear them to shreds. The certainty of this settles on her like a promise.

Still, she looks wildly around for some way to escape. Anything, rather than just standing here in the clearing, awaiting their fate.

Aethon's weariness drops from his shoulders like a garment, his body tensing in readiness, his movements lithe. In a flash, his bow is in his hands, arrow nocked and, to Luna's astonishment, an eager, almost joyous expression on his face.

He steadies himself and waits, eyes focused as though he and the wolf are all that exist in the world. Luna feels her own body tense as the wolf bursts into the clearing, devouring the distance between itself and them.

*Twang.*

Aethon's arrow flies. His aim is precise. Flawless. The arrow hits the wolf in the eye but instead of piercing, it bounces off harmlessly and twirls into the underbrush.

Luna draws in a sharp breath.

Another arrow appears in Aethon's hand as if by magic. By the time Luna can track his movements, he's already taken the shot.

The wolf is much closer now and the arrow hits it with much more force. This time it doesn't bounce off; it *splinters*. It may as well have been driven into a wall of stone.

Aethon reaches for a third arrow, but it's too late. The wolf leaps. The bow and arrow fly from his hands, skittering uselessly across the dirt floor of the clearing, as the wolf slams into Aethon. They hit the ground together with a sickening thud.

The wolf's snarling teeth snap a half inch from Aethon's face as he drives the heel of his hand into its throat, pushing it upward with a mighty shove. Its claws tear at his shoulders, leaving deep gashes. Blood mats the fur on the wolf's forelegs. Aethon's blood.

Luna looks around for a stone, or a tree branch — anything she can use as a weapon. There's nothing.

*Except...*

Her eyes settle on the arrow, where it landed near her feet. She reaches for it but stops, remembering the way the arrows shattered against the wolf's hide. It won't do any good. *Nothing* will do any good.

Even so, she can't just stand here and watch. Aethon has somehow, miraculously, stayed alive beneath the wolf's razor claws and snapping jaw, but surely he can't for much longer. Already his face and arms are slick with blood.

There's nothing else to reach for, so Luna settles on the only thing at her disposal. With a running leap she hurls herself at the wolf's side.

She hears the bone in her upper arm crunch as her body collides with the wolf's. She bounces off it just as the first arrow did and rolls once or twice, coming to a stop on her back a few feet from where Aethon lays. Pain from her shattered limb radiates up into her shoulders and down to her fingertips, sucking the breath from her lungs.

"No!" she hears Aethon gasp. Dizzy with pain, she turns her head to look at him.

Whether from the force of the impact or only the surprise, her assault appears to have thrown the wolf off balance, if only momentarily, and it has stumbled off of Aethon. It gathers itself up and looks at her. She can read the creature's eyes as clearly as words in a book. It isn't wounded, simply indignant. It is furious at her brazenness, enraged that she would dare to attack it, however unsuccessfully.

The wolf turns, crouches, springs. Aethon reaches for it vainly as it vaults his body, aiming this time for Luna. Frozen in place, she watches, eyes wide, waiting for the impact.

*Thwap.*

The wolf's full weight lands on her, driving the air from her lungs as several of her ribs crack.

She steels herself for the claws that will come next, for the tearing of its teeth, but nothing happens. She can feel its ragged breathing, but it doesn't move.

Luna hears a scrambling sound, not from Aethon's direction but from the other side of her, and feels the weight of the wolf being rolled off of her.

She squints into the sunlight as two startled looking women stare back at her.

# CHAPTER TWENTY-ONE

*I*t's been a long time since Aurora handled a bow. In her youth, she was a skilled archer, but the earl did not see the need for a countess to maintain such a skill and forbade her its practice.

When she picks up the bow in the clearing, she doesn't wonder if her hands will remember what to do. The moment she stepped into the clearing, time had slowed to a crawl, distilling every detail of the scene before her: the bow, the arrow, the blood-soaked boy in the dust, the dark-skinned girl cradling her arm to her chest.

And the red wolf.

The wolf that has haunted her for eighteen years now stands only feet away; real, solid and preparing to pounce.

Aurora reaches for the bow and nocks the arrow before her thoughts catch up. Her hands remember their work before her mind does. It feels natural — like coming home. She draws, the bowstring biting into the fingers of her right hand, the left maintaining a relaxed grip, her fingers barely touching the bow.

The wolf turns, crouches, leaps. Her body adjusts instinctively to the wolf's movements, as her fingers release the string, her right hand falling gracefully back as the arrow flies. It strikes the wolf in the chest, arresting its momentum. The beast writhes and falls gracelessly. Aurora winces as it lands directly on top of the girl. She hears the gasps of Sarah and Violet behind her.

They rush forward as one, Sarah and Violet reaching the wolf before Aurora does and using their full bodyweight to roll it off the girl's body. Aurora runs past to where the boy, bloodied and torn, watches in wide-eyed astonishment.

There is no question in her mind about his identity. Even covered in blood and dust, even with those eyes like a starless night, she would know him anywhere. She has to hold herself back from embracing him, realizing at the last moment that he will not know her so easily.

Instead, she kneels beside him, examining his wounds. There are long, ragged tears in his arms and chest from the wolf's claws, and a flap of raw skin hangs from his cheek, but he is alive. She turns to call for help to stop his bleeding, but freezes mid-turn.

The wolf's body is writhing grotesquely in some unholy metamorphosis. After a few endless moments, its new shape takes form. It's a woman, naked, her pale face standing out in stark relief against the deep red hair pooled around her head.

Aurora grimaces but there's no surprise in her horror. Hasn't she always known that Watho and the wolf are one?

Watho looks at the arrow protruding from her chest as though it were a foreign thing, her face a mask of dumb shock. She pushes herself up to her elbows, then grasps the arrow shaft with one hand and yanks hard, screaming as it comes free.

She stares at it for a moment as if trying to solve a difficult equation, then utters a shaky laugh. She turns to the boy and brandishes the arrow as though it were a private joke between them.

"You put it back in the quiver. I should have realized." She laughs again.

Aurora glances at the boy and sees dawning comprehension on his face.

As Watho casts the arrow away in disgust, Sarah removes her traveling cloak and steps tentatively forward, arm outstretched to offer it to the dying woman. Watho recoils, not in fear, Aurora thinks, but in anger.

"You think I don't know who you are?" she hisses. Sarah takes a startled step back at the force of her venom. "Spare me the charity of a chambermaid."

Sarah's face changes in an instant. She steps forward again, ignoring Watho's contorted features and kneels next to her.

"Not to worry, ma'am," she says as she tears a strip from the cloak and presses it to the hole in the witch's chest. She folds up the rest of the garment and tucks it beneath Watho's head. "I think you'll find none of us is feeling overly charitable toward you."

"These children are wounded," Aurora says. "We need to get them back to the castle."

Violet disappears from the clearing and returns a moment later leading three horses.

"Can you stand?" she asks the girl.

"I may need a little help," the girl says, and Violet readily complies, reaching out a hand to pull her up. The boy stands up on his own, but sways as soon as he's on his feet and nearly pitches forward again, until Aurora catches and steadies him.

She can barely breathe. Her own son is in her arms at last. She thinks her heart might stop.

Before it has the chance, Violet takes his other arm, and together they help him onto one of the horses, where he slumps forward, exhausted.

"Should we take the witch as well?" Violet asks.

Aurora looks at Watho, considering. However cruel the woman is, Aurora cannot bring herself to condemn her to die alone and naked in the woods. Still, she's unsure Watho will come willingly, and she will not make her son bleed to death while she struggles to wrestle the witch onto a horse.

"You take them. Leave one of the horses and I'll follow with the witch."

The thought of letting the boy out of her sight again, only minutes after first laying eyes on him, causes a physical ache in her heart, but she trusts Violet to care for him as though he were her own son. She is certain Watho is not long for this world and she wants to speak to her before the witch's soul departs.

She takes over for Sarah, pressing the now blood-soaked cloth to Watho's chest as the chambermaid climbs into the saddle behind the strange girl, and she and Violet steer their horse's heads toward the castle. Watho has ceased resisting aid, but her eyes are still stormy with defiance.

Aurora looks into the familiar face of the woman she once thought of as her friend, and remembers how they would laugh together over wine and books in the sunlit balcony room of Astarsaga Castle.

When she speaks at last, her voice is unsteady. "Tell me something."

Watho seems to consider, then nods slowly. *Go on then,* her look says.

"Why my son? Have I sinned against you in some way that you had to exact vengeance?"

The witch smiles weakly, almost sympathetically, and Aurora knows the answer before Watho speaks it.

"You were most convenient."

So that was all. There was no personal injury to atone for, no generational sin to avenge. If there had been, the witch's elaborate trap and the kidnapping of her son could at least have served some purpose, however unjust. But this? This is impersonal, unearned cruelty. Somehow, that makes it more unbearable.

Aurora feels her expression harden. She can leave the witch here to die alone and no one will be any the wiser. She can say that Watho wouldn't come. That she died struggling against Aurora's attempts to wrangle her into the saddle. After all, what lifesaving efforts does such a monster deserve?

Watho returns her gaze placidly, as if she can see the struggle in Aurora's face and feels only curiosity about how it will be resolved. Then, suddenly Watho's eyes flicker past Aurora and widen in alarm.

Aurora whips around, guilt settling like a rock in her gut. If Violet has returned already, she'll see right through Aurora. Excuses are already forming on her lips as she turns.

It isn't Violet. Aurora freezes, all thoughts of moral conflict gone in an instant as she meets her husband's eyes.

THE MAN who steps into the clearing is familiar, though Watho has never seen him before. She's seen the arrogant tilt of his jaw on other faces. Her own husband had the same haughty assurance in his step. Her father boasted the same immaculate precision in his manner and dress.

So this is Aurora's lord and master. Watho remembers Aurora's fear concerning the baby's sex. She never expressed the reason for her apprehension, but Watho had guessed that the earl was responsible. At the time, the understanding had stirred up a twinge of guilt, but Watho had suppressed it easily enough.

Now the feeling resurfaces as she watches him march into the clearing, ready to take command. He stops and confusion registers on his countenance as he takes stock of the scene; Watho, lying in a pool of blood, Aurora kneeling by her side. Whatever he expected to find, it wasn't this.

"What have you done?" he demands, looking back and forth between the two women. Watho feels his eyes rake her body and revulsion roils in her gut.

Aurora winces and opens her mouth to speak, but nothing comes out. She's searching for an explanation that will absolve her. Watho feels a wild urge to laugh. What can Aurora say? *She was a wolf when I found her?*

The earl looks at Aurora as if he's never seen her before, incredulity slackening his features.

"Have you... did you *murder* Lady Watho?"

Now, Watho really does laugh; a harsh, rasping sound.

"Not quite yet." Her voice sounds weak and unfamiliar in her own ears. The magic in the arrowhead is wending like poison through her veins. The magic her own hands wrought. She ought to have known Aethon would take the arrow with him. She ought to have predicted that her magical defenses would be useless against a weapon infected with the same magic.

"*Why?*" the earl asks. "I knew you were mad, Aurora but..." he gestures to Watho, speechless. His righteous indignation does not, Watho notes, inspire him to make any move to help her.

Gone is the self-assured Aurora who shot a raging wolf moments ago. Now she looks confused, as though she is uncertain how she came here.

"She kidnapped our son." She looks up at Sir Hugh, now frantic, plaintive. "Our son didn't die! She kidnapped him!"

The earl's jaw drops. He looks back and forth between the women again. For all his astonishment, his eyes are calculating. He's not at a loss for words, Watho knows. He's deciding. Browsing the possible responses in his mental closet before trying one on.

At last he comes to a decision and his face transforms. He pulls pity over his features just as Watho might pull stockings over her knees, and tilts his head in concern for his poor, addled wife.

"Aurora," he says softly. "Let me take you home. Your grief over the child has driven you mad. I'm sorry I didn't see it sooner, but now, let me help you."

"Help me?" Aurora looks back at Watho. "Help me how? The duchess is dying."

"No one has to know," Sir Hugh says soothingly. "I can protect you."

"Protect me?" Aurora shakes her head, as if trying to dispel a fog.

Suddenly, her eyes clear and her expression hardens. She stands, turning slowly to the earl. "And who will protect me from *you*? Who will protect our children from you?"

The earl's head jerks back as though she slapped him.

"Don't be foolish," he snaps. "I've given you everything. Your life has been nothing but ease and comfort. I'm offering you protection from the consequences of your own foolish actions and *this* is how you respond? You'd rather be hanged as a murderess?"

Watho remembers her own thoughts this morning. *I've given them both a comfortable enough life, haven't I?* The sentiment sounds pathetic coming from the earl's mouth. She wonders if she ever cut as contemptuous a figure as he does now.

There's a new steel in Aurora's voice, her shoulders drawn back and defiant.

"You call locking me in my chambers *protection?* Sending away my only friend? Visiting me only to take what you want when it pleases you?" she snarls. "I can do very well without your protection, thank you."

The earl's eyes flash and he takes a step forward. Watho can see Aurora resist the urge to step back and she finds herself smiling.

It infuriates her to feel any kind of sympathy for this woman who has been so long her enemy; from whom she has stolen without remorse, who Felnys taunted for pleasure, who she once tried to kill with an earthquake, and who only moments ago planted a fatal arrow in her own breast.

Yet, as Aurora's spine stiffens and the earl looms over her, Watho feels a wild, protective impulse.

Sir Hugh's gloved fingers are curled tightly around a horsewhip, but he doesn't raise it. Watho's eyes move up to his face and she finds another familiar expression on his countenance. Her own boiling fury at having lost control of what was hers is reflected in his eyes. *He's more dangerous to Aurora now*, Watho thinks, *than he has ever been before.*

"What choice did I have?" he hisses. "I was burdened with a

wife who could not even *pretend* to show me the honor I'm due. Who didn't bother to represent me with respect at court. Who killed my first son and did nothing but pity herself for the next eighteen years."

Aurora slaps him hard, leaving an angry red mark on his cheek. The earl steps back, shock and indignation chasing each other across his features.

"My son isn't dead," Aurora says in a low voice. "But you are wise to consider him so. Why would I murder the duchess? I ought to thank her for keeping him out of your wretched grasp."

Watho can't help but laugh again at the absurdity of this statement, the words hanging in the air over the arrow wound in her chest. They both look down at her as if they had forgotten she is there.

The earl is calculating again. Cajoling didn't work, so now he'll try a new tack. It's a pattern Watho has seen a hundred times before. He scans Watho, his lecherous eyes like beetles crawling over her skin.

"You know that I abhor violence," he says at last. "However, considering the circumstances, I find myself compelled to act."

Aurora says nothing, but neither does she waver in her resolve.

"I discovered that my son and heir was alive and that my wife had been hiding him from me," he begins thoughtfully. He's piecing together the story he will tell at court later. Watho rolls her eyes. "I found you here," the earl continues, gesturing again toward Watho, "in a highly compromising situation, having just attacked the duchess, presumably to protect your secret now that the boy has come of age. I was forced to intervene. In your madness, you flew into a rage and I had no choice but to kill you to protect her ladyship."

He turns a sympathetic gaze to Watho and sighs.

"Tragically, I was too late to save the duchess." He shakes his head, sadly.

*It's not a bad plan*, Watho thinks. A little stale for her taste, but he'll have the sympathy of the court. No doubt there will be a new countess in Aurora's place soon enough.

"If you've been following me, you know I didn't come here alone," Aurora says. "If you kill me now, there are others who will know what you've done."

The earl smirks. "Ah, yes, the servants you manipulated. Their testimony will not hold much weight in court."

This much, Watho knows, is true.

"Perhaps not," Aurora allows. "But in the public square, what will they say about you? The chambermaids will whisper. The lady's maids will know. You'll never lure another unsuspecting baroness into your bed."

The earl steps toward her again, menace twisting his features. "My dear, you are very persuasive. I had planned to let your little servant girls live, but perhaps I should reconsider. It's not as though they'll be missed."

He wants her to beg, if not for her own life, than for theirs. Silently, Watho finds herself cheering Aurora on. She's beginning to wonder, albeit a hair belatedly, if her understanding of power has been entirely correct. She has taken it for granted that her father was right — that power is domination of the weak. At this very moment, however, Watho thinks there is more power in the defiant set of Aurora's shoulders than there ever has been in the earl's iron fist.

"You've been a burden on me long enough," he snarls. "Since the day I took you in, you've brought nothing but shame to my house."

"Took me in?" Aurora scoffs. "I *stooped* to marry you. Your association with my family is the only reason you haven't sunk into oblivion long before now."

The earl's indignation reaches its boiling point. He raises the fist that holds the horse whip, but Aurora catches his wrist and steps closer.

"You will *never* meet your son," she hisses.

Sir Hugh twists his wrist to free it from her grasp and swings the whip. It's an awkward movement and the blow lands with less force than he intended, but enough to make Aurora flinch as it strikes her across the shoulders.

His arm draws back to swing again, this time with nothing to stay his momentum. His lips are pulled back in a furious grimace, but Watho thinks he's been looking forward to this part.

Aurora moves nimbly out of the way of the first and second blow, but the third lands with a stinging crack across her lower back, the whip wrapping itself around her waist. With a vicious jerk, the earl pulls it back toward him and Aurora stumbles to her knees.

Sir Hugh's lips begin to curl in a victorious smile, but it's premature. Aurora is back on her feet in seconds, dancing out of the way of the next blow. Watho's glad to see a flinty determination in her face.

They face each other, circling slowly, and Watho feels laughter welling up inside her again. Of all the ways she has pictured her own end, watching a nobleman and his wife square off like fighters in a ring next to her dying body was not a possibility she had considered.

The laughter dies down, however, as the realization settles on her that she and Aurora will likely be buried here together.

The countess is holding her own, but she's unarmed and entirely on the defensive. Watho doubts she'd have the stomach to kill the earl even if she could. Sooner or later, Sir Hugh will come out the victor.

Aurora's eyes are glued to the whip in the earl's right hand, so she doesn't see his left hand wrapped around the hilt of a dagger in his belt. Watho watches that hand, pushing herself up to her elbows, though the movement sends waves of sickening pain coursing through her body. Aurora is backing away, but the earl closes the distance between them in a single bound. In a flash, he has her backed against a tree, the dagger pressed to her throat.

Watho presses her palm into the earth. She doesn't know why the arrow that killed Felnys has not yet extinguished her as well, but however slowly it's working, she *is* dying. There's no need to preserve her magic now. Nor does she have any desire left to avenge herself on her enemy. Aurora has already suffered a lifetime at her hands, and after all, it was never personal to begin with.

As her hand connects with the warm earth, she feels the last of her power drain through her fingertips. Blood starts to drip from Aurora's neck where the blade cuts into her skin. The earl is taking his time, apparently, relishing her helplessness. Watho presses harder, pushing her magic into the ground. The earth begins to tremble and part beneath her fingers, a jagged fissure forming that races toward the earl's boots.

Sir Hugh glances back over his shoulder just as the earth splits beneath his feet. Aurora places her hands on his chest and shoves him backward, just enough to free herself and dive to the side. The earl tries in vain to regain his footing, but it's too late; the crack widens and he topples ignominiously into it. Watho hears his body smack the bottom of the newly created pit, even as the earth underneath her own body crumbles away and she feels herself falling into the chasm after him. Then she, too, slams into the hard earth.

She feels only a flash of pain before darkness descends.

WHEN AURORA STUMBLES out of the woods, a few hours later, she is greeted by a party of armed horsemen riding toward her.

These must be Watho's men. Her mind races, looking for an explanation to give them. If she tells them their mistress is dead, they may kill her on the spot before she can find out what's become of her son. Before she can even learn his name. Her chest tightens with fear.

*Spirits,* she thinks. *Don't let me have come so far only to die here.*

The head horseman, a tall, bronze man, reigns in his horse as he approaches. Aurora tenses, but the horseman makes no move to draw a weapon.

"Lady Aurora?" he calls.

Aurora nods, her throat too dry to speak.

"His young lordship sent us to find you," the horseman says. He motions to one of his men and another hunter rides forward, leading a riderless horse behind him.

"Are you well enough to ride?"

Aurora can barely breathe for relief. She nods gratefully and swings herself into the saddle.

"These men will take you to the castle," the huntsman says. "I must go and find my mistress. I take it she is dead?"

"Yes," Aurora says. "But my husband the earl may not be. You'll find them together at the bottom of a chasm."

The huntsman's eyebrows arch. "Lord Aethon didn't mention an earl, my lady."

Aurora feels frozen. Is there some other lord of this castle to whom the huntsman is referring, or is it her son of whom he speaks? A surge of jealousy shoots through her at the thought that her own son's name, which she has never known, can pass so easily through this stranger's lips.

"Aethon? Is that what he is called?"

To his credit, the stranger understands enough to look ashamed. "Yes my lady."

"Do you know what it means?"

"The lad himself says it has something to do with sunlight in his veins."

The tumultuous mix of emotions that well up at this cause her voice to catch as she whispers her thanks and turns her horse toward the castle.

She stops after a few steps and twists in her saddle to face the huntsman. He's sitting still on his horse, watching her.

"If you find the earl," she says, "I would rather that... Aethon..." she pauses, the name feeling strange in her mouth. "He will need medical treatment," she starts again. "If he must be brought back to the castle, I would prefer that my son does not see him, or know that he is here."

The huntsman nods once, then turns to head into the forest. Two of his men accompany him, while the rest remain with Aurora.

When they reach the castle, she slides out of the saddle before the horse has come to a full stop. She rushes through the front doors, where they must be expecting her, for a servant leads her unquestioningly to the little used great hall.

The room is brightly lit and sparsely furnished. Soft couches have been hastily moved in from other rooms to accommodate the hall's current occupants: Violet, Sarah, Aethon, and the strange, beautiful girl with the luminous eyes.

Aethon and the girl are stretched out on couches near each other, having been carefully washed and bandaged by Violet, Sarah and the castle staff.

When Aurora enters, Aethon sits up, concern creasing his brow. Aurora pauses, feeling suddenly awkward. A hundred questions she wishes she had thought to ask her escorts parade through her mind.

How much has Aethon been told? Will he know who she is? Who is the brave girl who saved his life from the wolf? The worst question comes last: what if he hates her for leaving him here?

Before she can speak, however, Aethon jumps to his feet, wincing with the pain of sudden movement.

"Thank the spirits!" he cries. "You were gone so long, we began to think the wolf came back! You're bleeding! Are you injured?"

He's at her side now, wrapping her in his arms. Hot tears pour down her cheeks and dampen his bandaged chest as dry, racking sobs escape her lips.

"Goodness," Violet's calming voice says from over his shoulder. "Someone get her some water."

THE WOMAN who rushes into the hall, wild-eyed and bloody,

looks so much like the female version of Aethon, that Luna wonders how she ever mistook Aethon for a girl.

She's known who the woman was since the moment she saw her in the clearing, but for the first few hours after the two other women brought her and Aethon back to the castle, there was little time to think about it.

The two women, who introduced themselves as Sarah and Violet, had set about tending to her own and Aethon's wounds with a speed and efficiency Luna had never before witnessed. There was no need for such skill in her lackadaisical life with Falca in the dungeon. She was still looking around in wonder at how much of the castle she had never seen when she found herself gently deposited into an ice bath to reduce the swelling in her ribs, while Sarah washed her face and neck with a warm, scented cloth.

Then they bound her broken arm tightly to her and servants she'd never met came in and out, bringing her spiced wine sprinkled with hellebore for the pain, and a thick warm soup.

She tried to ask several of them if Falca was alright, but they only scurried nervously away, never meeting her eyes. A knot of dread tightened in her chest each time this happened, but she swallowed it down. *It's just the rush of things*, she told herself. *They'll have news soon enough.*

Sarah had asked her if she wished to rest in her own room, but Luna had recoiled so violently at the thought of returning to those lightless quarters that they nearly had to set her arm again.

Thus, a space was made for her and Aethon together in the great hall, where Violet and Sarah flitted about anxiously, seeing to their needs but avoiding their questions.

"You are owed as thorough an explanation as anyone has

ever been given," Violet told them, "but Lady Aurora will want to be here when it's given."

"Lady Aurora is my mother isn't she?" Aethon had asked. Violet had relented and acknowledged that much at least.

Now, as Aethon leads his mother to where Luna rests, she feels a stab of pain. If Watho told her the truth, her own mother is dead. She does not begrudge Aethon the chance to meet his, but grief washes over her all the same. In a way, the grief is like the ice bath — a pain that also brings relief.

There are tears shining in the lady's eyes as she kneels next to Luna's couch. The woman looks like Aethon in every respect, except the eyes. These are the same deep blue as Luna's own.

"I saw what you did in the clearing," the lady says. "If not for your bravery, I may have been too late. I am forever in your debt."

Luna casts around for some appropriate response to this, but when she opens her mouth, the only words that come are, "we have the same eyes."

Aurora's laugh sounds like music and feels like her first glimpse of moonlight.

"Indeed we do," she says.

"I noticed that too," Violet says. "It's uncanny. But how can that be? Unless I'm very mistaken, Luna is Lady Vesper's child."

Aurora studies her a little longer, her face becoming serious.

"Watho has done us both great harm," she says at last. "Maybe one of the mysteries of the world is that the wicked become an unwitting tie that binds the good to one another."

Luna considers the implications of this long after everyone else has fallen asleep. She lies awake on the soft couch, under the warm glow of the hall's lamps, listening to the gentle breathing of her companions and considering.

If Watho's wickedness, she thinks, linked her to Aethon from birth, giving her his mother's eyes, might it not have worked the other way as well? Could it be that when Aethon turns his dark, laughing eyes on her, it is her own mother's eyes she sees?

# CHAPTER TWENTY-TWO

*A*urora and Violet are arguing theology again. It has taken Luna some time to become accustomed to the sharpness of their banter, but now the sound of their laughter over the dinner table sets her soul at ease, like the music of a gentle rain on a moonlit night.

She thinks she will never tire of hearing Aurora laugh. In the three years since they met, Aurora has become like a woman on fire, lit from the inside by her profound freedom and the return of her long lost child. Luna still sees weariness in her from time to time, however; she still grieves for her estranged younger son, even while rejoicing in Aethon's adoration.

Aurora moved to Astarsaga Castle almost immediately after Watho's death. She returned to her old home only once during the earl's convalescence, accompanied by Fargu and his men, to retrieve her things.

During the inquest, Luna had been afraid that they would all be evicted and the castle seized by the king. The earl's testimony about Watho's murder had been colorful, detailed and, for a short time, persuasive enough that Aurora's friends had feared for her life.

Dozens of witnesses had come forward to testify against Watho, however: servants who had been held captive by her magic for years, and even some who had glimpsed the red wolf around the castle, though no material evidence of such a creature was ever found.

Falca had been found in Luna's rooms, her neck broken from the force of Watho's wrath on the day she cast Luna out into the sunlight, but only Luna had witnessed the event. The memory of that violence, the ache for her old friend's companionship, and her guilt at having provoked Watho still grips Luna's heart in cold fingers and keeps her awake many nights. Even now, when she understands Falca's complicity in her own imprisonment, she feels the loss acutely. The memory of the apology on Falca's lips only sharpens the pain.

The final piece of evidence presented at the inquest was the mysterious death of Lord William and the subsequent disappearance of Lady Vesper, both of whom were well thought of in circles much higher than Sir Hugh's.

The earl had counted on his noble status to grant him the favor of the court over women and servants, but he had forgotten that Aurora was a prince's daughter. The king was not inclined, in the face of compelling evidence, to put her to death on the word of an unpopular country earl. Thus the king had awarded the castle to Aethon and given Luna her parent's estate. Though she spends a good deal of time at Astarsaga, reveling in the company of her friends, she has come to think of the estate as her home. Having a haven of her own to which she can retreat when she pleases takes all the sting of captivity out of Watho's former fortress.

Now, she looks around the table where they all laugh and talk — Violet, Sarah, and Aurora are always here but tonight they have guests. Violet's cousin, Alyvia has come to visit, as well as a shy young man whom Sarah has brought to be questioned and approved of by the other ladies. Once things had settled down and the heat of Aurora's fear had subsided, she had been quick to establish peace with Alyvia. It had been, after all, the tavern mistress who had caused the clouds over Aurora's life to finally break. She has reassured Alyvia many times since then that she blames no one but Watho for the witch's crimes.

Aethon was here for dinner, but his chair is now empty — he must have slipped away before the cakes were served. Something has been weighing on him all day. His moods are so vivid, Luna can almost see the colors of them: the bright golden glow of his enthusiasm when they race together on horseback across the plains; the fiery orange of his bouts of anger, though these occur less and less often these days; the silvery blue of his contentment when he's reading poetry in the gardens; and the deep, aching green of his pain. Today, for the first time, he has been unreadable.

Luna lingers at the table for a while longer, soaking in the gentle warmth of companionship and smiling at the poor young man's attempts to impress, before she quietly makes her own escape.

She wanders through a side door into the gardens, where she knows she will find him. She takes her time, enjoying the scent of fresh flowers and the song of crickets on the crisp night air. After a moment she spots him, sitting on his favorite stone bench by the pond, studying the reflection of the moon in the water's still surface. To her amusement, Nox is curled up in his lap. The two have been fast friends since the day they met, though it took Aethon some time to learn how to treat a creature that did not need to be conquered.

He smiles when she slides onto the bench next to him, but doesn't look at her.

"Hello Dryad," he says.

She wonders what kind of a night it is. Sometimes, Aethon comes here to sit in quiet gladness. Other times, it's pain that drives him here.

He feels the loss of Fargu as deeply as she feels Falca's, though Fargu is only banished. Aurora asked for clemency for him, since he was bound to Watho's service by magic, but the huntsman had testified against himself.

"However much I loved the boy, it was I as well as the witch who kept him from his mother," Fargu had said.

"But are you not as much a victim of the witch's plots as the boy himself?" the inquisitor asked him encouragingly.

Fargu shook his head, "No."

"But if you had broken the terms of your magical contract you would have been harmed or killed, isn't that true?"

"Aye."

"Then you were as much at her mercy as the child, were you not?"

"But I *wasn't* a child. That's the difference. Spell or not, I should have been willing to sacrifice my safety for his sake."

In the end, the king could hardly argue with this. He had sentenced Fargu, along with Lucy, to exile in Kolb. Aethon had wept bitterly when they said goodbye and promised to visit him.

*Perhaps*, Luna thinks, *it is time to make the trip at last.*

"What are you thinking about?" she asks, studying his face in the shimmering glow of the moon. His cheek is twice marred now, once by the boar, again by the wolf — the only visible sign of the scars they each bear on both body and soul.

Aethon tilts his head back to examine the night sky, his expression veiled.

"I'm thinking about moonlight."

*How much he has changed,* she thinks. There is nothing left of the cowering boy she met on the riverbanks, moonburned and terrified. They have each made peace with their enemies, he the tender night and she the glorious day. Now she sometimes thinks that Aethon even prefers the moonlight to his beloved sunlit moors.

"I was worried you might be thinking of the earl."

Sir Hugh has written to his son repeatedly, trying to convince Aethon to join him at his estate, if only for a while. To meet his father and see his inheritance. Aethon has never answered one of Sir Hugh's letters and rarely mentions them, but Luna suspects they cause him pain.

"The earl?" Aethon turns laughing eyes on her. "What earl? How could I be thinking of any earl when the moon goddess herself is at my side?"

Luna laughs in return. She and Aethon have always shared a blessedly unselfconscious friendship. She can tell when his teasing is genuine and when it is used to deflect; tonight, his good humor is real.

"Was it not his steward who came to see you today? A bit unusual for him to appear in person wasn't it?"

The unpleasant man had arrived in the late afternoon, asked to speak to Aethon in private and left immediately afterward, despite the inadvisability of beginning such a journey in the evening. As though he could not endure the freedom and happiness of Astarsaga Castle for one second longer than necessary.

Aethon had been preoccupied since his departure and spoken little. Now, the corner of his mouth twists in an ironic smile. "It was indeed. My father has challenged me to a duel."

Luna's head jerks back in her surprise. So the earl's pride has gotten the best of him at last. Having been unable to win his son's attention through bribery or flattery, he means to crush him through violence rather than bear the indignity of being ignored.

"He... what?"

"To the death." Aethon sounds amused, but not distressed.

Luna is afraid to ask about the source of his apparent ease of mind. Is he merely confident that he can best his father?

"Will you accept?" she ventures after a pause.

Aethon laughs and shakes his head without hesitation. "Certainly not."

Luna only realizes she's been holding her breath when her lungs expand again in her relief. "Won't it be a mark against your honor?"

"To accept would be a far greater stain on my honor than to decline. I will not become my father's murderer. Anyway, if he is not worthy of my regard, or my mother's, he is less worthy still of my wrath."

"The nobles will call you a coward, you know."

That word which, when they met, would have sent him into a fury, now makes not the smallest ripple in his apparent serenity.

"Then they understand cowardice as little as I once did," he says. "A coward is a man who would rather die, or worse, would rather kill, than suffer injury to his pride."

*What a miracle the moon has wrought in him,* she thinks.

"Alright then," she says aloud, unable to hide the gladness in her voice. "I am satisfied it is not the earl. So what about the moonlight gives you that faraway gaze?"

He's silent for so long she begins to wonder if she spoke aloud, but the silence is not heavy.

"I was thinking," he says at last, "that I love the moon more than I ever loved the sun."

The directness of this declaration surprises her. When she looks back at him, his face is still upturned, the silver light anointing his features like oil.

"*More* than the sun? You had better be careful. A few more such declarations and I shall think that my friend has been replaced by an imposter," she laughs.

He takes her hand in his, as he often does when they talk like this. His grasp is friendly, affectionate, a reminder to them both that the bonds of their isolation have been cast off. "I loved the sun for what she gave me. For how she made me feel. I still do, really. Riding in the sun feels like thunder in my blood."

A long pause follows. Luna wants to press him to continue, but she waits patiently while he collects his thoughts.

"But I love the moon like a mother," he says at length. "Because she's *your* mother. She taught you at her knee. *You* love her and without her I wouldn't have you."

Tears threaten but do not swell as she looks back into his dark eyes — her own mother's eyes. He knows how she aches for the lack of what he has with Aurora. He knows what he's just given her, and it's all the more meaningful because it cost him to do so. Aethon is still learning to be comfortable laying his heart out so plainly.

"I think I know what you mean," she says. "I once thought we could never be friends, the sun and I. Now I want to sing her praises every day."

The smile that lights up his features now is the same one that was so alien to her the first morning of their acquaintance. Now, when she sees daybreak on his face, she understands why the morning light means hope and strength for him.

She has come to see it in much the same light. What she once thought could only bring cruel death is now a song of increasing glory. Of richness and warmth. When she rides out with him, as she did this afternoon, she feels the same thrum of excitement, the same pulsing of hot blood as their horse's hooves beat steadily beneath them.

She has gotten in the habit of going to the balconies sometimes to watch the dawn, even when she's at her own estate. It seems strange that so much was stolen from both of them for so long, and she wants to drink in as much of the world as her body can hold.

They sit for some time in comfortable silence, punctuated by the occasional calls of bullfrogs, their fingers loosely linked.

"How strange," Aethon muses after a while, as they watch Nox chase fireflies by the edge of the water, "that the day should be so much brighter with the moon in it."

"Who knows," Luna says, "there may be yet another kind of day, brighter even than my sun and your moon, ahead of us still."

# AUTHOR'S NOTE

This story is a retelling of my favorite of all fairy tales, *The Day Boy and The Night Girl*, by George MacDonald. I cried the first time I read MacDonald's version (and pretty much every time since). When I initially considered writing my own retelling I found the whole idea daunting. It felt like hubris to believe I had anything to add to such a beautiful story, written by such an incredible author. In the end, I wrote *Oh Wretched Moon* not to improve upon what MacDonald wrote, but simply as my own love letter to it.

Those who are familiar with the original version will note that I preserved quite a bit of that story in my version. Since this is a somewhat obscure fairy tale, I focused more on expanding the story and exploring its many layers than on giving it a new twist, as can be so cleverly done to some of the better known fairy tales. Whether you are a George MacDonald fan or not, I hope you have enjoyed my humble attempt to pay homage to his brilliant work. Thank you for the time you've spent with Luna, Aethon, Aurora, and even Watho. They and I wish you many sunny days and moonlit nights.

# ABOUT THE AUTHOR

Kate Ramsey lives with various siblings, nieces, and nephews in Oklahoma where she drinks copious amounts of tea and coffee, runs a birth photography business, and writes whatever wants to be written.

Follow Kate's work at TalesMustBeTold.com

Sign up for Kate's newsletter to read *High Magic*, a companion adventure to *Oh Wretched Moon*.